I0788534

Praise for Charley's Novel

"This long-lost treasure is a glimpse into the lives of the very rich and the very poor and how quickly one can become the other. Charley poignantly describes greed and its dire consequences. Readers will get a glimpse of life in the 1879-1880's, with its trials and triumphs."

- LINDA GASS, Archives Assistant, Carson-Newman University, Jefferson City, Tennessee

"Mr. Peck has opened a portal to another time by bringing this long-forgotten publication to light. A finding such as this should encourage us all to look into our family histories for treasures untold."

- RYAN JOHNSON, Library Director, BA Historical Studies, MA Library Science, O'Fallon, Illinois

"Anyone desiring to better understand the post Reconstruction era should consider reading this book. Filled with stories related to ore mining, slavery adjustments, and the lives of the poor and rich in the southern states, this book brings a depth to the reality of the time that compliments any other narrative."

- JUSTICE BRATTON, 11 years old, homeschooled in Kathmandu, Nepal

The Pecks of Mossy Creek

The Pecks of Mossy Creek series editor, Andy Peck, seeks to bring the Peck Family together through books, information sharing, and family gatherings. If you descend from the Pecks of Mossy Creek, please email andy@crossmountainbooks.com for more info and updates. The photos above were taken in July 2021 at Mossy Creek Station, Jefferson City, Tennessee. Special thanks to Linda Gass, Teresa Collins, Kim Stapleton, Downtown Mayor Frank Brown, and the Mossy Creek Foundation.

The Pecks of Mossy Creek

The Pecks of Mossy Creek series highlights the founding family of Mossy Creek (now Jefferson City), Tennessee and their ancestors and descendants. Adam Peck, Sr. and his wife Elizabeth (Sharkey) Peck pioneered west from their home in Fincastle, VA and floated down the Holston River on a flatboat. They settled Mossy Creek using a land grant of 5,000 acres Adam earned for his service in the Revolutionary War. As one of the Overmountain Men, he helped win the Battle of King's Mountain in 1780, and eight years later founded Mossy Creek. Adam and Elizabeth initially moved into an abandoned fort, and then built their own log cabin. He built a grist mill, which was the first mill in the area. At his wife's request, they built the first church in Mossy Creek and named it Elizabeth's Chapel in 1790. The Pecks had a number of slaves, and Elizabeth taught them to read and write along with their 12 children. One of these slaves was named Uncle John, and they installed him as the first preacher. Rev. John Peck was called "the best human being there ever was," and the old log chapel became the foundation for the Methodist and Presbyterian churches in Jefferson City. In addition to the monument that says "Adam and Elizabeth Peck: Pioneers to the west from Virginia in 1788," the family burial plot in the Old Westview Cemetery in Jefferson City features a plaque that reads, "Pioneers of 19th Century Methodism at Mossy Creek."

The Pecks of Mossy Creek series seeks to highlight notable Peck family members and their stories and writings through the years. Some notable Peck family members are:

- Jacob Peck, Sr. (1723-1801) – Adam Peck, Sr.'s father and Revolutionary War Veteran
- Lydia (Borden) Peck (1728-1800) – Adam Peck, Sr.'s mother and daughter of Benjamin Borden II and Zeruriah Winter
- Judge Jacob Franklin Peck (1779-1869) – Adam Peck, Sr.'s son, TN Supreme Court Judge, State Senator and Geologist
- Judge James Hawkins Peck (1790-1836) – Adam Peck Sr.'s son, War of 1812 Veteran, U.S. District Judge for Missouri

Cross Mountain Books is a proud supporter of the **Mossy Creek Foundation**. A portion of the proceeds from each book sold will be donated to the Mossy Creek Foundation in its efforts to revitalize the Historic Mossy Creek District in Jefferson City, TN. Learn more about this great project by visiting **mossycreekfoundation.org**.

Charley's Novel: Mary Anderson and Peacock the Mineralogist, The Bad Luck of a Young Southern Girl

Charles Talbot Peck
16 Nov 1857 – 22 Feb 1882

"This story was written in the month of April [1879],
during my idle hours."
~Charley

Charley's Novel

Mary Anderson and Peacock the Mineralogist, The Bad Luck of a Young Southern Girl

Edited by
Andy Peck

The Pecks of Mossy Creek
Andy Peck, Series Editor

Cross Mountain Books
Scott Air Force Base, Illinois
www.crossmountainbooks.com

Published by
Cross Mountain Books in Scott AFB, IL

Manufactured in the United States of America.

First Edition.

Cover & Frontispiece: Photograph from Peck Family Collection

Signed copies available. Books also available in quantity for promotional or premium use. For information, email <u>info@crossmountainbooks.com</u>.

www.crossmountainbooks.com
Facebook: fb.me/crossmountainbooks

Unless otherwise indicated, all definitions presented in the book are taken from Merriam-Webster.com Dictionary, https://www.merriam-webster.com/dictionary

Publisher's Cataloging-in-Publication Data

Names: Peck, Charles Talbot, 1857-1882, author. | Peck, Andy (Thomas Andrew), 1981- , editor.
Title: Charley's novel : Mary Anderson and Peacock the mineralogist, the bad luck of a young southern girl / Charles Talbot Peck ; edited by Andy Peck.
Description: Scott AFB, IL : Cross Mountain Books, 2021. | Series: The Pecks of Mossy Creek ; 2. | Includes 89 illustrations: art work, photos, chart. | Includes bibliographical references and index. | Summary: Reputable mineralogist, Mr. Peacock, enchants Mary Anderson, a wealthy Southern girl. Her family's trust in him, and her father's lust for gold, nearly lead to family ruin. Includes author's biography, 19th-century paintings and poetry, history of Morristown College and the Ku Klux Klan in East TN, and primary sources for study of the 1870-1880s American South.
Identifiers: LCCN 2021919030 | ISBN 9781955121163 (pbk) | ISBN 9781955121170 (hardcover) | ISBN 9781955121187 (ebook) | ISBN 9781955121194 (audiobook)
Subjects: LCSH: Peck, Charles Talbot, 1853-1859. | Peck family. | North Carolina—History. | Tennessee, East—History. | United States—History—Civil War, 1861-1865—Fiction. | BISAC: HISTORY / United States / 19th Century. | HISTORY / United States / State & Local / South (AL, AR, FL, GA, KY, LA, MS, NC, SC, TN, VA, WV). | FICTION / Historical / Civil War Era.
Classification: LCC F442.1 P433 2021| DDC 975 P43--dc23
LC record available at https://lccn.loc.gov/2021919030

For my boys:
Justice, Hudson, and Noble

I love you so much.
May you be inspired by Charley's
creativity, and commitment to faith,
perseverance, and providence
in his novel.

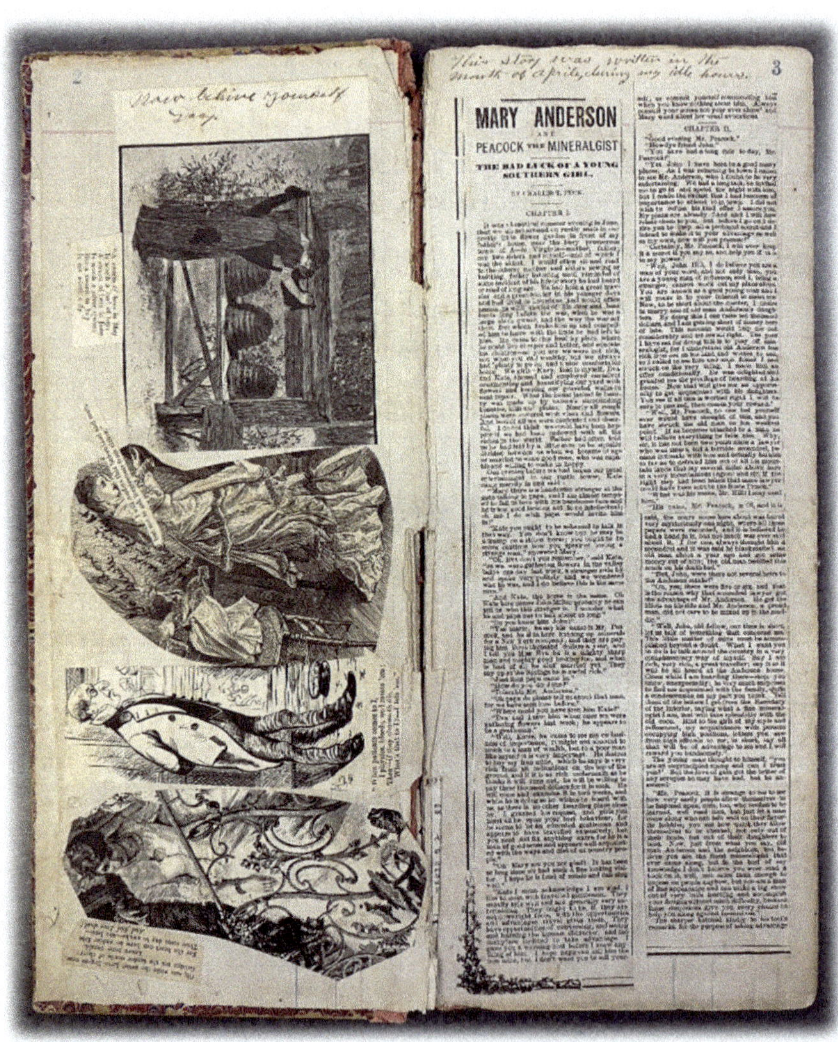

Figure 1 - *Inside front cover and first page of Charley's novel, first published in series in a newspaper, see Appendix for illustration details*

CONTENTS

FOREWORD

Historians often look at the writings from times past to gain a snapshot of the period from which an author wrote. *Charley's Novel* provides an excellent glimpse into the world of a young man, and those people, places, and events which shaped his life.

In modern terms an "Easter egg" is a part of a usually electronic medium that is a small hint or hidden message to an inside reference. While electronic mediums were distant from the time of Charles T. Peck, he has nevertheless provided "Easter eggs" for us throughout his story. We are introduced to characters who bear names of family members both lost and revered like Ada and Ashby, his older sister and younger brother. Charley's characters reflect his perceptions of the people he knew and mourned, and now bear tribute in written word.

Here we also see the influence of his parents and the respect of individuals of tremendous ability. We see a family of well-traveled men and women who proved very capable of expressing themselves vocationally, and also in written word. We see in Charles a young man who respects and admires strong women. Andy's previous book, *Ada's Journal,* shows how capable his mother Emma and grandmother Louise were, as Emma wrote the incredible journal and letters, and Louise wrote spectacular letters full of fun phrases and expressions. We also see the influence of his father - Dr. Isham T. Peck, a man of many talents and abilities. Though he was an established physician, he was also a military officer, writer, farmer, traveler and more.

Charles was a young man surrounded by a talented family, but he also lived in a period where liberal arts was the primary means of education. Public schooling in that day meant more than an introduction to math, ancient languages, and classic literature. A new vision of education emerged after the Civil War, which placed great importance on instructing the total mind, body, and spirit of an individual. Charles' parents emerged from the Civil War bruised, but not broken, and still had some means. This allowed them to provide Charles with extensive travel experiences, which made his learning experiential, and helps us understand how he could have written such a masterful story that far exceeded his years of life. Through the lens of his novel, we see a young man who has traveled far, yet carefully remembered his home in Mossy Creek. Charles also wrote about other locations in surrounding Southern states, each place helping tell his family story. One can imagine the Peck family members sharing about the places mentioned here at family gatherings.

Charles is truly an author who allows us to see a New South in the post-Civil War Era. The South was seeking to redefine itself economically, and mineralogy was a way that its resources could be redefined and valuable in an Industrial Age. Southern states were in a new era of virtue, not defined by battle or conquest, but by standing for a righteous cause and helping others. This time-period novel also gives us a glimpse into the language and discourse of the time period, as we see how people speak and interact.

In this work, Andy brings to life Charles T. Peck's long forgotten story, and introduces us to the 1870's. He shows us a life that knows not only joy and happiness, but also heartache and sorrow. In *Charley's Novel*, we find Easter eggs to his time period, and despite the 140-year gap, we discover people quite similar to us.

Whether a student of history, or someone simply looking for an engaging and interesting read, I would certainly recommend this novel to you. Because *Charley's Novel* can reach all of us on so many levels, I'm confident you will enjoy reading and learning in the pages to come. As you begin this glimpse into the past, and meet the characters in this fictional novel, what can you learn about our history, and more importantly, what will you discover about yourself?

Finally, thank you to Andy Peck for his research and Cross Mountain Books for publishing *Charley's Novel* and *The Pecks of Mossy Creek* series. Each book helps us better understand the history of Mossy Creek (modern-day Jefferson City, Tennessee) and its surrounding communities.

David Needs
Carson-Newman University Instructor
Mossy Creek Historian
President of the Lakeway Civil War Preservation
Association

(Photo Courtesy of Carson-Newman University)

Charley's Novel is a novel written by Charley Peck in April 1879, published in series to a local newspaper, likely *The Morristown Gazette*. As it was published, Charley cut out each column of newspaper print and glued it into a tall, skinny, ledger book. The front cover is shown to the right. The inside of the front cover has images and quotes clipped from newspapers, magazines, and Charley's handwriting. The last two pages of the ledger book include a handwritten poem attributed to W. Little (*W. Lytle*), see Appendix. Finally, the inside of the back cover has the clipping of a pencil sketch of Sarah Bernhardt drawn by Georges Clairin in 1879. Charley's accompanying handwriting makes it clear that he was enamored with Ms. Bernhardt; but it is unclear whether he thought of her when he created his character, Mary Anderson. All front and back matter of the journal has been placed in the Appendix for inquiring minds.

Regarding the text of the novel itself, it has been retained in its original form. Notations of "to be continued" and "concluded" are left intact, so that one can study how a serial novel was published in that day. The transcription of the novel from the ledger book was made by me, the Editor. There were no maps or illustrations contained in the original newspaper printing of the novel, so all included here were additions to help bring color and context. My goal was to share original photographs and artwork from the time period. Because some of the words used in the text have fallen into disuse, definitions are added for ease of reading. I have also placed historical notations when it is clear that there is or might be a connection between a place or name Charley used. This should help you find some of the Easter eggs David Needs talked about above. Are there others that you can find?

My overarching policy for this publication was to keep the original. If a word was misspelled (according to modern spelling), the original misspelling was retained and a "[*sic*]" was placed beside the word, indicating *spelling in context*. Very occasionally, if it was abundantly clear that a misspelling was simply the newspapers' typo, I just corrected it. Original paragraphs, punctuation, and grammar were retained as well. I did add some commas and other punctuation, but always with brackets "[,]" to indicate that it was an editorial insertion. Original ledger pages are numbered like this, "[Page 1 End]".

Those with a keen eye will notice that there is no "CHAPTER X." It is not found in the ledger book, but the story does **not** seem to have a "missing" chapter. I believe that Chapter XI. should have been Chapter X., and so on, but the original numbering scheme has been retained.

Transcribing this epic southern tale was a labor of love. I am ecstatic to share it with you and everyone. Whether interested in time period novels, studying the 19th century in school, a lover of Peck family history, or otherwise, I hope you really enjoy *Charley's Novel*.
~Andy Peck, Editor

INTRODUCTION

For just over 140 years, this southern tale has been preserved by the Peck family. Rediscovered in 2021, photographed and transcribed, this epic novel written by Charles Talbot Peck is now made available to the public by editor Andy Peck. With themes of chivalry, integrity, honor, faith, and providence, *Charley's Novel* reveals a window into the world of East Tennessee and surrounding states just after the period of Reconstruction following the Civil War.

In *Charley's Novel*, we learn about the patterns of courtship for wealthy families. We see the meanness of and spousal abuse by "ruffians" as Charley calls them. We learn of the fortitude of women who bore up under such abuse, and were rewarded in the end for their strength, grace, and determination. Difficult subjects are covered as well in this time period novel including greed (the lust for gold and wealth), threats and coercion by the Ku Klux Klan, and the simple but difficult life of mountain people—with limited opportunities for education.

The pages here include a love story, and lessons for all of us to learn from. They also contain signposts to the history of Mossy Creek (modern day Jefferson City, TN), and to the Peck family itself. Charley inserts family names and history throughout the novel. What treasures can YOU find, that teach us about life in 1879?

ABOUT THE AUTHOR

Charles "Charley" Talbot Peck was born 16 Nov 1857 on Henderson Plantation in Louisiana surrounded by his mom's side of the family, and he died 22 Feb 1882[1] in Cincinnati, Ohio under the care of his younger brother and physician, Dr. Ed Peck. According to the Census taken in Civil District No. 1, Cocke County, Tennessee on 9 Jun 1880, Charles T. Peck was born in Louisiana and his occupation was "lawyer." He was 22 at the time of the census (though listed as age 21). In relation to the founders of

Figure 2 - Charles Talbot Peck Abt. 1880, Photograph from Peck Family Collection

Mossy Creek, Charles was the great-grandson of Adam and Elizabeth Peck, and grandson of Judge Jacob Franklin Clayton Peck.

His parents were Dr. Isham Talbot Peck and Emma Elizabeth (Henderson) Peck. Isham (1811-1887) was a physician in the military pre-civil war, serving U.S. soldiers as a physician in Mexico and stationed at multiple forts in America. He attended Greenville College (now Tusculum University) and was very well read. He was a writer, likes Charles, and his writings can be found in the upcoming book

---

[1] This date of Charley's death is more accurate than the one listed in *Ada's Journal*

Sawbones: The Life and Times of Dr. Isham Talbot Peck, published by Cross Mountain Books. He wrote numerous letters to the editor of *The Morristown Gazette* from 1874-1886, and people from around the country wrote to him using his pen name, "Sawbones." He grew up in Mossy Creek, Tennessee, but also lived for a time in Louisiana and Mississippi, before retiring to Wolf Creek, TN in the Blue Ridge Mountains between Newport, TN and Hot Springs, North Carolina.

Charley's mom, Emma Elizabeth (Henderson) Peck (1833-1900), was a writer as well. See *Ada's Journal and Emma's Letters: The Civil War Era Journal and Letters of Emma Peck*, by Cross Mountain Books. *Ada's Journal* is the written account Emma kept of life during 1853-1855 from the perspective of her first-born daughter Ada. It shares the adventures Ada enjoyed through her second birthday—riding in stagecoaches, traveling by railroad, and floating up and down the Mississippi River on steamboats. It also shares family stories including gifts, holiday traditions, and illnesses. *Emma's Letters* includes a series of letters written from Emma Peck to her best friend Emma Allen who lived in Wolf Creek, TN. The letters start in the 1850s and continue well into the 1890s, revealing life before, during, and after the Civil War. Emma was a gifted writer, as was Isham, and so it is no wonder that Charley developed a love for the written word at an early age. Emma's parents owned Henderson Plantation, a sprawling cotton plantation in East Carroll Parish, Louisiana that bordered the Mississippi River (north of Vicksburg and Milliken's Bend). A more detailed biography for Emma, including maps of Louisiana and East Tennessee, is found in the introduction to *Ada's Journal*.

Emma's mom, Louise Henderson, wrote this about baby Charley when he was just a couple days old, "Since I commenced [*writing the letter*] this a little stranger has made his appearance here by the name of Charles Talbot Peck. He was born on the 16th. Daughter thinks he is a great boy. and Willy is mighty put out because "Tarl" (for Charles) is not allowed to go to the table to eat of his favorite dish "Banes" (beans)."[2] In another letter, Charley's grandma Louise wrote this to Charles' Uncle Horace Prentice, Jr., "we have another little member of our house hold, who is not quite a week old, and is named Charles Talbot, he is a bright eyed little chap, Daughter [Emma Peck] sends her love to you, and she is very much pleased with the little Charley."[3]

Other biographical details can be gleaned from letters that his mom wrote to her best friend Emma Allen in the mid-1800s. Speaking of his natural abilities, Emma wrote on 27 Nov 1860, just 13 days after he turned three years old, "Charley spells remarkably well without knowing a letter." In the same correspondence, she said that Charley was much larger at three years old than his brother Ed was at the same age.[4] Before that, when he was just two, Emma said, "I never saw Willy and Charley so fat and healthy as they are now_ Charley is a great imprudent looking fellow_ calls out 'good morning' to strangers that pass him in the road, and has a funny way of saying bad words. He waked up soon one morning, and the first thing he said was_ 'I want to see Mrs Allen'. I asked him what I must tell you for him, and he said 'something pretty'."[5]

Charley attended the Reagan High School for Boys in Morristown, TN. In 1881, the school and its land were purchased and the building was then used for the Morristown Seminary College, which eventually became Morristown College. Morristown College was one of only two institutions for black youth in East Tennessee and its buildings were used until it was absorbed by Knoxville College in 1989, and doors permanently closed in 1994. Please see Appendix IX for more information about this amazing school and the story of Andrew Fulton, a Morristown hero. The institution of Reagan High

---

[2] See letter from Louise Henderson to Emma Allen (written 14 Nov 1857) in *Ada's Journal and Emma's Letters: The Civil War Era Journal and Letters of Emma Peck*, 2021, Pgs 75-77.

[3] *Ada's Journal*, 20 Nov 1857, Pg 85.

[4] *Ada's Journal*, Pg 60.

[5] *Ada's Journal*, 4 Dec 1859, Pg 56.

School became Morristown Male High School, then Rose High School, and is currently Morristown-Hamblen High School East.

During the 1874-1875 school year, Charles attended Washington and Lee University in Lexington, Virginia. While there he studied Latin, English, and Mathematics. He is listed as a first year in the college directory, but not listed for any of the subsequent classes of students. I have not found any record of his attendance at another college, but I believe he may have attained a law degree from another institution.

There was a love for newspapers in the Peck Family. Isham subscribed to "a number of leading papers", Charley's brother Ashby started his own Wolf Creek paper called *The Mountain Boomer*, and in May 1876, at the age of 18, Charley began his own weekly newspaper called the Mossy Creek *Independent*. The *Independent* was quoted in *The Morristown Gazette* and the *Memphis Daily Appeal*. It even got a hearty endorsement from the *Gazette* when it launched. Family friend and editor Henry Helms said this about Charley's paper, "The initial number of the Mossy Creek *Independent* has found its way into our sanctum. It is a respectable looking, 24 column sheet, and well filled with local news and miscellaneous matter. Issued weekly, by Chas. T. Peck at $1.50 per annum."[6] The *Memphis Daily Appeal* quoted the *Independent* on 2 Aug 1876, Pg 2 saying that a Mr. Banj. F. Franklin, of Jefferson County had a serious accident when his team [of horses] ran away and upset the wagon. Mr. Franklin's skull was badly damaged and they did not expect him to survive. In news more related to his **novel**, the *Gazette* quotes Charley's paper in this way on 24 May 1876, Pg 2, "The Mossy Creek Independent understands that the Federal Court will confirm the sale of the Zinc Works at that place July next. It is valuable property, and will be a safe investment to any party purchasing it."

---

[6] *The Morristown Gazette*, 24 May 1876, Pg 2

Charley sold the paper to his friend Capt Ed L. Owens, from Greeneville, South Carolina, in September 1876. The *Gazette* reported that Owens "has been assisting Mr. Peck in the editorial management of the paper for the last month or so. Mr. Owens said the title will be changed next week from the Independent to the Lancet. He shows the right colors on his mast-head, and deserves to reap a rich harvest of patronage. The *Independent* is much improved since the change, and ought to be sustained by the good old people of Jefferson."[7] But despite this planned sale, the Library of Congress says that the paper had a circulation through 1878. Contributor "Sam Slick" to the *Gazette* says in Feb 1877, "I am informed by Capt. Chas. Peck, that he is contemplating a revival of the *Mossy Creek Independent.* This is a step in the right direction!"[8] Slick's comments beg the question, had Charley joined the military? The only mention I can find of a Charles Peck in the military is in the *1879 Report to the Adjutant General to the Governor of Ohio*, where a Charles Peck is listed as a 1st Corporal. But it is unclear whether this is our Charles, and Corporal is an enlisted rank whereas Captain would make him an officer. Finally, regarding the paper, a poem published in the *Gazette* in July 1877 speaks with great pride about the *Mossy Creek Independent.*[9] After praising many other aspects of their town, the Squire says, "look at the Mossy Creek Independent that waives [*sic*] over the land of the frea [*sic*] and the home of the braive [*sic*] …". Many citizens appreciated Charley's paper.

In 1878 at the age of 20 he published a poem in *The Morristown Gazette* called *Every Day*, see Appendix X to read his striking poem. It is a poem that indicates a discontent within Charles…a longing for something more, something greater, and a life filled with the extraordinary. Charles filled this need with grand trips overseas, of which we have a definite record of one, and a possible record of

---

[7] Ibid, 27 Sep, 1876, Pg 2
[8] Ibid, 28 Feb 1877, Pg 2
[9] Ibid, 18 Jul 1877, Pg 1, 4th of July poem by Squire Simpkins

another. Ashby's Wolf Creek *The Daily Boomer* says this in its 10 Jun 1878 issue, "The Hon. Charles T. Peck postponed his lecture on account of the inclemency of the weather."

A few months later, in Sep 1878, there is record that a Charles Peck, 21 years old and listed as a student, traveled from Liverpool, England on a Cunard ship called the Bothnia, and landed in New York City. This could have been our Charles, travelling to Europe and back, getting away from the "every day" activities of home.

In Sep 1879, just four months after writing his novel, he transferred 500 acres of his land in Cocke County to his brother Ed.[10]

At the age of 22, Charles took the trip of a lifetime to South America, and the local paper captured it this way, "Prof. Charles T. Peck, formerly of Mossy Creek, gave us a call last weekend on his way to visit his father's family at Wolf Creek after a protracted tour for the benefit of his health, during which he visited and traveled through many of the South American States, returning by way of San Francisco and taking in the Golden State and intermediate territories. We are glad to say that the object of his trip was accomplished, as he returns in vigorous health."[11] The article generates some questions…why was he called Professor? Was he teaching law classes where he studied? What was it like to travel to South America in 1880 and did anyone go with him? The same article said that Charley's younger brother, Dr. Ed Peck, returned home around the same time from New York after having "perfected his medical knowledge under the supervision and training of the most learned and famous doctors." It does not seem like a coincidence that Charley and Ed came home to visit their family in Wolf Creek at the same time. They shared another moment together just two years later, though this one much more somber.

---

[10] *Knoxville Daily Chronicle*, 14 Sep 1879, Pg 1

[11] *The Morristown Gazette,* 3 Mar 1880, Pg 2. See Appendix I for a clue about one of the countries Charley visited during his epic journey south.

The following account from *The Morristown Gazette* (Morristown, TN) on Wednesday, 1 Mar 1882, Pg 3 provides a great deal of information about Charley and his death.

The text reads "Mr. Chas. T. Peck, son of Dr. Peck, of Wolf Creek Tenn., who has been engaged in business at Cincinnati, O., was stricken with an apoplectic fit [*a seizure*] in that city on the 18th inst., and prostrated in the street. He was taken in charge by physicians, and his brother, Dr. E. J. Peck [*the editor's 2nd Great Grandfather*], of Atlanta, Ga, telegraphed to. On account of a delay in trains, the doctor did not reach Cincinnati until a few hours before his death, Wednesday night. The death was from congestion of the brain, and Dr. Peck thinks he could have saved him if he had reached there twelve hours sooner. The remains were brought home and interred at the old family burying ground, at Mossy Creek, last Saturday. Charley formerly was a student of Reagan High School of this place and has many friends who will lament his sad and untimely death. He was a promising young man with a bright future before him. We extend our sympathy to the bereaved family. *Requiescat in pace.*"

Charles was just 24 years old when he died in Cincinnati, OH. This article attributes his death to "congestion of the brain" but another article calls it suicide. *The Daily American* (Nashville, TN) dated

Wed, 30 Nov 1887, Pg 2 reads, "THE SAD SEQUEL. **Ashby Peck's Father Falls Dead Upon Hearing of His Son's Suicide.** *Special Dispatch to The American.* KNOXVILLE, Nov. 29.—Ashby H. Peck, of Wolf Creek, Tenn., committed suicide at Jacksonville, Fla., yesterday, and his aged father, Dr. Peck, *one of the most extensive* land owners in Tennessee, fell dead on hearing the news. **Two of young Peck's brothers committed suicide. One was found dead in his room at a Cincinnati hotel about two years ago**, and the other killed himself on a Louisiana plantation about five years ago." [*emphasis added*]

THE SAD SEQUEL.

Ashby Peck's Father Falls Dead Upon Hearing of His Son's Suicide.

Special Dispatch to The American.

KNOXVILLE, Nov. 29.—Ashby H. Peck, of Wolf Creek, Tenn., committed suicide at Jacksonville, Fla., yesterday, and his aged father, Dr. Peck, one of the most extensive land owners in Tennessee, fell dead on hearing the news. Two of young Peck's brothers committed suicide. One was found dead in his room at a Cincinnati hotel about two years ago, and the other killed himself on a Louisiana plantation about five years ago.

No mention was made to suicide in the initial article by *The Morristown Gazette*, so it is curious why *The Daily American* newspaper would claim so matter-of-factly that Charles took his own life. To note, Charles' father Dr. Isham Peck, and sons Ashby and Louis Sharkey Peck, were friends with the previous managing editor of *The American*, Maj. Henry Heiss. They even went on fishing trips together. Notably, though, Maj. Heiss retired from the paper in the winter of 1881, and died in June 1885. So, he was not the editor when the story was published in 1887. Regardless, with the close family friendship to the paper's former editor, one couldn't imagine the paper printing the story that Charles had taken his own life, if the family did not believe it in fact. If true, it is a tragedy of epic proportions. One paper shared that Charley was "well known through East Tennessee, where he had many friends, who will hear of his death with regret. He was engaged in business in Cincinnati, and had a bright future before him. A younger brother [Louis] is a student at Goodman's Business College, in this city."[12] Did Charles take a lethal dose of laudanum like his brother Willy and eventually his brother Ashby? Whatever happened, he fell ill on the 18th and died four days later on the 22nd. Ed brought Charley's remains back to Mossy Creek on the train, and the family buried him in the Peck area of the Westview Cemetery in Jefferson City, next to his siblings Ada and Willy. A photo of his gravestone is found is Appendix IV.

Isham was 71 years old, and Emma 49, when their son Charles died in Ohio. It had been 11 years since their son Willy took his life.

Interest in Literature

The Appendix of this volume is full of Charley's notes, poems, quotes, and lithograph cutouts. These were found in the same form book where he pasted the newspaper clippings of his novel. He was a very well-read young man. He read *Scribner's Monthly Magazine: An Illustrated Magazine for the People*, which included stories, illustrations, and news from around the world. He loved poetry, and he read and quoted the works of Lord Byron, Russian poet Michael Lemontov, English poet and hymnist William Cowper, Anglican archbishop and poet Richard Trench, British novelist and teacher Amelia E. Barr, and others.

If you desire to learn more about Charley and the time in which he lived, spend time looking through the Appendices in this volume. I'm confident that you will come away knowing more about Charley, but also the tumultuous landscape of the 1870s/1880s that formed the backdrop for his novel. You also get to learn about and see the woman he had a crush on, French stage actress Sarah Bernhardt.

I truly hope you enjoy *Charley's Novel,* or as he titled it: *Mary Anderson and Peacock the Mineralogist, The Bad Luck of a Young Southern Girl* by Charles T. Peck.

---

[12] *Knoxville Daily Chronicle*, 24 Feb 1882, Pg 4

Charles Talbot Peck Family Tree

Biographical Information

Father = Dr. Isham Talbot Peck (23 Feb 1811 – 28 Nov 1887)

Mother = Emma Elizabeth Henderson (1833 – 9 Aug 1900)

Children of Dr. Isham and Emma Peck

1) Ada Louise Peck (25 Jul 1853 – 27 Mar 1859)

2) William "Willy" Henderson Peck (30 Nov 1855 – 1 May 1871)

3) Charles "Charley" Talbot Peck (16 Nov 1857 – 22 Feb 1882)

4) Dr. Edward Jerome Peck (14 Oct 1859 – 7 Jun 1927)

5) Ashby Henderson Peck (1862 – 27 Nov 1887)

6) Louis Sharkey Peck (15 May 1865 – 27 Jun 1937)

7) Paul Eve Peck (23 Mar 1869 – 22 Nov 1922)

8) Helen Emma Peck (24 Nov 1871 – 27 May 1887)

9) Robert Lee Peck (29 Apr 1874 – 10 Jan 1938)

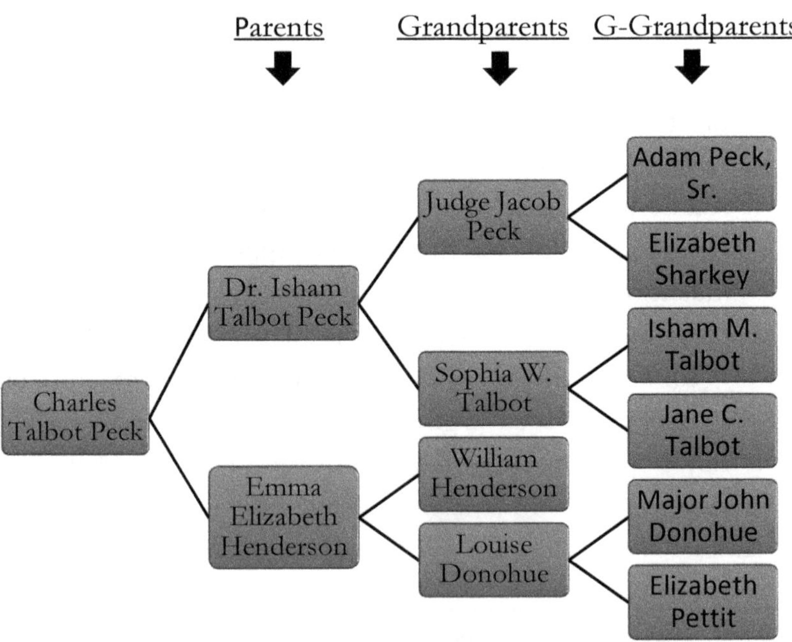

CHAPTER I.

It was a beautiful summer evening in June, that we all sat around on rustic seats in our pretty little flower garden in front of my father's house, near the busy prosperous town of A—in Virginia—mother, father; my two sisters and myself—and of which I was the eldest, I would often sit and read to the others; mother and sisters sewing or knitting, father listening until reminded of some incident of his life or story he had heard or read of long ago.[13] He had been a great traveler and a great hunter in his younger days and had lived in Louisiana, and would often amuse us with stories of his deer and boar hunts long before the war, when he was a large slave owner, and the way the war set them free which broke him up and compelled him to leave with the little he had left to him.[14] He came to this healthy place where he could live cheaper and better, and educate his

---

[13] "A—in Virginia" possibly refers to the town of Abingdon, Virginia, just across the state line. 101 years prior to Charley writing his novel, his great-grandfather Adam Peck, Sr. gathered with other patriots from Virginia and North Carolina at the Muster Grounds in Abingdon to begin their 300-mile march to Kings Mountain, South Carolina for the Battle of Kings Mountain.

[14] This description of Mr. Anderson closely resembles the life of Charley's own father, Dr. Isham Talbot Peck, who lived and owned plantations in Louisiana and Mississippi, and left the area permanently and moved to East Tennessee after the Civil War. See *Ada's Journal and Emma's Letters*, 2021, to learn more about conditions around the Henderson Plantation in the years just after the Civil War. See especially the letter from Emma Peck to Emma Allen, 24 Nov 1867, Pg 68.

children—so you see we were not rich, not what you call wealthy, but we always had plenty to go on and a nice comfortable home. We girls—Mary, that is myself, Eva and Kate, amused and employed ourselves ornamenting and beautifying our yard with flowers and keeping our graveled walks in neat repair. What the house lacked in beauty was made up by nature's surrounding beauties, hills and plains. Nearly all rough places were covered with vines and flowers. And best of all we were contented and cheerful. I do not think we could have been happier if we had been endowed with all the riches in the world. Father had often told us he had laid by a little sum to be equally divided between us when we became of age or married to some good man, who was capable and willing to make us happy.

One evening before we had begun our usual entertainment in our rustic bower, Kate came merrily in and said:

"Mary there is a handsome stranger at the gate talking to papa, and I am almost tempted to fall in love with his handsome face and he is too good looking not to be intellectual; oh me I do wish papa would invite him in!

"Kate you ought to be ashamed to talk in that way. You don't know but he may be a tramp on a stolen horse; you ought to be more cautious how you speak of loving a strange man," answered Mary.

"Oh, Eva don't you remember," said Kate, "as we were gathering flowers in the valley below one day last week, a stranger rode by and spoke very politely and we wondered who he was, and I do believe this is the same man."

"And Kate, the horse is the same. Oh Kate here comes John Miller probably he can tell us who this stranger is. I wonder what he and papa has to talk about so long."

"Do you know him John?"

"Yes marm [*sic*], he say his name is Mr. Peacock, and he is in here hunting up minerals for a New York company, and they are paying him three thousand dollars a year, and I tell you Miss Eva he is a mighty

sharp man and mighty good looking too, and what is best of all he aint'
[*sic*] married yet. They say up at the Springs he is awful rich."[15]

"Just then papa came in."

"How do you do John?"

"Tolerable Mr. Anderson."

"Oh papa do please tell us about that man, for we have seen him
before." "Where could you have seen him Kate?"

"Eva and I saw him when once we were gathering flowers last
week; he appears to be a gentleman."

"Well, Katie, he came to see me on business of importance, it
might not amount to much to a man of wealth, but to a poor man like
myself it is very important. He desires to buy my iron mine, which he
says is very rich from all indications on the top of the ground, and if it
is as rich underneath as he thinks it will turn out, he will be willing to
pay three thousand dollars for it in cash.[16] He will come and examine
it in two weeks, and while he is doing so he wishes to board with us,
as there is no other boarding place close by. I granted his request, and
girls you must all be upon your best behaviour, for he seems to be an
educated gentleman and appears to have travelled extensively, but you
need not fix anything extra for he is a man of good sense and appears
well acquainted with the ways and diet of us country people."

"Oh! Mary are you not glad? It has been so long since we had such
a fine looking visitor, I hope he is fond of music and can sing well.

"Kate I must acknowledge I am glad, I like to meet with travelled
gentlemen. They usually talk well and are generally very entertaining.

---

[15] "The Springs" may refer to Warm Springs, North Carolina, modern day Hot
Springs, North Carolina, where a prominent hotel welcomed guests from around
the country, and where many wealthy people resided. See Figure 3 (Pg 36).
[16] Both Dr. Isham Talbot Peck (Charley's father) and Judge Jacob Peck
(grandfather) had an interest in geology. Judge Peck owned mines and the family
would travel to visit him occasionally at his gold mines. See *Ada's Journal* and also
Appendix VII. Peck Family Geology for newspaper coverage of their interest in
minerals, iron ore, and even the land called "Peck's Iron Mountain."

They ought to be, if they are not downright fools, with the opportunities and advantages travel gives them. They have opportunities of conversing, and seeing and learning the human character, and too many are inclined to take advantage. I gave you a warning hint before I knew anything of him. I hope papa can sell him the iron mine, but I don't want you to sell yourself; or commit yourself commending him when you know nothing about him. Always consult your senses not your eyes alone" and Mary went about her usual avocations.

CHAPTER II.

"Good evening Mr. Peacock."

"Howdye friend John."

"You have had a long ride to day, Mr. Peacock?"

"Yes John I have been to a good many places. As I was returning to town I called to see Mr. Anderson, who I found to be very entertaining. We had a long talk, he invited me to go in and spend the night with him, but I made the excuse that I had business of importance to attend to in town. I did not wish to refuse his kind offer I assure you. My plans are already fixed and I will now relate them to you, but before I go on I desire you to keep all a profound secret and I intend to make it to your advantage as well as my own, now will you promise?"

"Certainly, Mr. Peacock, I will ever keep it a secret if you say so, and help you if it is in my power."

"Well, John Hill, I do believe you are a man of your word, and not only that, you are a young man of influence, and I, being a stranger, cannot work out my plans alone. You are known as a good young man and I will make it to your interest to assist me. Now to be short about the matter, I desire to marry one of old man Anderson's daughters. By doing this I can raise ten thousand dollars, and I am getting short of money here of late. This amount would help me out considerably and set me all right. The plan I have set for doing this is to play off mineralogist, for I understand old Anderson has rich iron ore on his land and wishes to sell, so I called to see him and soon found I had struck on the very thing. I made him an offer conditionally. He was delighted and granted me the privilege of boarding at his house. Now that will give me an opportunity to get acquainted with his daughters. You see if all this is worked right I will be sure to succeed, then comes your reward."[17]

"Well, Mr. Peacock, no one but yourself ever would have thought of this, and you have struck the old man on his weakest point. If he becomes attached to a man he will believe everything he tells him. Why, sir, it has not been two years since a lawyer who was smart, but a terrible scoundrel, became intimate with him and actually led him so far as to defraud him out of all his mountain lands that lay several miles above here in a very mountainous region: and sir, if the right step had been taken that same lawyer could have been sent to the State Prison."[18]

"What was his name, Mr. Hill? I may need him."

"His name, Mr. Peacock, is Ol, and it is said, the court house here about was burnt very mysteriously one night, where all those papers were recorded, and it is believed he had a hand in it, but not much was ever said about it. I for one, always thought him a scoundrel and it was said he blackmailed an old man about a year ago and got some money out of him; the old man testified this much on his deathbed."

"But, John, were there not several heirs to the Anderson estate?"

---

[17] Possible name correlation for "Peacock the Mineralogist"...Charley's great uncle, Adam Peck, Jr. and family, settled in Dahlonega, Georgia and were involved in gold mining. In 1900 there was a man named Edward Peacock, an assayer and expert mineralogist, who helped with a gold mining company. Info gathered from the 21 Jan 1900 edition of Savannah, GA's *The Morning News* on page 9.

[18] During the 1800s, Judge Jacob Peck and his children amassed tens of thousands of acres of mountain lands. But as time went on, lawsuits, tax issues, and corporate business deals caused them to lose all but a few acres of their land.

"Oh, yes; there were five or six, and that is the reason why that scoundrel lawyer got the advantage of Mr. Anderson. He got the idiots on his side and Mr. Anderson, a proud man, did not care to be mixed up in the muddle."

"Well, John, old fellow, our time is short, let us talk of something that concerns me. This little matter of mine must be accomplished beyond a doubt. What I want you to do is to talk around the country in a very complimentary way of myself. Say I am rich, very rich, a great traveller; say it so it will be all heard at the Anderson house. Come while I am boarding there—stop, you know, unexpectedly; be very much surprised to find me acquainted with the family, quite a condescension on my part you think. Tell them of the letters I get from the Secretary of the Interior, saying what a fine mineralogist I am, that will take splendidly with the old coon. Hint to the girls of my style and refinement, my acquaintance with persons occupying high positions, letters you saw from high officials to me; in short, say all that will be of advantage to me and I will reward you handsomely."

The young man thought to himself, "you are an unprincipled scamp and can I trust you?" But the love of gain got the better of any scruples he may have had, but he answered [:]

"Mr. Peacock, it is strange to me to see how very easily people allow themselves to be imposed upon, men, too, who profess to be learned, well read men, but just let a man come along who can talk well on their favorite hobbies, you see how quick they allow themselves to be cheated, not only out of their lands, but out of their daughters to boot. Now just from what you say, old man Anderson and the neighbors, too, believe you are the finest mineralogist that ever came along, but to the best of my knowledge I don't believe you ever read a book on it, well, not more than enough to impose on people anyhow, but you are a man of fine appearance and can make a big show out of very little learning and accomplish your designs without much difficulty, because these simpletons give you every chance to help you along against themselves."

The sharper listened kindly to his tool's remarks, for the purpose of taking advantage [Page 1 End] of him when the time came round and to discover his other weak points beside the love of money and his wish to be noticed. But he had the mortification to feel that the creature could read him too plainly and he was studying how to say, but not too plainly, that he must find out others and not criticize [*sic*] him. His vanity had made him believe he was impenetrable. He thought, "Well, I shall see that he gets no chance to betray me," but spoke aloud in his deceitful tones:

"Well, John, you have made me your friend and good will come of it, I hope. I thank you for your frankness and kindness. You know if you didn't talk to me I could never know you so well. It is getting late and I must be going, so good-night, old fellow, until I see you again."

"Good night, Mr. Peacock, and good luck to you."

',Well, Peacock is gone and I can't tell why, but I like him and like to talk to him though he thinks he is better than I am. He has certainly traveled and has been rich. I don't think it will be any harm to help him, and I may be helping myself too, so I will try on the Andersons. Mary will have no chance for marrying better, but her friends will pity her before she has been married long. But I must live and to live by one's wit is now the order of the day. I will help him, be it as it may, good or bad."

CHAPTER III.

"Oh, girls, are you not glad? I have just had a note from Mr. Ashbury. He will be here to-morrow [*sic*] to tune the piano and it needs it. I would be ashamed for that stranger to hear you on it now as it is."

"Mamma, I am glad. I was thinking how badly it needed tuning while I was practising [*sic*]. Kate and I have been practising "Pinafore,' and we do it up splendid. Now that Mr. Whatever-his-name-is need not suppose he is coming among ignoramuses or yahoos. We want to surprise him. Eva, just wear your every day manner and that will be sufficient to inform him you are a lady."

"But, mamma, it makes me a little anxious and nervous, knowing a handsome, travelled gentleman is coming to see us."

"I see papa and John Miller coming in from work," said Mary, "and they look warm and tired."

"Oh, they have been in their dear celery patch," cried Kate.

"Well, girls, is dinner ready? I am tired and hungry. Eva, fetch me a glass of cold water. Mary, wash this celery and have it for dinner, quick. After dinner I must go to town on a matter of business and come back by my iron vein and get some specimens. I think that little patch is going to bring me out all right and then we can live in a little more style. I will get a carriage for you all to go to church in."

"Papa, thanks; that will be better than going in a wagon."

"Yes, Eva, much more stylish too. And I will get that lovely blue silk at Barnes' to add beauty to style," said laughing Kate.

"Well, you may get the lovely dress and I will get a fine cluster diamond ring and won't it sparkle at the country dances and the girls will think I am engaged to some foreign cabob."

"Papa, dinner is ready.

"Mary, that is the best news I have heard. Come, Miller, I know you are hungry. We dine on the back porch [in] this warm weather, screened from the sunlight by roses and vines. Mary, I know Mr. Peacock will be pleased with the way we dine, and this dinner is good enough for anybody; roast beef, quail on toast, green peas, lamb, celery and everything good. Now, if Mr. Peacock is not pleased with this dinner or our way of living, Queen Victoria could not please him."

"Oh, now if we had a fine house," said Eva, "everything would be complete."

"Eva, you are so hard to please. Papa, here comes Sammy Rollins."

"How d'ye Sammy, how do you do, and how are all at home?"

"All are well. I fetch a note for the young ladies."

"Read it Eva."

" 'Compliments of Mr. and Mrs. Rollins to Mr. Anderson and family and requests the pleasure of their company at a picnic to be given in honor of their son's birthday, at the big spring in Shady Grove, June 18th.' Papa will you go?"

"I am very busy, but I suppose I must go. Yes, we will be there, Sammy." And Sam takes his departure.

"Now," continued Mr. Anderson, "I will leave you to talk and make preparations. Miller, you can go to work in the garden. Leave no weeds and grass. So good-bye till you see me."

"Mary, what will you wear?"

"Something neat and suitable."

"Mary, it is given in honor of the eldest son corning of age. He will be a beau now."

"But none of mine, Kate."

"Mamma, will you go?"

"No, Eva, I must remain to receive Mr. Ashbury."

'But dear mamma wouldn't you rather go. [?]'

"No Mary, I do not care to go, I will send my young representatives and they will be sufficient, and the pleasures they enjoy will be compensation enough for use. I will assist you in any arrangements of your toilets you may need,"

The proposition was joyously accepted and a merry and busy evening passed.

"Mamma, here comes papa and some one is with him. Girls, hurry away with your finery and sweep up your scraps. Mamma, it is Mr. Ashbury. Mr. Ashbury, had I known it was you I would not have rushed away with my sewing."

"You took me to be a beau I suspect, Miss Katie."

"Papa, what is the news in town?"

"Not much that I heard. The only excitement is on politics, and you know Mary, I care little about politics now. There is too much dishonesty. Well, I did hear something of our young mineralogist. I met Mr. John Hill, a young man not easily imposed on, and he says he has been a good deal with him and has a right to think him a first-class gentleman and man of wealth and influence, and he himself saw letters to Mr. Peacock from high officials, the Secretary of the Interior and others, all of the most complimentary kind. They speak in high terms of his knowledge of mineralogy; I heard others speak of his agreeable manners and his fine conversational powers. Now girls, you will have a good chance to improve yourselves. I am glad I invited him here.

"Ah! husband, we can tell better when we become acquainted with him ourselves."

"We have no right to judge a stranger harshly until he gives us cause."

"You are right there, Mr. Anderson, I for one am glad to see men of intelligence and wealth coming into our country. Our mineral and timber lands are valuable. We only need capital to develope [*sic*] the wealth of our lands. We are too poor and broken up to do anything ourselves.

"That is all fine, Mr. Ashbury, and I will do what I can to forward any movement towards the improvement of our country."

"Mr. Ashbury, you will excuse our presence to-morrow for we are invited to a picnic and must go."

"Very excusable, Miss Katie."

"Mamma will remain at home. She does not wish to go."

"I hope not on my account, Miss Mary, I can tune the piano while you are all enjoying yourselves."

"Well, it has to be as Polly says, as she runs the household. Be ready by times in the morning, girls, good night. Mr. Ashbury, I will show you to your room."

CHAPTER IV.

"Girls, are you ready? Breakfast is on the table and we are waiting."

"Yes ma, we are coming, will all be ready in time for the wagon."

"Kate, I look horrid this morning, what is the matter with my complexion? I wanted to look my prettiest to-day."

"You are looking well enough, Eva, and the day's just begun."

"Well, go on Mary, and we will follow, you are all right."

"Girls, you are slow this morning."

"But not too late papa, for I suspect we will yet have to wait for you."

"Not long, as soon as you are ready we will go. Polly, you need not fear but I will keep a good watch on these wild girls of yours. Good-bye until evening; good morning Mr. Ashbury."

"Papa, this is a lovely day for the occasion. The flowers look prettier and the birds sing merrily this bright day. All nature is bright; I could not help feeling happy."

"Yes Mary, look where we will every-thing is beautiful, you girls too, as well. We will soon be in sight of the spring, it is just over that hill. See what a splendid view we have. Look! see what a crowd is coming. Now we hear the music; very good in Mr. Rollins to hire the band."

"We will have dancing now."

"Kate, don't you cut me out with the heir."

"Mary, there comes Ada Rollins; how beautiful she is!"[19]

The friends met, they laughed and talked, More [*sic*] persons came, the crowd increased to a multitude. Ada said in a low tone:

"Mary, I am so glad to see you. I want to talk to you away out of this crowd with no one near us. I have not been happy for a long time and have often wished for the solace of your kind sympathy; you know our hearts will ever turn toward one we call friend."

"That is true, Ada, we can bear our troubles better if we have a kind friend to sympathise [*sic*] with us. But I am afraid I am not capable to give advice."

"It is not advice I want, I want to know if you think people will be influenced by the reports against father. This electioneering has brought out so much rancor against all my family, I am sorry father became a candidate. I would rather have died than have passed through the humiliation of all this abuse. Ridicule and abuse have been heaped on us, and I suppose you have heard it all, Mary."[20]

"If I must tell you, I have, but loving your family as I do, I did not believe it."

---

[19] Charley's older sister, Ada Louise Peck, died when he was just two years old. She was their parents' firstborn, and she was very well loved. Through the years, numerous Peck family members were named Ada or some variation of the name. Charley's brother Ed named his daughter Adalaide (who then gave her daughter "Adalaide" as a middle name), and his brother Ashby named his daughter Ada Elizabeth. See *Ada's Journal* for more about Ada's life.

[20] The Peck Family were not strangers to public office. Charley's grandfather, Judge Jacob Peck, was a State Senator from Greene and Jefferson Counties. He was also a Tennessee Supreme Court Judge—so there would have been plenty of "eyes" on the family as Charley was growing up. And he may have heard stories from his father on this topic as well. Notably, two of his uncles, Wiley Hawkins Peck and William Raine Peck, held prominent office in Louisiana. Charles' great-uncle, James Hawkins Peck, was the first federal judge for the district of Missouri.

"Judge Page, our old neighbor, is very severe on father. You have heard him and he can make people so readily believe him."

"Ada, you must not let all this distress you so much. Let us drop this; our talking can't help the matter. Come, let us go and see how they are all enjoying themselves."

"Yes, and you must have some dinner. There is my father now, about to make a speech,"

"Just then came a shout: "A speech from Col. James Rollins, who has kindly consented to deliver us short address on the topics of the day."

The day's festivities came to an end [.] When going home Mr. Anderson wanted to know why Mary and Ada remained by themselves. "You were selfish and there were so many good-looking young men present. Well, Kate and Eva enjoyed themselves.

"Ah, papa, remember Ada and I are old friends and schoolmates and our opportunities to be together are few."

"Mary, I hope you and Ada did not go off to talk about your sweethearts."

"Oh, no, Eva, nothing was said on that subject." [Page 2 End]

"I heard papa reporting around amon[g] the girls that we were going to have a handsome young mineralogist to stay awhile at our house, and we would have some dancing parties, and I do believe some of them envy us."

"That is bad, I thought I was telling them something pleasant."

"Oh, papa, they were sorry they had not the honor to entertain Mr. Peacock. Some of them said it was a pity he had not a better name[.] But here we are at home; good-evening mamma, oh, we have had a splendid day!

CHAPTER V.

"Papa, what has become of Mr. Peacock?"

"To-morrow is the day he is to visit the iron mine, girls must fix up and have a fine dinner for him."

"Mamma will tell us how to do; so never fear, papa."

"Eva, here comes your beau, Mr. Smith, to have that game of croquet you promised him."

They not only had their game, but had music and something they called conversation. There was certainly something wrong in the atmosphere around about in that region, for while the laughing and nonsense was being carried on in the parlor, old aunt Betsey came with her budget of news, and making herself comfortable on the back porch where Mrs. Sanders and Mary were engaged preparing nice things for the next day's dinner, relieved her mind of the village gossip she had gathered.

"Aunt Betsey, it is evening and not morning."

"Dat's a fact, Miss Mary, but you know dis ole nigger's mem'ry aint' good no way. I tell you, Miss Anderson, there was a big row in town last night. You knows dat Dr. Philips as has dat drug store, and it's close to dat pretty white widow ooman's house. Mis Philips has been watching dem. Last night she listened, and she picked up a board and went for dat white ooman. Dat white man didn't stop to explain, but went outen de door like he had been struck by lightnin'; didn't stop till he had got inside dat drug store. Miss Philips bein' a big stout ooman, soon knocked down dat wider ooman. Folks came in and parted 'em. Lor massy! Look, Miss Mary, dar is a buggy coming right to your gate, and sure dar is your daddy with a man."

"Mary, go and see. I do believe the strange gentleman is hurt."

And he was. Mr. Smith was called out to assist in helping Mr. Peacock to his room. A doctor was sent for. The whole family were sorry and were devising remedies to relieve the intense pain he complained of. While his workman and assistant was digging for the best iron vein, unfortunately Mr. Peacock was underneath an embankment and the whole mass, rocks and all, fell in on him. The doctor made his examination and used remedies to relieve his patient: but thinking there was no serious hurt, wondered that he complained. But somehow Mr. Peacock convinced the whole family and the doctor too, that his delicate constitution, acute sensibility and the fine texture of his nervous system had received a severe shock, and pain with him, was so hard to bear.[21]

"Papa, how is Mr. Peacock now?"

"He is better, but very weak. The hot toddy[22] you made, Mary, revived him very much. I am afraid he will be confined to his room for several days. But, girls, this accident need not prevent your going to the dance to-morrow night. Mr. Day will be sure to come for you,"

"But, papa, I think I ought to remain with you and mamma."

"No, no necessity at all Mary, I can assist your father, and I want you to go with these madcaps, Eva and Kate. They are too wild to go alone, they will run on with too much foolishness."

---

[21] Both Charley's father, Isham, and brother, Ed, were physicians.
[22] Hot toddy = A hot toddy, also known as hot whiskey in Ireland, is typically a mixed drink made of liquor and water with honey (or, in some recipes, sugar), herbs (such as tea) and spices, and served hot. (Source: Wikipedia)

"Now mamma that is too bad to send Mary to keep us in check. We will only flirt the more."

"I have decided Eva and Kate."

"I have been thinking of trying to catch this handsome stranger, but I am afraid it will be useless as long as sensible sister Mary is in the way."

"Eva how you run on nonsense, and you a school girl."

"But I will not go to school any more, I know enough, I am old enough to have a beaux, and they all tell me I am pretty."

"They are as shallow pated as you are, and a pretty concern you would sit up with any one of them."

"Oh, mamma! Papa was she any smarter than I am when she was of my age, and am I not as pretty as she was?"

"Man's vanity will make papa say you are the prettiest, as you look like him, Eva."

"Well girls when you go to this party, I hope Sam Quills will not introduce another stranger to his wife as a single lady and then get up a fuss about it when he found they two were well pleased with each other, and were talking love in earnest. I will go and see how Mr. Peacock rests and then we will retire for the night; so good night girls."

CHAPTER VI.

The next morning did not promise to be fair, but it would have been happier for our party if it had rained in torrents all day and all night too. Dark as the morning was it did not prevent a visitor coming to see Mr. Peacock. Mr. John Hill hearing of his patron's mishap—but which he thought was purposely gotten up—hurried over to Mr. Anderson's house to see him. The kind attention he gave the invalid made all the family have respect and affection for him. Mr. John Hill was not idle. Whenever opportunity presented [,] he sounded the praises of "the best man in the world," and "the wealthy and accomplished gentleman traveler and scholar." His hearers listened eagerly and believed. Poor old Mr. Anderson thought the millennium [*sic*] had come, and he hoped Mr. Peacock would be pleased with Mary, and oh! if they should marry! What visions of future greatness rose up in his mind at the thought! But they did not prevent his going out to gather the vegetables, and help John Miller hunt for iron ore—specimens to show Mr. Peacock. The female portion of the family were very assiduous in their attentions to both Mr. Peacock and his friend, and listened, without doubting, to all the fine stories that either of them told.

Mr. Peacock was now one of the Anderson family. His recovery was slow; he could at times leave his room, and a lounge in the parlor was prepared for him. Very interesting he looked with his high, pale brow denoting intellect; but no one seemed to notice the cruel curve of the lip, or see the evil stare he gave when he thought he was unperceived. Those—his kind and honest-minded entertainers—never thought of analyzing a face that was agreeable to a superficial observation. The whole family rejoiced in his recovery. Mr. Anderson, in fact all the family, would say, "I like him better and better and better every day." He gave them his mother's letters to read, which they very much admired, and she wrote to May thanking her and her family for their kindness to her son. "Oh, Mr. Peacock was a great man, surely." One morning he told Mrs. Anderson that if he should take a drive it would be a benefit to him. The evening was appointed and he asked the pleasure of Miss Mary's company which she readily granted, provided her mother had no objections. Of course [,] none were made. When the time came round his buggy was at the door. Mrs. Anderson asked if his spirited looking horse was gentle.

"Oh, Mr. Peacock, you know mothers are timid."

"Mrs. Anderson, it is because you never experienced the raising of wild boys."

"That may be. I will not detain you any longer, good bye and a pleasant drive," says all of them. "Now, Polly, they are a handsome pair. I am thankful I met with him. If we get nearer connected he will save me a deal of trouble getting our iron lands worked."

Just then they were a happy family.

Mr. John Hill was an almost constant inmate there too, he always had something good and pleasant to tell of Mr. Peacock and he did not neglect to be very gallant to Miss Eva and Kate. The neighbors began to predict there would be two weddings soon at Mr. Anderson's. All of them had picked out Miss Mary for the wealthy Mr. Peacock.

"Miss Mary, your lives have been cast in a beautiful country with a delightful climate," said Mr. Peacock. "In Vermont, where I had my home from early boyhood, it is too cold and bleak."

"Mr. Peacock, we have very cold weather here."

"But your winters are not so long or so cold as there where we are frozen up the winter through."

"Here we have a cold spell, but have soon again some weather that is warmer."

"I don't like those changes, they are not healthy."

"I enjoy them very much. I think that is the delightfulness of our climate. We are not worn out with one kind of weather, and never having been sick I never think of sickness."

"How is it then your very presence seems to relieve the tedium of a sick room? My aches and bruises were not so painful when I could see you, but I fear, Miss Mary, my heart will have to pay the penalty for the enjoyment I had in seeing you."

"Mr. Peacock, I would think the advantages you have had in travelling and seeing so much, would save you from being very impressible, and please do not try to make me believe what is impossible."

"Miss Mary, I did think you were too good to doubt my truth, my sincerity. Amid all my wanderings I never met with one like yourself. I saw you twice by chance. You did not seem to see me, but even then you threw a spell around me. Since I have seen you without ceremony, domiciliated as I have been in your house, you have realized my beau ideal of female loveliness; lovely in form and feature, in sweetness and gentleness of character, and with all, a firmness to defend the right. Indeed, I already love you devotedly."

"Mr. Peacock, you embarrass me: I had no idea of hearing such sentiments from you."

"And why should you think I have not the feelings I try to express. I am no hypocrite, Mary, but I did try to conceal from you all I felt— the joy of your coming in, the despondency when you left me. One day you came and said I had been idle, because I had not read the book you gave me; but, Mary, I had not been idle, I was forming to myself an ideal world. I was building up an earthly paradise with you by my side. Will you encourage the belief? Will you not give me hope? Say something that I may cling to as a hope. If you cast me off, shipwrecked indeed will I be then. All my hopes of future happiness will be gone, you—you alone can save me, can give me happiness, to live for your love and to cherish you above all earthly love. Your love is all I ask for on this earth," and Mr. Peacock looked his love in his eyes as he talked to the poor girl by his side. [Page 3 End]

"Mr. Peacock," said the bewildered Mary, "this is a subject I never thought much on, you must allow me a few days before I can give an answer. You must let my father know the subject of your conversation to me. We have no secrets in our family, Mr. Peacock."

"Mary, I then will hope. I will live on hope. I will speak to your father, and oh! I hope he will not disdain to give his jewel into my keeping. What would life be to me without you, my Mary?" She softly raised her pretty eyes and said:

"Mr. Peacock, you have not been indifferent to me. You interested me the first time I saw you and my sympathy was awakened from your sufferings. I must own there was something peculiar in our acquaintanceship, something out of the ordinary course."

"Oh! how happy you make me, my Mary. I see we are in sight of home, can you not give me a few moments to ourselves this evening?"

"Our little parlor is where we meet of evenings and it is there where all are expected to be."

The pair were met by all the family, hoping Mr. Peacock was better and that Mary had a very pleasant ride.

CHAPTER VII.

Morning dawned in sunshine and beauty. Mr. Peacock was feeling quite happy over the progress he had made with the one upon which he had centered all his thoughts and hopes and the treasure he now considered within his grasp. His heart beat with joy. Mr. Anderson was sitting on the front porch enjoying his pipe as usual.[23] Mr. Peacock approached in his usual pleasant manner.

"Fine morning., Mr. Anderson."

"It is indeed, Mr. Peacock, and how are you feeling after your drive?"

"Quite well, except a pain from the hurt that still remains, but I gain strength fast in your bracing climate. It will be but a short time before I am quite well, I think. Mr. Anderson, I feel it my duty to approach a subject in which I am deeply interested and to the interest of one I hold dearer than any earthly treasure, and for whom I would sacrifice every earthly pleasure. That person is your charming daughter, Mary, with whom I have recently had a conversation on the subject and having received some encouragement, I deem it my duty to inform you before proceeding farther, hoping from the bottom of my heart it

---

[23] Charley's father, Dr. Isham Peck, was known to always be smoking his meerschaum pipe (and reading his newspapers).

will meet with your approbation. The love I bear her is deep and unalterable."

"Well, Mr. Peacock, the subject comes to me so suddenly, I hardly know what to say, but as to yourself I can find no fault what-ever. 'Tis true, you are a stranger in this country; but your actions prove you to be a gentleman, and the letters you have from prominent men fully attest your worth and standing, not only at home, but abroad; and now turning to my daughter Mary, it will be hard to give her up. Her services and advice are felt throughout our little household. She was always my favorite daughter, but I must remember that the first duty of a parent to his children is to look to their interest and not stand back on personal feelings. One word of this kind might blast the future hopes and peace of our children. I shall never say one word, Mr. Peacock, to disappoint their hopes, for I love them too dearly. I know I must soon die and would feel better satisfied if I knew my daughters were comfortably situated in life, and I wish my children to make their own choice with those they expect to spend their lives with. I will further say, if you and Mary can agree I shall not object in the least."

"Mr. Anderson, I shall do my best to make your daughter happy. My every thought shall be devoted to her. I will also try and be a son to you in affection and respect. My mean abilities will always be at your service. I shall try to be all you and your admirable family desire in a member of your household."

"Mr. Peacock, I believe you, I do from my heart."

"I know you feel badly at the idea of giving Mary away, but then you will gain a son." So they shook hands heartily on it. Just then a man passed on down the road. "That is the old gentleman that keeps the little country inn or hotel half a mile or so below here, what is his name?"

"Mr. Peacock, his name is Agen. He is an old friend of mine. I met that family before the war and we have always been good friends.

He has two aged sisters and they are mighty fine women. I visit them every day and always find them the same thing."

"I have stopped there," said Mr. Peacock, "They are talkative and easy of approach, are they not?"

"Yes, they are not proud."

"Well, Mr. Anderson, I heard them speak in high terms of you. Stranger as I was, they also showed me a pipe which you gave one of them. True, I suppose?"

"Yea, Mr. Peacock, it is true. The pipe was sent as a Christmas present to me by my daughter Kate; but, Mr. Peacock, you know there is nothing like making friends with outsiders and I gave the pipe to one of them. Kate was mighty mad and hurt at what I did. There is the dinner bell. We will go to dinner, Mr. Peacock."

The dinner was good and Mary had the credit of preparing the nicest dishes. There is no better place for pleasant, social chat than at the table. Mr. Peacock took advantage of every turn to play the agreeable. He was witty and paid sly compliments to the ladies and to Mary in particular. With Mr. Anderson, he humored him to the top of his bent about his valuable iron ores. After dinner Mr. Peacock asked if the family had any commands for town—he was feeling so well he would go in on a little business he had to see to, and as he had to pass by Mr. Agen's hotel, would call there to see his gold specimens.

"He will be glad to see you and show you all of his specimens. I think he has found rich ore recently."

"Probably, Mr. Anderson, I can be of service to him, for the company I represent are the richest in the United States," and Mr. Peacock took Miss Mary's hand and whispered his good-bye, bowed to the others and left.

"This is a beautiful country," thought he, "mountains, hills and valleys with one or the other always in sight; flowing, clear streams on every side, and the blue, hazy atmosphere is enchanting. I must say nature has done much, man nothing: a field or patch here and there, but no energy is visible."

"Good morning, Mr. Agen, how do you do?"

"I am not well, Mr. Peacock."

"I see you do not look well, Mr. Agen. Are the rest of your family well, Mr. Agen?"

"No, sir, they are all 'complaining.' "

"Mr. Agen, my friend, Mr. Anderson, told me you had found a gold mine on your place?" "I say, I say, I gad! I say I have found the pure stuff. I have found it just as sure as you are a living man," and Mr. Agen, rummaging [*sic*] in an old sack full of rocks, got out two or three which glistened with yellow specks, and Mr. Peacock knew at a glance they were what the New York Sun called "fool's gold," nothing but pyrites of iron, but in appearance of sincerity, he exclaimed,

"Why, Mr. Agen, these are the finest specimens I have seen. Can the land be bought?"

"Mr. 'Peacock, I say, I gad! I think it could."

"Well, sir, do you know where the land is?"

"I know all about it, but I don't intend to let any one know where it is until I get it secure."

"Well, Mr. Agen, I would advise you to secure it at any price. It will be a fortune to you. I am sorry I have to go to town to-day. I would rather stay and talk about this fine specimen. Good-day."

"I say, I say, 'gad! Ninthy, I have found the pure stuff now. I showed it to the mineralogist. He says it's gold beyond a doubt."

"Well, White, I want you to make all the money you can. That is what makes us so great. It's our money."

"I gad! Ninthy, I must go feed my hogs. I say, I must talk more about it."

CHAPTER VIII.

"Well, John, old boy, I have not seen you for several days."

"I am happy to see you, Mr. Peacock, and congratulate you. You, like the great Julius, came, saw and conquered. Take a seat and tell me the news."

"Many, many thanks, John, for the assistance you have given me, and, old boy, it will not lead to anything that will lay us up in lavender. I have good news for you. I first talked to Mary and she referred me to her father. It is all right now. I struck fast while the iron was hot and won. That was the time. No faint heart ever won a fair lady or anything else worth having. Now, John, visions of gold begin to loom up in my mind and how you and I can have it all our own way among these sons of the mountains. "

"Mr. Peacock, I had no idea you would succeed in so short a time."

"John, I will want you to help me again, I will see the Anderson family and have the day set for the marriage. Then on pretence [*sic*] of business North will leave them; and don't you leave a stone unturned that will benefit me. Of course, my going North will be to procure the money for putting up large iron works on the Anderson property. All this I will tell before leaving."

"Mr. Peacock, that is the plan. Now I will know what to do, but why don't you extend your plan and take in that old opinionated Agen. He is too conceited. Do you know him? He brags that he knows you."

"I know him and a glance made me acquainted with the whole batch of them. Too stuck up on too little. Old man Anderson likes them to brag on their acquaintance with him. It is strange how some men will swallow flattery. Anderson will like any one who brags on him and flatters him. If he can't find the man refined he will fall back on the Agen sort."

"In one way they are pretty sharp, Mr. Peacock; if it had been them you were dealing with, you would have had to show some thing more substantial than mere letters. More money with them. You call them old fogies. A sharp old fellow who wanted a home and money and who was nearly a hundred years old came courting Miss Ninthy. She read him and sent him the way he came. She valued her money too highly to share it with him."

"Ha, ha, John, old fellow, I don't think they could have baffled me in any plan I should have had. I must look over their land and see if it is as valuable as people say. I don't know that I shall want it, but you know I will take all I can get. But first let us see what disposition I will make of it."

"I can use it, Mr. Peacock."

"Yes, John, I will see that you share my good luck.'"

"I must be going now, Mr. Peacock. Good bye until you see me again."

"You must come over pretty often. Do all you can to glorify me."

"He is gone and now I will plan."

"Mr. Anderson, I desire to have a talk with yourself and wife. From a letter I got to-day from the company, I find it my duty to go North, as they desire to see me on important business and they also wish to know what discoveries I have made in this delightful region. I am satisfied I can effect [*sic*] much more through conversation than writing. I am anxious they should put up large iron works on your premises. It would add to the country and be such a great benefit to yourself."

"I hope you may succeed, Mr. Peacock, in all your undertakings, for I take great interest in you, and a great deal more in my dear daughter's welfare." [Page 4 End]

"Well, Mr. Anderson, I desire to say this to yourself and wife, that if agreeable to you and to Mary, I would like to have the day set for our marriage, for then I can have an idea when to hasten my return and to fix my business accordingly."

"Well, Mr. Peacock, I am willing to leave that to you and Mary. Well, Mary, what do you say?"

"Papa, I am perfectly willing to await Mr. Peacock's wishes. He knows his business better than I do. I will leave it to his convenience and what time he thinks best."

"Well, as far as I am concerned," replied Mr. Peacock, "any time that will suit yourself will best suit me. Business alone prevents me from begging for an early day, and what do you say to the tenth of August? This is June. A long time for me to wait, but the company will be expecting me soon. On that day you may expect me promptly, dear one. Will you take a stroll with me?"

"Most certainly, Mr. Peacock."

"Well, Polly, I think this is one of my happiest days. To think and realize that our Mary is to be married to a man of wealth and influence. She certainly deserves it all, for she has ever been a dear, good child. You can all enjoy yourselves at dinner to-day without me. I am going to see my old friend, Mr. Agen."

"Girls, I feel very badly to-day. I do not like to see Mary get married."

"Why, mother?"

"Well, for sound reasons. I do not like Mr. Peacock as well as your father does, and I do really believe Mary could have made a better choice; but as it is settled now I will make no objection, for if I should be wrong in regard to it I would ever be blamed for being a fool."

"I hope, mother, that it will all turn out for the best and no one will have to be blamed in any way."

"Well, Mrs. Anderson, Mary and I have had a pleasant walk and I feel better from talking and listening to her. I regret very much that I must leave in the morning, for every link I move from her I feel the weight of my chain more severely."

"Well, Ninthy are you the housekeeper today. [?]"

"Yes, Mr. Anderson, they always put that on me while they are enjoying themselves. How are all your folks?"

"I believe they are all well, Ninthy."

"Well, we are the same here. Tell me the news, Mr. Anderson."

"Well, I will, Ninthy, and I will tell you something in regard to our young mineralogist."

"Sure enough? I hope nothing is wrong."

"Oh, no; to the contrary, it is very good. But I don't want you to tell it to any one at present, for my daughter is concerned in it."

"Oh, me, what can it be?"

"In short, my daughter Mary is to be married to Mr. Peacock in August. He starts North in a few days for the purpose of procuring money to put up large, iron works on my property. I assure you I am sorry to have him leave, for I like him, and he talks a great deal in regard to myself, He says I am a man of very fine sense and judgment. I tell you, Ninthy, it makes me feel proud and grand. Then I tell him of my adventures and he is well pleased to listen to me; takes in every word."

"Well, does Mary like Mr. Peacock as well as you do?"

"Oh, yes; fully as well."

"I am satisfied it will be a good match, Mr. Anderson. I hope Mr. Peacock will succeed in putting up large iron works on our lands. It will improve the country so much, and I really think White has found gold. If so, it will attract rich people to come here and they will leave money behind them. Mr. Anderson, they say dinner is ready; walk in."

"Miss Ninthy, have you lettuce and fish?"

"Oh, yes, sir."

"Then, to be sure I will go dine with you." Just at this moment a woman's voice was heard crying:

"Oh, Mr. Agen, save me, for God sake!"

"Why, what is the matter, my dear woman?"

"I have taken paths through the mountains to save my life from a drunken brute who is following me, and trying to force me into another State to live with him."

"I say, Igad, I say, are you his wife?"

"Oh, no sir, I am not; and I hope you will save me that I never may be, for he is a very bad man—the vilest of wretches. He thinks if he forces my little child from me that will force me to marry him; he knows I cannot give up my child. My husband died last year, and since then I have been destitute of a home. I only ask your protection until I can leave on the train. I wish to leave this country to escape this brute."

"Well, I say, Igad, I say, madam, I don't wish to see a fuss in my house, and I say, I think it would be best for you to leave. I say, Igad, I say, you had better leave."

"Oh, Mr. Agen, for God sake, don't drive me off. Have mercy for a poor helpless woman and child."

"I say, Igad, I say, Mr. Anderson, come out here."

"What is the matter, Mr. Agen?"

"Why, this woman says there is a man who threatens her life if she does not give up her child to him."

"Mr. Agen, you know my dignity will not let me get into fusses of this kind. It would be better if she would go at once to the train."

"Oh, Mr. Agen, yonder he comes at full speed. Don't turn me away! don't turn me out to be at the mercy of that drunken wretch."

"I say, Igad, I say, you must go. Go out the back way to the depot."

The poor woman had just time to get into a back yard when the wretch came charging up with pistol in hand, and demanded the woman and child. Agen, much frightened, had recourse to his favorite expletive more vehemently than usual.

"I say, Igad, I say, I have seen no woman; I have no woman concealed from you."

"You are a liar and a fool besides!" thundered the man, "I have traced her here;—bring her out, and her child, too, or I will blow your head off."

"I say, Mr. Anderson, what am I to do?"

"Agen, rather than have a fuss and run the risk of being shot, if I were you I would give her to him.

"I say, Igad, I say, I will go and find her.'

The woman was hiding and in mortal fear, holding on to her child, and both were crying.

"I say, Igad, I say, come outen them bushes this moment; I ain't going to be killed for you; I ain't, I say. Oh, Ninthy, come help me!"

"Oh, you wretch, for you to come here and make my brother run the risk of getting killed for you."

"Miss Ninthy, have mercy, I pray!"

"Come on, I haven't a word for sich as You. Take hold of her, White, and we'll take her to him."

The woman screamed, but in vain; they were strong as mules, and succeeded in dragging the woman and child in sight of the man, who said:

"Oh, I have got you now!"

Then he slapped the woman over and yelling in fury at her— clutching up the baby boy by the leg and dangling him about, head down, and threatening those present with dire vengeance if they interfered. Presently a quiet looking gentleman, with delicate form, rode up. His face as mild as a woman's, inspired the swearing bully with no fears. The mild looking gentleman took in the situation at a glance—the unprotected woman and little child, the time-serving brother, and sister, the timid old man and the armed ruffian who had them cowering before him. Mr. Hill, for it was that gentleman who had come, alighted from his horse and walked up to the woman and asked what was the matter?

"Oh, please sir, save me and my poor child from that bad man."

"Is he your husband?"

"Oh, no sir," then she screamed as she saw her child swung through the air and the man swearing he would kill both child and the mother.

"Oh, sir, save us, I have done no wrong, and yet Mr. Agen and that old man nor Miss Ninthy will protect me."

A fresh scream from the woman, as she saw a new danger. The ruffian was pointing his pistol at Mr. Hill, who turned to him and ordered him to hush his swearing, and to put up his weapon, and to put the child immediately down."

"You dare not take up this matter, you simpleton! Just you do and I will kill you. Fool, leave me, or I will kill you."

"I will make you put down that child, and free this poor woman from your vile clutches first; put down that child," and Mr. Hill attempted to catch the suffering boy. The ruffian dropped the child and struck at Hill with his pistol and then shooting at him, barely missing him; striking again he hit Hill a tremendous blow on the face which made him stagger for an instant, but regaining self-possession he drew his revolver and fired! The fellow fell, struggled a few moments and ceased to breathe.

"He is dead!" cried Ninthy.

Hill dropped his pistol and casting his eyes upon the body exclaimed:

"God forgive me for this act; I have now the blood of a fellow man upon my hand, still I feel I have done no wrong!"

The woman kisses her child, then timidly approaches Hill, fearing she knew not what, dreading his displeasure but begging his forgiveness for implicating him, praying he will forgive her, and to receive her deep and earnest thanks for the protection he gave her. Hill in his quick, earnest manner told her not to distress herself about him, that he was only defending his own life, he desired to give himself up to proper authorities; a party was dispatched for the Coroner, who was an old Dutchman that lived a short distance off to hold an inquest over the dead body. Soon a large crowd assembled about the place and none seemed prejudiced against Hill, but he said:

"Gentlemen, I am very sorry I had to do such an act, it was not only done in self-defence [*sic*], but I was trying to protect a woman and child from brutal treatment by a vagabond. I regret that it occurred, I regret the termination of my attempt to do a charitable act. I saw no protection given by Mr. Agen, and he could have given the woman shelter, and shut his doors against the entrance of a vagabond, and I must say it was a surprise to me to see such cowardice. A true man would scorn to be guilty of such conduct."

Hill's brow looked very much changed since he rode up with that innocent face, he now looked as if he could face cannon balls without a single fear. Just then the old Dutch Coroner, Otawer, came and immediately summonded [*sic*] a Jury. After hearing the evidence, and what had to be said, a verdict was brought in that the man came to his death by a wound received from a pistol in the hand of John Hill— and we do further say, that it was done in self defence—and we do most honorably acquit Mr. Hill. At this a loud cheer went up, that sounded through the woods. The old Coroner at hearing all this and the noble qualities of the young man, went up and kindly offered his hand, which was grasped in thankfulness for his acquittal. Mr. Otawer was fond of meeting strangers, for he thought it would be quite an honor to relate something in regard to his family; so he proceeds as follows: [Page 5 End]

"Well, Mr. Hill you "air" one of the finest young men there "air," and I would like very muchly for you to come up and see me and meet my family, for there air our Jossie, she air just one of the finest gals there are and then there are Hester, she air just a plum belle, but sar my darter "Elloon" she are just one of the most business gals there are in the whole country, she, by-gad can cotch a horse and ride it just the same as any other boy, and there air Catherine, she air a splendid wife, for she makes zarves and jams."

"Well, Mr. Otawer, I know your family must be very interesting, and I shall be delighted to call the first opportunity; it is getting late and I must leave now. Gentlemen, let me thank you, and bid you good evening."

"Well, Mr. Anderson, won't you stay longer and talk all this over?"

"Mr. Agen, I don't want to express any opinion on the subject of this difficulty, you know I never like to lose the good will of any one," and Ninthy said:

"Why, Mr. Anderson I heard a beautiful, and rich young lady from Mississippi say she thought Mr. Hill a grand looking gentleman, now she will say he is a hero; she was very anxious to make his acquaintance, and as he is now going up to the Springs she will now be sure to do so. Mr. Anderson, you must be on his side now. I will go see what became of that woman."

"Sit longer, Mr. Anderson?"

"No, Mr. Agen, I will go home. You must come to see me."

Figure 3 - Patton Hotel, Warm Springs, NC, Circa 1880. Warm Springs changed its name to Hot Springs on 3 Nov 1891. Image courtesy of NC Collection, Pack Memorial Library.

Figure 4 - Bethlehem Steel Works, Bethlehem, Pennsylvania, May 1881, by Joseph Pennell (1857-1926). https://www.loc.gov/pictures/item/9517130/, Library of Congress, Public Domain, accessed 28 Aug 2021

Figure 5 - The Iron Rolling Mill (Modern Cyclopes), German "Eisenwalzwwerk", Oil on canvas, by Adolph von Menzel (1815-1905), Public Domain

Figure 6 - 1885, The Iron Foundry, Burmeister and Wain, Danish "Fra Burmeister og Wains jernstøberi, Oil on Canvas, by Peder Severin Krøyer, located at the National Gallery of Denmark in Copenhagen, Public Domain

CHAPTER IX.

"Polly I wish you would have some coffee made, my friend Agen will be up to see me on a matter of business; in fact to see me in regard to his gold mine, he wants my advice, he likes to hear me talk on mineralogy. He believes he has a rich gold mine, not only in the rocks, but the very bottom of the creek to be full of it. I will walk down now to see how Miller is getting along with his work."

"Mary, you look real sad; Mr. Peacock's leaving has had a bad effect on you, come rally, you must not grow serious, sis Mary."

"Oh no, Kate, I was merely guessing over the future, and wondering what would be the end of all this; I feel as if I was in a dream; but I must try to make all happy around me, and I will try to make life as useful as possible. Kate, there is Pa and Mr. Agen, we will put the chairs on the porch."

"Mr. Agen; have a seat, it is more pleasant out here than in the house," and they made themselves comfortable in their big cane rocking chairs on the gallery. Their comfort was provocative of chat on this bright cheerful day. Mr. Agen felt like talking gossip, and said, "Mr. Anderson I suppose you like Hill better now; and what does Kate think of what he did?"

"She has not said much, and I think I shall do as I have heretofore done, still refuse my consent to his marrying Kate, I think Agen, I have good reasons for not giving my consent."

"Well then maybe he will court and marry that Mississippi girl up at the springs, they say she is in love with him."

"Well I am glad if she takes him off my hands. I heard she said you and I were arrant cowards, and Hill a hero."

"Mr. Anderson, Ninthy you know is powerful to find out news, she thinks Hill is gone to see that rich girl. But I want to talk to you; Igad I believe thieves are stealing my gold?"

"Agen, where is this gold?"

"Well, I say igad, a man brought me some specimens the other day he said he got it up the creek; I believe it is on your place and mine. What I wish to suggest is this, I think the entire creek is full of gold, ought we not have a guard there to watch it, Mr. Anderson?"

"Agen, I am satisfied it would be the very plan, we can get a trusty fellow."

"Mr. Anderson, I do not think we could get a better person than old Kiley Lawson. I don't think he would steal, and we could give him orders to report on others."

"Well Agen employ him and tell him not to let any one know his business."

Agen had gone to see Lawson. Hill and a young friend made a plan to fool the old creature. They got up a pound or two of old brass, filed it up like gold dust and placed it under a shelving rook in the creek. By this time Lawson came and had been stationed at his post to watch, the sum of ten dollars per month was to be given him; the mischievous friends knowing this, got a mountaineer to go and look for gold, but to be very cautious and not be seen, and they would give him an interest in the gold. While the old soul was finding and washing what he supposed to be gold. Agen and Lawson comes up on him before he sees them.

"Ah," says Agen, igad, I say, I have you now and will have you tried in a court of justice for this sin, igad, I say, I will."

"Oh, kind sirs, I meant no harm. I was only trying to see what I could find."

Mr, Agen proposed a compromise with him, he would test it himself and pay him five dollars, provided he would never say anything about it in any way, to anybody, which he at once consented to do. He left Agen and Lawson talking it over.

"Lawson, igad I say, I will pay you the amount of a month's wages and let you go, for I don't want a single person, I say, igad, I say, to know where this valuable place is," and Agen went to see his dear friend, Mr. Anderson. He was much excited.

"Mr. Anderson, I say, igad, I have found the pure stuff, and it is in a public place on the creek. I dare not attempt to work there in daylight. We must work there by moonlight and no one will know of it. I believe from indications I can work out a hundred dollars a day."

"Great Lord! is it possible, Agin?"

"Yes sir! Anderson, you must not tell a soul."

"Oh, no, no, not for the world."

After dark[,] Agen gets a pan and starts for the place where he thought thousands of dollars were hidden from human eyes. He passed on very cautiously and at last reached the place. He looked cautiously around him to be sure he was alone, then rolled up his sleeves and waded in up to his knees, reached under the rock and brought out a handful of the shining metal that he had so longed for. When he had finished one panful the quantity seemed inexhaustible and greater than he had expected. He became excited and often repeated igad in the fullness of his glad heart.

"Igad, this is the fortune that I long thought I would have; now that I have got it in possession my heart is overflowing with joy."

After getting something like a pint cup full he started for the house in triumph, visions of imaginary importance filling his mind. He slipped, cold and wet, into his room and softly deposited his treasure under lock and key. If it had not been for his want imaginings he would have felt the cold to be painful, but up in the seventh heaven of his desires, he disregarded in a measure physical pain until he had a very strong reminder of his rheumatism. In the morning at breakfast[,] he complained of it--could hardly move. Ninthy was uneasy and said it was because he was out in the cold the other day, trying to protect that woman. He and Ninthy disagreed about some patent medicine, but she carried the day, and he expressed himself as somewhat relieved.

"Ninthy, I have found it, sure enough."

"Found what? White, what do you mean? You are not losing your mind, are you?" she exclaimed.

"The very gold itself, and in such quantities."

She walked briskly while he hobbled on to show her his precious treasure.

"Oh, White! this room is too public to keep this in."

Just then a gentleman walked up, looking very tired. He had a haversack thrown over his shoulder and said he wished dinner, and that he was a mineralogist and desired to know if that was a specimen of the lands he was holding in his hands, and what was it?"

"I say, igad, I say it is pure gold itself and I know where I got it."

The man examined some or it for a few minutes and asked where he got that stuff. "I say, igad, I say, I will not tell; I don't intend to tell any one, for I can wash out thousands myself."

"Thousands of what, my dear sir?"

"I say, igad, I say gold, sir."

"Well, sir, let me say if you call that gold you are badly mistaken. Why, sir, that is nothing but filed up brass. Some one has been putting a job on you. Here, take my glass and look at it and you will soon find I out it is not in a natural state."

Agen looked, and his countenance fell from the brightest anticipations to the saddest reality.

"Well, I say, igad, on my word I have been fooled again. I say, igad, I say they have not only played off on me but on Anderson too, and have caused me to take my death of cold. I say, I do believe it has run into asthma, and it has cost me and Anderson money to hire men to guard the creek."

The mineralogist did not retain his politeness but burst out laughing. He laughed so long at the lugubrious[24] face of Agen that he got mad and Ninthy was mad too, to think how White was treated, and maybe by those who had eaten of her dinners. That was too bad. White, who was manager of farm and hotel, had caught cold and had both asthma and rheumatiz [*sic*] and probably would die and then she would be left alone to be robbed of her money.

The mineralogist composed himself enough to offer sympathy and hope it was not so bad as she feared, but she would not listen to sympathy or reason. She still lamented the ills, but the loss of the mine was the last drop that overflowed the cup of her sorrow. She was like Rachel, she would not be comforted. Agen had various fears to distress him. He knew of the ridicule that would be rained down on him when it became known, and there was the money given away in hiring men to keep guard, but the worst was the terrible loss of all that gold. "Oh, me, I shall never get over this!" [Page 6 End]

---

[24] Lugubrious = exaggeratedly or affectedly mournful : dismal

Figure 7 - "We have it rich." Washing and panning gold, Rockerville, South Dakota. Old timers, Spriggs, Lamb and Dillon at work. 1889, by John C. H. Grabill. Library of Congress, https://lccn.loc.gov/99613951, accessed 28 Aug 2021.

CHAPTER XI.

Miss Bessie Laurette; the young and beautiful heiress from Mississippi, had expressed herself in love with Mr. Hill for his bravery, handsome face and fine presence, she shocked her father by her undisguised praise but he had indulged her in all her whims and laughed at her fancies. He pretended now to chide her but ended in agreeing with her.[25]

Mr. Hill was very much flattered, and most agreeably surprised, at the news his friends brought from the springs in regard to himself. So he resolved to make the young lady's acquaintance and in a few days after the catastrophe went there, dressed in his best style and with good taste. He received a warm reception from the hospitable proprietor, pleasant salutations from friends and acquaintances that he met on the way to his room. After adjusting his dress and fixing his hair, he

---

[25] Name correlation: There was a well-known young widow named **Bessie** Rumbough who lived in Hot Springs, North Carolina at the time Charley wrote his novel. Her husband, Andrew Johnson, Jr., the son of ex-president Andrew Johnson, died on 12 Mar 1879, just one month prior to Charley writing the serial. Notably, Bessie hosted a luncheon at her home after Charley's brother Ed's funeral in Hot Springs in 1927. And when Bessie died in 1930, she was most likely staying at the home of Charley's brother Louis's in-laws, the Perkins, in Jacksonville, FL. Bessie's home in Hot Springs was called "**Loretta**," which sounds very similar to "Laurette." Her family owned the Warm Springs Patton Hotel and Charley's father, Isham, was close with her father, Col. James Henry Rumbough. See 10 May 1882 entry in *Sawbones* by Cross Mountain Books for details.

determined to see the proprietor and learn something about the young lady.

"Are you well enough acquainted,'" said he, "with Miss Laurette to give me an Introduction?"

"Oh, yes, Mr. Hill; she is the belle of the springs; and not only that but quite wealthy, worth a million, I have heard."

"Good Heavens! a million? I am afraid now to ask for an introduction; that will put a stop to all I desired,"

"Why what can that be?"

"I wished to make her acquaintance."

"Your desire shall be gratified if it is in my power. Remain here and I will see you again in a few moments."

Mr. Hill was seated where he could look into a private parlor where there were a number of ladies, some middle aged, some older, some in their teens and a few just entering into the twenties, but of all in the crowd there was one little sprite, who seemed to set order and dress at defiance, and who had a fascination for Hill, he never before felt. He sat and looked like one entranced, but it was the fairy-like figure, bright-eyed, talkative, and, merry little lady that charmed him. He wished he knew her. At a little distance sat a stately young lady reading, she was regal looking in black velvet and diamonds, and Mr. Hill selected her as the heiress. How much now he dreaded the promised introduction. Mr. H. the proprietor, entered and he and the group of ladies were soon having a merry tune laughing and talking— the carelessly dressed little lady appeared to be high priestess of fun and wit, presently he approached the lady that was reading, some few words were said and Mr. H. left. He came to Mr. Hill—who had moved his seat near a nice looking gentleman, with a portfolio of landscapes— and informed him that the lady would be happy to be introduced to him after supper. He wished to ask about the little beauty, but all at once felt his usual self-possession desert him. Mr. H. invited him to walk round and see the improvements lately made.

"This house we are now leaving was the first building put up here, but all the rest are new. The two Ls running back her fountains in the centre."

"But, how do you get the water, or the power to throw the water to such an immense height?"

"That is easily explained, you see our water courses rise at least one hundred feet to the mile, I have my pipes to begin on the side of yon mountain, which is at least two hundred feet above us; that being the case, you understand, we are freely and plentifully supplied. Here is my garden, but the bell will soon ring, we will return."

While Mr. Hill was smoking after supper he soon entered into conversation with the gentleman he had seen with the port-folio, and who was a landscape painter, who informed him that he had that morning sketched the "Lovers Leap," and thought it the finest effort of his life.

"I prize it for its beauty, and the romance affects me. Standing where the lovers stood, I thought what a pity people should be such fools."

"I never heard the story, and I hope you will tell it to me?" said Mr. Hill.

"Well, they say a young, talented, and handsome man, came to this region years ago; was said to be of a haughty and imperious family, aristocratic in feelings, prejudice and blood. This only son they had built high hopes upon. He had been elected to is high position while others of his age had scarcely finished an academical course. While here he saw a young lady, his equal in beauty and talent, but not in birth and wealth—they loved, and engaged themselves to marry. Then the young man wrote to his parents asking their consent, but there came a wail from his far off Southern home, begging and imploring him, not to disgrace himself and them; and they never would give their consent. The son knew too well the implacable resolution of his parents to say more to them, his resolve was to die if he could not marry the one he loved so well, the lady said she would not marry without the consent of his parents, he knew too well it would be useless to apply again to them, he met the lady soon after receiving the fatal letters; she saw in an instant—with love's eyes—that her doom was sealed.

"James, oh, James, what can be the cause of your turning away from me?"

Figure 8 - Kate May (Bessie) Safford, 1891, Ready to meet Queen Victoria, when she was presented at the court of St. James, from "Hot Springs of North Carolina" by Della Hazel Moore, p64, published 2002.

Figure 9 - "Lover's Leap" - In the heart of the Blue Ridge Mountains - A Scene at Hot Springs, NC (Photo Asheville Post Card Co., Asheville, N.C.)

"I cannot tell you here, will you walk with me? Will you go with me to that high point on the mountain off yonder, just facing the river?"

"Anywhere you wish me, you know I would James? How, distressed I am to see you look so sad, and pale, what has caused this?"

"I will tell you up yonder."

They walked on mostly in silence; the place was reached, and both seated near each other and near the edge of the cliff. There they must have formed the fatal resolve for the flowers they had gathered were left on the rocky seat, a scrap of paper was written in pencil said, "We will die together: Farewell earth."

They were locked in each other's arms when found two hundred and fifty feet below that high cliff. To this day the place is called The Lovers' Leap."

Just as the story was ended Mr. H. touched Mr. Hill on the shoulder and said:

"The lady will see you in the parlor."

Mr. Hill went, a cold chill on his heart. Short as the distance was[,] he had pictured the reception he would meet at the hands of that scornful but queenly-looking woman.

"Why did I have the temerity to accept after seeing her? On the very book she held in her hand she looked in disdain, and what am I to expect, a poor, nameless nobody?"

As they entered the thronged room[,] he first caught sight of the bright-eyed little lady who had so charmed him. She was richly and tastefully dressed and was lightly holding to the arm of a gentlemanly-looking man who appeared to be an invalid. How much Mr. Hill did wish it was to that party be was to be presented, and he was almost speechless with surprise when Mr. H. did stop immediately in front of them. The affability of father and daughter somewhat reassured Mr. Hill, who was not easily non-plussed, and he acquitted himself very creditably. Somehow his unaffected manner and sensible replies to questions asked by the gentleman in regard to the country around them, made a good impression. He told them of many beautiful spots they had not heard of. After awhile the gentleman said:

"We will take a turn in the gallery and enjoy this bright moonlight."

The lady asked questions too and she encouraged Mr. Hill to talk. Belles and beaux joined in the promenade and conversation, or rather, the light, gay talk we all like so well at times. Mr. Laurette at length remarked that his twinge of rheumatism reminded him he must leave them. His daughter was turned over to her elderly relative, but the beaux soon spirited her out of her charge and all repaired to the ball room, where gaiety reigned supreme. Mr. Hill danced well and often, but somehow his conscience reproached him, he thought with shame of his intercourse with Peacock and before the festivities of the ball room were ended[,] he walked up and down one of the deserted parlors and pondered on many things.

CHAPTER XII.

Mr. Peacock was supposed by all to be in the far North, in the State of Maine, but he was only in a secluded place among the mountains of West Virginia, which he was satisfied was too remote to be found by any one who knew him. From there he wrote frequently to Mary through a friend in New York, who sent the letters to her. He described how busy he was in completing his plans among capitalists in New York, their future home, brightened by her presence, his impatience to see her dear self and what delight her letters gave him. Her letters were forwarded through the same channel as his to her. The postmaster of this little, secluded office reported among his simple neighbors that that air stranger must be a great man, as he got lots o' letters from York City. Peacock never let opportunities slip and he soon took advantage of their good opinion, and would often chuckle the mean man's laugh over the imposition he had so easily practiced upon the Anderson family. "I couldn't have done it though," he said to himself, "if I had been left to play my game alone with those women, but that vain, egotistical old Anderson helped me so well, the-verdant old fool! I will first get the three thousand dollars, and then for the land! I will then soon be myself again and be paid for all my past trouble. A few years ago I was wealthy and had friends, plenty of them, but as my dollars vanished from my pocket my friends vanished from my sight; now I am living among people scarcely a remove above the beasts of the field. By Jove! I will make something out of them. I can't waste my time by this sacrifice of every comfort, they must pay for it. This old man's land is valuable and railroads will be made here, but not, as he thinks, through my endeavors. I cannot be put on an equality with such ignorant people without making them pay the piper. To lose some of this land is the penalty this old man must pay, and why can't I make him believe I will marry his "darter" as he calls her."

So the fascinating Mr. Peacock set about bamboozling the old mountaineer and his "gal," as the neighbors called her, and succeeded in getting a good share of the old man's land deeded safe and lawfully to him, and speedily he cajoled some men into putting him up a comfortable little house. He exhibited but little money, but made them believe it was inexhaustible. The old mountaineer was the busiest among the busy ones —helping to destroy himself—and Mr. Peacock walked among the poor deluded fools like a lord of all he beheld. To that fraudulently gotten land and house he was going to bring poor Mary, to use her as a tool to get money from her father. Under his sole control, unassisted by any one, she would not dare to rebel against his authority. The merciless wretch in thinking over his cold-blooded plans, often congratulated himself on knowing how to use men.
[Page 7 End]

"No voice divine,

No light propitious shone,"[26]

for poor cheated Mary. He could plan her ruin as well as that of the poor, ignorant mountaineers who were singing the praises of that "best and kindest man in the world."

"What virtue can we name, or grace,

---

[26] Quote here from the last stanza of William Cowper's poem *The Castaway*, written in 1799. See Appendix V for the full poem.

But man, unqualified and base,
Will boast it in their possession.
The richest gems are ever counterfeited most."

The noble Mr. Peacock's time was drawing to a close. He must have more money. He tried his hand on his friend in New York. That man had believed his story of mineralogy and now he was secretly buying up good lands for rich and sure capitalists; the money came and plenty of time given to repay it. Mr. Peacock, in the thankfulness of his heart, and Micauber-like,[27] hoping something would turn up so he could keep from paying back that borrowed money. John Hill he had not heard from lately.

"If John Hill has played me false, and told that he knew nothing about me except what I had said myself and that I had gotten him to blow my loud-sounding trumpet, well, I will"— and Mr. Peacock ruminated gloomily and did not say what he would do. The friendly old mountaineer stood in the doorway and said he "hed come for to tell him his darter sed supper was about ready and she had bought some coffee for him to eat, as the sassafrac tea had gin out."

Peacock had little to say as to what they had to eat, but talking to them he tried to make himself as agreeable as possible; and with his very pleasant ways, made them nearly idolize him. All this was something they had never before experienced; he let them be on as free a footing with himself as was safe. While he himself would be familiar, he rather checked their too near approach. The old mountaineer considered himself a good deal smarter than any of his neighbors, and they were willing to be led by him. He liked to discuss his bravery; he had no equal on that score in his own estimation. He had, according to his own account, never met a man that could out-

---

[27] Micauber = Wilkins Micawber is a clerk in Charles Dickens's 1850 novel David Copperfield. He is traditionally identified with the optimistic belief that "something will turn up." https://en.wikipedia.org/wiki/Wilkins_Micawber

hunt or out-fight him, until he had the "good forten to meet the captin thar," pointing to the invincible Peacock, who had related to these around him of his many hair-breath escapes and wonderful exploits; the fame he had won on the battlefield, etc. The old man's family called themselves very religious. Mr. Peacock would escort the young lady to the little log house they called the church.[28] The girl sincerely believed she was to be Peacock's wife ; but he was preparing to leave soon to fulfill his engagement with Mary. He had succeeded so well that he felt triumphant. But let the guilty ever fear—that sword suspended by a single hair is ever hanging over their heads. One bright day, Mr. Peacock in his imagined safety, thought he would go to the office—he got no letters, but got papers. Whilst looking over them a gentleman in a hunting suit and a gun over his shoulder, rode up and alighted near the postoffice [*sic*], and was talking to those on the outside. Peacock saw his face and heard his voice, and knew him. His first impulse was to remain and listen, and find out what brought him there; but he concluded he had best wait and ascertain some other way. Prudence admonished him to conceal himself in the little back room; and whilst there he overheard the stranger ask if there was good hunting and fishing anywhere about there, and stated that he and a party had been on an expedition of that character, and had enjoyed themselves immensely—caught splendid trout. He was in fine humor with the fun he and his companions had experienced. After awhile the remainder of the party came up, all in glorious good humor. They talked about the "wild-cat whisky" they had been supplied so plentifully with; and, to Mr. Peacock's great annoyance they said nothing about leaving. "Great heavens! are they going to remain here longer?" he exclaimed, large drops of perspiration standing on his brow. The talking and

---

[28] Charley's great-grandparents, Adam and Elizabeth Peck, built the first church in Mossy Creek, a small log structure that was called Elizabeth's Chapel. It was rebuilt in 1850 on the same location, and was used as a Field Hospital for federal troops during the Battle of Mossy Creek on 29 Dec 1863.

laughing went on. Mr. Peacock execrated them in his soul's wrath. They were keeping their spirits up by pouring spirits down,—and there was no sign of their going away. The hilarity continued for a long time; but all things must come to an end. As there were neither "wild cat" nor good fishing near by [*sic*], they all mounted their horses and left, to the great relief of prisoner Peacock. In former and wealthier days, Peacock had a business transaction with the gentleman who first rode up, and had cheated and swindled his too-confiding friend, who swore dire vengeance against him for his rascally conduct. Peacock knew full well he would carry out his threat if the opportunity offered, hence his hiding. When he emerged from his place of concealment, the post-master said, "Oh, Mr. Peacock, I didn't know you were here; thought you had gone; we have had so many nice gentlemen here; I am so sorry they didn't have a chance to see you, I would have had you out if I had known you were here."

It is well Mr. Peacock's heart and thoughts were not visible—the man would have seen fear, hate, shame, fully and foully displayed. Peacock made his excises; he had verdigo [*sic*], was subject to it, and had gone in the little room for quiet and had fallen asleep.

From that day Mr. Peacock lost favor; he was suspected not to be the great man he had represented himself to be. He himself felt very badly over all these little incidents. He left the post office and walked leisurely towards what he called the miserable hut where he was staying and receiving the free hospitality of a people be had such contempt for. The poor simple people always hear him speak of the place as home, and it was in fact the only home he had. But he was living in hope; he thought everything would be allright [*sic*] as soon as he secured Mary, and that time was fast approaching, and he had told his hospitable entertainers already of that fact, and probably, when he returned he would fetch his sister with him, and he asked them to put some little furniture in the new house and fix it up nice by the time of his return. They expressed, in their homely language, a deep regret at his leaving, and promise that he would find them all at his return his warm friends. Mr. Peacock returned his thanks, expressed deep feeling of friendship towards them all, and in such heart rending tones, that it made the old grandmother shed tears. Mr. Peacock was a regular Sunday school attendant, and was often teacher; his big words gave him fame in this department. The mountain belle, that he had made believe he would marry, was one of his scholars; she was docile and obedient, and sometimes when Peacock heard her, in her simple and unaffected manner, praise him for being so good and kind, the little speck of conscience he had, would reproach him for his base imposition; but alas! his selfishness and indolence would get the better of any reeling apart from himself. (TO BE CONTINUED.)

Figure 10 - Unknown. An Old Photograph of an Old Time Mountain "Moonshine" Still. Retrieved from the Digital Public Library of America, https://exploreuk.uky.edu/catalog/xt7x696zwx82_1_1266. (Accessed August 29, 2021.)

CHAPTER XIII.

The Anderson household were in great joy at the return of Mr. Peacock. They had received a telegram the day before announcing his coming. Every preparation was made to receive him with honor. He had been gone some months and returned looking very well. He had been smart enough, not only to get the money from his friend, but to request he would fill a small bill for him—nice suits of clothes for himself, nice lace shawls and so forth for Miss Mary. He was pleased and gratified with the reception he met with from Mary and the family. He produced his presents after waiting for an opportunity to give them. After retiring to his own room for the night, he congratulated himself for completing his plans so well.

During the day the visitors who had come in, congratulated him on getting such a fine girl as Miss Mary. She was so "beautiful and good." The next day he went to see his friend, John Hill, who was in his office hard at work. He did not perceive Mr. Peacock until he gave him a slap on the shoulder and exclaimed:

"Why, John, old boy, it gives me pleasure to see you again. Your pleasant countenance is a treat."

"The same to you, Peacock," and a hearty shaking of hands until both were seated.

'Why, where have you been? I have had but one letter from you, Peacock. I couldn't imagine what had become of you."

"Well, John, I will tell you the reason I didn't write to you oftener. I had so much business on my hands I had hardly time to write to my Mary, but, John, old boy, all, or much of my success is due to yourself. Oh, you are a noble man! I can take your hand and say, 'Here is one who will not betray a friend.' But my gratitude is not to be shown in words only. Something more substantial than that. Now let me know in what way I can assist you, or do you need me now?"

Mr. Peacock, in his mind, was not altogether sure of John, and besides he wished to see if any change had come over John Hill. He knew if he could get him to talk unreservedly, it would be probable he could give a guess about him and his designs.

"Mr. Peacock, where do you intend to establish yourself after your marriage?"

"Oh, I have fixed all that! I have rented a house on Broadway in New York. My office will he there too."

"Oh, Mr. Peacock, I am sorry to hear you say that!"

"Oh, it is a money-making business I am going into. John, I intend the cotton exchange as my next venture. I will get a splendid salary. But what have you been doing here? What adventures have befallen you?"

"And you want to know, do you, Mr. Peacock?" [Page 8 End]

"Oh, yes, certainly I do."

"Well, I got in a sort of a scrape that may yet make my fortune," and Mr. Hill related his encounter and killing of the drunken man, his acquittal and the praises of the heiress in regard to the affair; his introduction to the lady and to her father, their kindness to his poor, humble and unknown self.

Mr. Peacock listened attentively to all his friend said, but did not look friendly into John Hill's face, indeed, did not look into it at all. There was a change in tone and look. He had been thinking, "I have been too hasty. This all might have been mine, now I am sacrificing myself for a few thousand dollars, too few to do any good." He was very much dissatisfied, all about himself now looked so paltry. That den of mischief—his brain—was set in motion, but he got hold of nothing tangible to catch at to change his own plans. John Hill had an idea his story had not pleased his friend, and the averted face made him think envy was at work, and both knew they viewed each other with jealousy and distrust. Mr. Peacock made some attempt at jocularity, but John, in his heart, thought he made a lamentable failure and Mr. Peacock said he would bid him good-bye [*sic*] and return to his Mary. John had promised to be at the wedding and remarked. "Anderson would not die of grief if I missed."

The preparations progressed finely. Mr. Anderson wished it to be grand and a surprise to the neighbors. All were told to hold themselves in readiness. The Agens wanted to create a sensation on their "own hook." They prided themselves on being the richest in the neighborhood and were to act accordingly. Mr. Peacock had almost turned Mr. Anderson's head, describing the style and state of Mary's future life. "These lands here must be developed too. Shafts must be sunk to fetch to light this rich iron ore. I am arranging everything, Mr. Anderson."

The wedding day came round and Mary in her maidenly shyness avoided meeting her affianced. The guests arrived. Ninthy in the tightest of pinbacks. Her self-complacency and her wise sayings, made one think she considered herself the pink of fashion and an oracle of wisdom. She had been for sometime thinking if there was such a thing as a young man of sober and temperate habits she would marry him and partly endow him with her wealth. During the wedding festivities she thought she had found him. She made fearful assaults with the hope of capturing the heart of Mr. Jack an old bachelor. The company were all assembled. It was said, "They are coming," and perfect silence reigned. The doom was spoken; and then began the merry congratulations and hearty good wishes for the doomed Mary. Some envied her seeming, good fortune, but there was too much gaiety for any to indulge long in any feeling but high good humor. Why was that shadow, or shade of a shadow on Mary's pale face—always until now so radiant and joyoas [*sic*]—why did her hand involuntarily press on her heart and she, whispering to herself, "Oh, heart, be still!" Why now was all this, as the last words were spoken had a spirit given her a silent warning? Mary thought so from the chill that seized upon her heart. God sets no mark in vain. The best could not stand beside the basest without the heart's being charged with a prophetic sadness.

Laughter, and talk with the aid of wine, was indulged without intermission. The pleasures of the evening continued until a late hour, but the hour of departure came, and silence soon reigned where idle mirth had been with all but one.

"All whose life is sure, their life is calm,
Silent the light that moulds and colors all things."[29]

As Mary repeated those words she had an instinctive dread that her life was not to be what she had promised herself. The next morning early, Mr. Peacock had a long and private conversation with his friend, Mr. Hill. Mary was with her mother and sisters and all grieving that they were to part so soon. Eva and Kate telling her not to forget or be ashamed of them when she got among Mr. Peacock's fine, fashionable friends and in her palatial mansion. The mother's heart was too full to talk much, or to say any but the dearest and kindest words. To part with her child was like tearing body and soul apart. The father took consolation in the proud thought of his daughter's success.

---

[29] *Vesuvius*, by Richard Chenevix Trench, Anglican Archbishop in the Church of Ireland. See Appendix VI for the full-length poem.

The dreaded farewell was spoken. And Mary started into the wide world with the man she did not know. The man boasted of the pleasant places they would visit on this bridal tour; he would else, visit his mother in his far off home in Maine who was longing to clasp her new daughter; then for our home in New York. And Ninthy, she for awhile did not know what was the matter with her. She could not rest well the night she got back from the wedding. She was wondering how the Anderson family could put on so much style, and the way Mary had married such a fortune. She would grit her teeth in envy. She then came down on poor Jack for not paying her more attention, but could be amused with those chits[30] of girls like Eva and Kate. She got up in the morning in a bad humor. She met up with White, the first one she saw.

"Now, look here, White, I am going to have things changed here."
"I say, igad, I say, Ninthy, what do you mean?"

"Why, I say, I mean to use our money to better advantage than I have done. Why, look at that Anderson family who are not half as rich as we are, carrying on the style they do, and look at Mary who has cut out every rich girl in the country, and now has gone on a bridal tour all over the world, and then going to live in New York. Well, I am glad that breakfast bell has rung at last." Ninthy was furious because White was absent.

"White knows breakfast is ready, but this is the way he always treats me. Jenny, get them pigs out of the kitchen. Goodness sakes, alive! have you let that cornbread burn up?"

"I did'nt [*sic*] do it," the cook replied.

"Now, look here Jenny, you sha'n't jaw me. If you don't do better than that I will send you home. You know, Jenny, I have always told

---

[30] Chits = facetious or derogatory, a pert, impudent, or self-confident girl or child: *a young chit of a thing*. Collins English Dictionary – Complete and Unabridged, 12th Edition 2014 © HarperCollins Publishers 1991, 1994, 1998, 2000, 2003, 2006, 2007, 2009, 2011, 2014

you better than that. Oh, Jenny, there's that devilish pig again. Kill it, Jenny. Oh, I wish every hog was dead?"

Now comes White dragging His feet along.

"Goodness sakes alive, White! what do you mean? But this is the way you always treat me, and being we are waiting breakfast on you. Oh, lordy! I don't expect to live much longer anyhow. Get your chair and set down, White, and don't keep us waiting any. longer. Oh o, I do believe this cough will kill me. Hand me the fat meat and grease, White. Don't keep me waiting. Don't be so slow about it. There!"

"Ninthy, you are so hard to please. You are so headstrong. You won't let me do nothing."

"Now, White, shut your mouth!"

"I say, igad, I say, Ninthy, I must go and feed my hogs. Open the closet and get me my bridle and I will ride," turning the closet bolt it caught Ninny's fingers.

"Now, White, dog gone it! let go the bolt. Quit turning it. Oh, White, you have mashed my finger nearly off. You haint got a bit of sense."

"I say, igad, I say, Ninthy, I didn't mean to do it."

"Now, White, shut your mouth. You have nearly killed me. Go away and let me alone! You won't let me have any peace! Oh! oh! I don't know what I can do with White. Jenny, have you fed them chickens, and got them beans for dinner. O git out! fly. Shoo fly! Oh, I wish it was winter. These flies bother the life outen me. Oh, Jenny, Jenny! you black devil, you have let that coffee burn up! Now, Jenny, you know I have always treated you like my own child; you must do better, Jenny, or I will send you home; I will, Jenny. Now, just look here and see what White has done. That man will worry the life outen me—cough, cough! Oh, this cough will kill me! Jenny, be in a hurry with them beans. They ought to be on now."

White comes in with a bile, as he calls it, on his finger.

"Ninthy, have you got an, patent medicine Mobelian?"[31]

"No, White, but go to the store and get some of the extract."

"No, Ninthy, I would rather go get the weed and make it, and that will save money, so I will go out to the old field and look for it."

He hunted for three hours and came back without it. Then Ninthy came down on him.

"Hunting for hours when he could have got it at the store for five cents."

Just then one of her old beaux came in and her countenance cleared up like the sun passing from behind a cloud. She went to laughing and shaking her fat sides as if nothing had ever disturbed her. Ninthy was hospitable to those she liked.

---

[31] This may refer to a Red Mobelian Potato Plant.

CHAPTER XIV.

John Hill was satisfied that on his last visit to the springs he had made a good impression on Miss Laurette, and he began to think his chances good. At first his motive was somewhat mercenary, but not so now, he loved her solely for herself. She occupied all the best feelings of his mind. So he resolved to return to the springs and spend a month. In that tune he would have the opportunity of finding if he was anything to her, and resolved to win if possible, his little beauty, the goddess of his idolatry. He felt it was not blind idolatry, but the best and truest feelings a man can have for woman.

In regard to that immense fortune, he had heard too it was not quite so immense—what would she and father want with it all? what use have they for so much? "Do they expect her to marry a rich man just because she is rich? Nonsense! I am poor but if I had a chance[,] I would soon outstrip these who are rich now; but they have not the assurance they will keep it. With no business capacities they squander in dissipation what they will never restore. I have business qualifications. I could take one hundred thousand dollars of this money and make it double itself every year. Now, if the father and daughter only knew me well enough to trust me[,] I don't think they would complain of me. This transaction with Peacock is my only blemish. The tempter found me without friends or any kind of employment. My poverty made me an easy prey, and I almost, know now he is deceiving me in regard to the business he says will be so profitable to me. Well, I will get leave of absence from my boss this evening and to-morrow will get my fast horse and go up to push the matter in earnest."

His request was granted. He had a beautiful day for his ride, which was twenty-five miles, it being the time of year the farmers were gathering in their fodder. He would often stop and talk to them on the roadside; and the merry boys who were hard at work were glad to see him. At one place, seeing a large brick house in the distance, he inquired of one of them who lived there. He was told, to his surpise [*sic*] that it was Mr. Oteger, the old Dutch coroner.

"Is he rich?"

"You might call him rich for this country, young man. He owns rich bottom farms, and has some pretty gals. If you want to please him just brag on his gals." [Page 9 End]

"I would think you boys would have a desire to please him in good earnest."

"I tell you, sir, we are pretty thick up in that direction."

"And how far do you call it from here to the springs?"

"Well, I s'pose it is about seven miles."

Mr. Hill thanked them for the information they had given him and rode slowly along, as the day was very hot, and the merciful man has mercy on his fine beast, he had no idea of riding him down, for he intended riding out with Miss Laurette.

It was nearly dinner time as he approached the Oteger mansion and he resolved to dine with his new acquaintances, invited or not; but he felt assured in his mind that he would be a welcome guest. At a little disdance [*sic*] he met the old man. It was a pleasant recognition on both sides. He was hospitably invited, not only to dine, but to stay all night; from this he excused himself on plea of business at the springs.

"Why, Mr. Hill, I'm the gladdest to see you."

"And Mr. Oteger, I am delighted to meet with you. I assure you my sentiments towards you are of heartfelt gratitude, and I have been wanting to come and see you, but pressing business has until now prevented me."

"Well, I am powerful glad to see you. Walk in, and let me introduce you to my daughter Jossie.[32] She are the gal I was telling you about."

While the old gentleman was attending to Mr. Hill's horse, Sorcerer, Miss Josie and Mr. Hill entered into a lively conversation, and to his astonishment she moved her chair very close to his and while showing him some photos, she would very familiarly rest her hand on his shoulder, which pleased his fancy and assured him hospitality. But he feared the old man's coming, as he might think they were too friendly on so short acquaintance and in his dread he began to think she never would get through showing them the photographs.

"But," he thought, "she is much prettier than I expected to see, to have such a looking daddy."

At length dinner was announced and Mr. Hill was presented to the rest of the family. He had the satisfaction of trying Catherine's "zarves."[33] The dinner was good and they had a merry time eating, laughing and talking.

"Now, Mr. Hill, you see this house; it is made of brick, all brick. Well, there are my daughters that are before you, and to tell you the truth, sah, they are the gals that carried every brick that built up this house."

"Mr. Oteger! is it possible? I am surprised to hear you say that. They are as useful as ornamental."

"Yes, Mr. Hill, they are the best girls in the country." All Mr. Hill saw and heard was new to him, which made him spend a merry and a

---

[32] It seems that the girl's name is Josie, but her father pronounces it "Jossie."
[33] "Zarves" is short for "preserves" and highlights the family's strong accent.

pleasant day. Now his thoughts began to wander off in the direction of the springs, and he would soon meet the little beauty he longed to see and whose affections he was going to strive for. Bidding his hospitable friends good-bye, he rode rapidly toward the springs.

In riding along the, beautiful river that bears the Indian name, Minnehaha—laughing waters—all at once in a turn of the road, he saw a party coming in full gallop towards him, and among the foremost he recognized Miss Laurette.[34]

All being acquainted they stopped short and began a merry conversation. Mr. Hill said he was going to the spring to stay awhile. Miss Laurette said they had gone far enough and would turn back, and as she was not riding with any one in particular, she and Mr. Hill would take the lead. Although they were riding at full speed, her tongue kept pace with wit and repartee.[35] Mr. Hill took the opportunity to beg the honor and pleasure of escorting her to see the beautiful view of the river and mountain.

"With pleasure, Mr. Hill, you are, in fact, the finest cicerone[36] I have met with. Your very descriptions are poetry itself, and besides you know where to find the sublimest views. The others I go with show me only commonplace sights."

"So much for being inspired by you[r] presence," said Mr. Hill. "Yourself alone is the cause of any poetry in me, Miss Laurette. While you are engaged in viewing the lofty mountains and the rippling streams or rushing rivers, my eyes are feasting on the highest type of the great Creator's handiwork."

---

[34] "Minnehaha" was made famous by Henry Wadsworth Longfellow's 1855 poem, *The Song of Hiawatha*. Minnehaha Falls are located in Minneapolis, Minnesota.
[35] Repartee = a quick and witty reply; *and* a succession or interchange of clever retorts : amusing and usually light sparring with words.
[36] Cicerone = a guide who conducts sightseers.

Miss Laurette knew and felt his meaning, his eloquent eyes and intellectual face bespoke his full admiration. She was pleased and felt there was no flattery, but true heart felt sincerity.

The next morning, directly after breakfast two splendid horses richly caparisoned, stood near the hotel door and were being admired by the passing crowd. Presently Miss Laurette with her escort, Mr. Hill, came out. Her father assisted, or at least stood by and looked on, telling her to be careful and not run a race. The two when fairly seated in the saddle presented a handsome sight—she in her well-fitting and rich riding costume, plumed hat and fresh, joyous face, was, as all said, a faultless figure on horseback. Her easy, skillful management of the bridle and fearless manner made her look bewitching. Her escort in his manly beauty was a fitting hat-off to her fascinations.

Gaily laughing at the compliments thrown after them they rode off full of life, charmed with themselves and all else about them. They rode rapidly along the river's side for several miles until they reached a beautiful spring, called Clinchdale[37], which was surrounded by high mountains towering to the clouds, the dale looked so beautifully inviting, carpeted with the leaves from the tall and swaying pine trees and other evergreens, the little wild flower peeped out, like some shy body, who considered herself as having no interest or connection with those mighty ones above her. Miss Laurrette said "the place was too beautiful and romantic to merely take a look and then leave, she must get down and pay, her devoirs[38] to the presiding deity of the place." She was gallantly assisted and conducted to one of the many rustic seats around them, and Mr. Hill said:

"There is a feeling of awe in all this grand solemnity," but he took a seat by the lady's side, and what he had so long thought, he now

---

[37] Clinchdale is another name for Bean's Station, TN, located 10 miles from Morristown (where Charles went to high school), and 27 miles from Jefferson City, Tennessee.
[38] Devoirs = a usually formal act of civility or respect.

determined to express, he had resolved to do his best, end as it might, good or bad, if bad I will be no worse off than I am now. Miss Laurette talking and, admiring all around her said:

"Mr. Hill, what is more beautiful than nature, look at it any way you will, it is the same, all grandeur, filled with lovely birds of every plumage, with their sweet melody enlivening us from early dawn to dewy night, and the murmuring of crystal streams that come rushing, or gliding along so sweetly, the sweet and gentle breeze that plays among the many leaves of these evergreen pines."

"Yes, Miss Laurette that is all true; and he would be a person of poor taste who could not admire it in every particular—but Miss Bessie there is something that dwells in my mind that is far more lovely than all this, and that is a true little woman, I think she is the noblest of God's works."

"Oh, Mr. Hill! how can you say that, while sitting here viewing that grand old mountain that towers up before us, and has stood firm in his majestic beauty through all time, has felt the whist winds of a thousand years."

"Well, Miss Bessie, that may be all true, but that mountain cold and grand as it is, could not alone make us happy. We admire it for its grandeur, I am thankful we have such sublime objects and such beautiful scenery to admire, but when we come to take a common sense view of it, all we find at last is, <u>that our real happiness exists between ourselves alone, we can either make each other very happy, or very miserable, a pleasant word; even a pleasant look, cheers up our spirits and makes us happier, to be with those we love is happiness supreme, while that grand mountain would ever remain the same, cold and far removed from us, and the merry streams that look so beautiful, is not the warm blood that flows through our hearts and makes us feel</u>

for each other. Miss Bessie, what I wished to say to you, is that I admire you very much."[39]

"Now, Mr. Hill, please, let us talk of something more important, not to sit here and talk of ourselves."

"I only ask you to listen to me, you have never treated me as if you disliked me, you said you admired me as a man, and I say from the deepest recesses of my heart I love you! I more than admire you as a lady, can you give me one encouraging word? one that will give me hope?"

"Oh! Mr. Hill, I think you are too good ever to be unhappy, you know I do admire you, and papa says you have interested him, and he likes you, and you know—here she was a little embarrassed—you know you have been so kind, well you know we have not been very long acquainted and I don't know how it is but I admire you."

At this Mr. Hill fell on his knee, took the delicate white hand and kissed it with the grace and devotion of a knight of the olden time."

"Miss Bessie, do you think you could ever think of me as something more than a friend, do more than admire me?"

"A far as loving goes or is concerned, I never gave that a thought."

"Well, do you think you could reciprocate the love I offer you?"

"Mr. Hill, I do not know what effect the future will have upon my feelings, but I will be plain now and say I do admire you very much indeed."

The little hand was still held and pressed, and many sweet words were spoken, and at length they remounted their horses and rode on rapidly to the springs. As they went on, Mr. Hill got her permission to

---

[39] Handwritten in the margin of the notebook where Charley placed his story, and next to the soliloquy by Mr. Hill to Miss Bessie, are these words, "This is fresh and sweet as a dream nestled beneath the petals of a wild mountain rose." Charley also underlined in pencil the words underlined above.

ask her father, if his addresses to the daughter would meet his approbation?"[40]

Mr. Hill's heart almost failed him, when he appeared before the father to make the request. "What had he to give in return—he would ask himself—they were born aristocrats and reared in luxury and refinement; and he, what was he, a poor man, and one who had never known the appliances of wealth, only at a very early period of his existence, when he was too young to know the advantages of wealth and position; ruin came upon his house before his tastes or habits were formed and he retained nothing of his ruined fortunes but memory— a bitter legacy sometimes—he had a will to rebuild his fallen house— and like the proud Hastings[41] was determined to have money to work with—those were his first feelings when he heard of Miss Laurrette, but the money was lost sight of in his love for the charming girl; now he dreaded that mercenary motives might be attributed to him. [Page 10 End]

He had now been spending his time very pleasantly at the Springs, took part in all the amusements and tried to make himself as agreeable as possible, but every one noticed a sad look on his face and could not imagine what the matter could be? The visitors would often say can it be that Miss Laurrette has refused him, and if that be the case they act very strangely, they are hardly ever apart. No! this was not the case.

Hill had a long conversation with that stern old aristocrat—who was a sly old fox—and had positively said no, thought his daughter much too young to marry. Hill then did his best to prevail on her to run away with him, but he failed in this for she said, she would not disobey her father. Seeing his case was hopeless he resolved to leave, notwithstanding he had received encouragement from her, and even

---

[40] Approbation = an act of approving formally or officially.
[41] Hastings = most likely refers to the Norman-French army of William, Duke of Normandy, who emerged victorious during the Battle of Hastings on 14 Oct 1066. William was crowned king on Christmas Day 1066.

from her father, he had only said she was too young, but Hill thought this was a ruse of theirs to keep clear of any engagement; they would give him no better reason, he almost knew they had heard he was nothing but a clerk. All this gave him pain and he resolved to return to his business, and see what the future had in store for him. But if Miss Bessie Laurette had only known what the future had in store for her, gladly and quickly would she have married Mr. Hill. She did not know old Laurette had taken her from an orphan asylum when she was too young to speak plain. He was a widower without children, but had claimed her as his, but he had never taken any steps towards giving her a legal claim upon his property. It was true he was rich, but at his death she could not inherit a dollar, and likely would be thrown again on charity as in her infant years, while the vast estate she now thought was hers, would go to distant relatives. [TO BE CONTINUED.]

CHAPTER XV.

Mr. Peacock dreaded to tell Mary where he was going. He could see from her face that there was something wrong. She felt that all was not as Peacock had represented and now feared she was bound to an impostor. Peacock knew he was nearing the station where they were to get on, and this was the nearest point to where he bad built his hut. From this place they would have to get through the mountains the best they could. Mary had a number of trunks filled with things her mother had given her as parting gifts. Eva and Kate had laughingly said, "Mary would be ashamed of them in New York."

Peacock was sitting in deep thought, but suddenly turning to Mary, said:

"My dear, since I left your father's I have remembered a promise I made to some friends to visit their country to see if there was any prospect to develop its mineral resources, I think it is to my advantage to do so, and as the country is beautiful it will be cool and pleasant and it is too hot to go to New York just yet anyway.

"Mr. Peacock, I am certainly willing to do anything that would be to your advantage; besides I think it would be pleasant to stop over as you suggest."

"Well, my dear, we are drawing near the station where we will get off, and from there we will make our way to the mountains."

It was eight o'clock in the morning when the train neared the station where the trunks were tumbled out on the ground. It was a dreary looking place, and it had been raining which made it look only the more gloomy. The place contained only a few shabby looking dwellings.

Mary looked around to see if there was a genteel looking person among the vagrant looking crowd that was standing about in the mud watching the departure of the train, but the only relief about the place was the creek, which was covered with moss and gave the place the name of Mossy Creek.[42] She was conducted by Peacock and an old man up to the hotel which was an old barn of a place kept by the old vagabondish looking person who went with them. He seated them on his front porch and told them to make themselves at home. Then the old man's wife came out and gave Mary a history of the place and the people, which was anything but favorable, and then left to fix Mary a room.

Peacock had walked up the only street in the place and joined in conversation with the crowd of roughs at the post-office, which was in the back end of a little grocery store on close to the depot.[43] The office was kept by an old fogie, who was a big man among them

---

[42] Charley's great-grandfather, Adam Peck, Sr., founded Mossy Creek, Tennessee in 1788 and helped draft the first state constitution. Though born on Henderson Plantation in East Carrol Parish, Louisiana, Charley was raised on the Peck family farm in Oakland, near Mossy Creek. Mossy Creek Station (constructed 2017) stands today in downtown Jefferson City, TN, and trains still travel through town. Visit www.mossycreekfoundation.org/festival-park for more information.

[43] In 1871, Charley's older brother Willy was caught hanging out with an "idle, loafing, riffraff gang of teen-aged boys at [the original] Mossy Creek Station. Their father, Dr. Isham Peck, led Willy back to the farm, scolding him and admonishing him to not do so again. That evening, Willy slipped into his dad's doctor bag and took a lethal dose of laudanum, a morphine-like substance. Charley was 13 years old when these tragic events took place. The grief nearly too much too bear for the family." (*People and Places of Jefferson County*, 1994, by Estle P. Muncy, Pg 81.)

because he was one of those knowing justices of the peace, usually called Squire, and would occasionally get off some vulgar anecdote at which all would laugh uproariously.

Poor Mary was tired from traveling and went to her room, where she was trying to go to sleep, but was soon awakened by the oaths of the landlady which satisfied her the tumbler of whisky she saw her take was now having its effect.

"Can it be possible," said she to herself, "that we will have to remain here any length of time? I do wish Mr. Peacock would come," and just then he came in; "Mr. Peacock, I am glad you have come, I have been frightened."

"Who dared do that, Mary?"

"Oh, no one meant it for me, but I heard the landlady swearing just across the hall, and not being used to such language it made me nervous. I wish we could get away from here as soon as possible."

"Mary, that is what I am trying to do. I have no desire to stay here, and I have tried all over the place to get a hack[44], but there is no such thing here. But I secured a wagon with a spring seat which I think will be just as comfortable."

"Mr. Peacock, I am willing to go in anything to get away from here. I hope we will go at once."

"I made the arrangement to leave immediately after we get our dinner and we will get to our point of destination in a day or so. We can find nicer places than this to stay at. I will go now and see if the baggage is all right, and immediately after dinner we will be off."

Dinner was over and the wagon was ready to take them to their desolate home. Mary had a fearful headache from loss of rest, and their stopping place had not added anything to her relief. She tried to be cheerful, but a presentiment of coming evil drove the smile from her lips and the careless, cheerful words upon her heart. She felt that her

---

[44] Hack = horse drawn wagon with higher capacity, a precursor to the modern bus

future happiness was gone, but now and then would ask herself, "why should I feel this way? There is surely nothing in our going out of the course I had expected. He has only forgotten this invitation. I must be in the wrong. I must get over this depression."

The travelers had fairly left the town, the road was good and they journeyed on in pretty good spirits. The pure, fresh air invigorated Mary's tired body.

At last the way became rough and then dangerous. The driver would advise them to leave the wagon and walk. So night came on. They began their inquiries for a stopping place, and were told the best place to stop at would be old man Beaver's. He sometimes took in travelers.

Mary, weary in body and mind, was glad when they arrived at the old man's house, who willingly took them in. She was soon in the little log room, where she fell asleep. Peacock seemed to be proof against physical weakness, and sat telling tales and adventures to his host and his family sitting out of doors in the bright moonlight.

He told them he was but lately married, and that his reason for coming out there was to discover if it would be favorable for building a railroad and it he found it profitable he might look for iron ore. He told them anecdotes which amused them very much. Then the old man told his anecdotes in return. They had a hilarious time of it, the old man and boys helping themselves from time to time to their favorite beverage "wildcat whisky."

Peacock had an object in all this. He hoped to escape paying for staying all night. No game was too little for him to play. He asked the old man to come and see him up in the mountains where he was going to spend his time during the hot weather, only twenty miles distant. Now and then be would take a drink with the blear-eyed old yahoo. Peacock handed him a cigar with as much grace as if yahoo had been a man of fashion. The creature took it and looked and then asked which "eend["] must be lighted. Peacock showed him and he puffed away highly pleased.

When at last Peacock left them[,] they talked him over. The ignorant are generally suspicious, and some of them thought he was after mischief; but they concluded he was a fine man after all.

The next morning when the travellers [*sic*] were called to a disgusting breakfast, Mary excused herself from taking much on the plea of headache. The old lady of the cabin then began a dissertation about the trouble her stomach gave her. She loved grease and "hit wouldn't love of her eating hit, and, mister, thar is my Jim and he has always had biles on his neck."

The old yahoo said to Mary, "Marm, jist let me gin you some of them ar corn dumplings. They ar powerful good."

Mary, of course, excused the greasy mess, and soon after left the table.

In time the driver was ready and she the satisfaction of getting again out in the fresh air.

Peacock did not like the look on Mary's pale face. He did not want her to die and he had the sense to know what a powerful influence the mind has on the body. He set about to cheer her up, and she would try to repay him for the attempt, but felt in her secret soul he had an object in doing so. She felt relieved when she heard they were near their place of destination and fervently hoped she would meet human beings. Those she had lately seen were scarcely human. The driver said, "only three miles now." They were then on a high precipice where they could look down several hundred feet. The horses took fright and ran the wagon to the edge, but before it went over Mary sprang out on the opposite side. Peacock, driver, horses and all went over, but very fortunately for Peacock, but very unfortunately for poor Mary, he caught to a strong limb of a tree and saved himself. Mary in her fright had fainted. Peacock, freeing himself, went to [Page 11 End] her and bathing her head in the icy cold water soon restored her to consciousness and to misery. Peacock then went to see about the driver and horses, but all were dead.[45] He thought with help he could save the trunks or their contents, but there alone he could do nothing. He got to the driver with difficulty and saw he was dead. He then thought if he has any valuable about him he would save it for his family. He found about thirty dollars in the poor fellow's pocket, but never did find the time when he could spare it to send, but said, "Mary may have something I can take and they will say what a liberal hearted man I am. I am kind to everybody. I can't bear to see distress. I don't think people ought to complain of anything where I am. They ought to know it is not so pleasant to me as to see them lively and making me lively. I love the beautiful and everybody ought to. What is the use of complaining? I never complain if things go as I want them. Now I will not it I am compelled to walk these three miles. I could not help the wagon going over and the driver and horses getting killed. But I must take a good hunt to see that nothing is lost out of the trunks. I think they are safe from the way they have lodged."

Thinking thus as he scrambled up a slight acclivity and swore dreadful oaths as he would accidentally scratch his hands with the briars that grew in the rocks. He went back to Mary and told her the sad news, but was very glad of his own safety. Mary was very deeply affected, expressed deep regret for the loss of the unfortunate driver.

"Mary, it is not far and we must walk to where an old man lives that I know and we will stay there awhile this summer. You will be in safety. We can remain there anyhow until we see what we can do with the poor dead driver."

---

[45] Charley's mom, Emma, related the following story on page 16 of *Ada's Journal* regarding the family's carriage ride over to Hot Springs from Mossy Creek, "The road is along the bank of the French Broad, all the way, some places it is so narrow there is barely room for a carriage to pass, between the wall of rocks and the river. . . Papa saw a horse and buggy fall off the bluff, once, and he was afraid for us to ride along it."

Mr. Peacock looked so much worried and troubled, Mary felt sorry for him and said nothing of her poor head or anything else to increase his cares, but consoled him as well as she could, when to her surprise he turned on her with anger to his face and said,

"I don't believe you have a bit of feeling, telling me not to distress myself as I could not help it. Do you mean to hint I did it? You will have to use a different kind of language to me, madam! Here all day one would think you couldn't talk, but as soon as you think you can blame me your tongue can run faster than a milltail.[46] I will tell you, madam, that I am a man that is not to be imposed upon. I have tamed lunatics, madam! Try your independence on me and you will see what will come of it! Try it! try it on me and you will see!"

Poor Mary was so bewildered with this brutal tirade, with horrid oaths interspersed that she stood and looked like one petrified, and he, seeing her fear, increased his abuse.

"I am not going to stand here all day waiting for you," he yelled.

"I am ready to go," she mildly answered. "Ready! you are ready, are you? Well, then, why did you keep me waiting?"

As she was about to answer, he told her she would rue[47] it if she gave him any more of her impertinence. Mary was uncertain what to do. If she attempted to make a move towards going, he would say, "Here I am, tired to death seeing after that man, and you have been sitting here doing nothing. You think you can have every thing your way, do you?"

After torturing the poor woman until he was out of breath, and seeing it was getting late, he at last started. With his long strides he soon got far ahead of the heart broken Mary. As she walked along she was thinking, "If he leaves me to find my way and I should make a

---

[46] Milltail = the water that flows from a mill wheel after turning it or the channel in which the water flows
[47] Rue = to feel sorrow, remorse, or regret

misstep and go over the precipice, my poor mother and all those at home would grieve, not knowing it was a release for their poor Mary."
(TO BE CONTINUED.)

Figure 11 - The 9:45 Accommodation by Edward Lamson Henry (1841-1919), 1867, Public Domain, (Courtesy of the Metropolitan Museum of Art, Bequest of Moses Tanenbaum)

Figure 12 - Southeastern Express Railway Depot, Jefferson City, TN, 1920, (Courtesy Tennessee State Library and Archives)

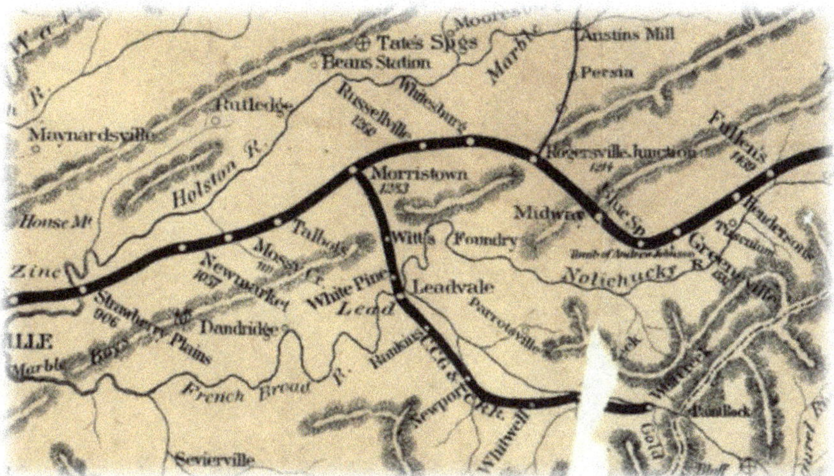

Figure 13 - Map of East Tennessee, Virginia & Georgia Rail Road (1880),
(Courtesy Tennessee State Library and Archives)

Figure 14 - Lithograph of Mossy Creek Farm with mill, farm buildings, and houses.
From J. Gray Smith's "Review of East Tennessee," 1842. A promotional tract of the East
Tennessee Land Company designed to encourage the sale of farm lands in the area.
(Courtesy Tennessee State Library and Archives)

Figure 15 - Edgar Brothers Family Groceries, located on the north side of the railroad tracks on Depot Street in Jefferson City, TN. (Diamond Jubilee Bicentennial Celebration)

Figure 16 - Post Office, Jefferson City, TN. First Mossy Creek Post Office was located in the Haynes / Mossy Creek Iron Works in 1816. Willie Blount Peck, Charley's great-uncle, was the first postmaster. (Photo from Diamond Jubilee Bicentennial Celebration)

CHAPTER XVI.

After a tiresome and weary walk they reached the old man's house, where Peacock expected to remain. He was still ahead of Mary as they approached the house. The old mountaineer and his family were delighted to see him. The girl who expected to be his wife was or pretended to be very bashful, but she made out to simper her joy at seeing him. Mary came up and they all stared at her, but said little. Peacock said:

"I want you to take charge of this lady, and I have some sad news for you."

"What is it, squire?" exclaimed the old man.

"Why, sir, we met with a terrible accident. Our wagon tumbled down the precipice and we barely escaped with our lives by jumping, but the driver and horses are killed. Our trunks are piled among the rock and brush."

They left Mary with the "women folks," as he called them and he and Peacock went to the scene of disaster. The women soon began to question Mary and to try and find out all about her. Mary soon knew what her future was to be and had but little to say to their questions. She did not know but what Peacock had two or three wives already in that country, from the general familiarity that seemed to exist between him and the people; for this reason she was cautious and kept her self-possession. When they asked her "if she and the squire was kin?" she merely replied, "distantly related." They wanted to know, "if he had fotched her all the way there?"

"Yes, to spend the summer or a part of it with him and you?"

They exhausted their efforts in "pumping" her, for she told as little as possible. The house was built of logs, with two small rooms. The floor was made of hewed slab: the sides of the house were daubed with mud; plenty of open cracks for the air, which was a needed relief. One room was kitchen and eating room; the other they slept in.

Peacock and his boon companion arrived at the fatal place, and after examining the poor driver found him dead beyond a doubt. The moon was shining bright and the two seated themselves on a log and began to discuss the best way of disposing of the body. The old yahoo says:

"I have a quart of the best corn whiskey you ever tasted in all your combustible life, and what is better than all, hit never paid the gover'ment a penny's worth of revenue. If you can stand it without sleep I can. Drink plenty of this ar and you can. We now will go about two miles further, where thar is an old man that makes coffins. We will make a contract with him to bury this poor fellow."

Peacock suggested they had better examine his pockets to see if he had money to pay the expenses.

The old man knew a short cut down the precipice.

They found some letters and five dollars in the man's pockets.

"This will bury him without interfering with our money," says Peacock.

After taking a long drink from the quart bottle, they started to see the old man; got to his house about ten o'clock, roused him up and told the sad story.

The man seemed sorry and agreed to make the coffin and bury him in his family graveyard.

Peacock considered all responsibility now off his hands, paid the charge of two dollars, then he and his friend left and went a mile further into a deep ravine where they found hid among the brush a "wild cat distillery." The men had a fire and were hard at work. The old mountaineer was one of the proprietors, so they did not fear the man he brought with him, but got down their bottles and an old greasy deck of cards, which looked like they had been through the war. They began to gamble at five cents on the corner, drinking hard all the time.

In the morning Peacock looked as mean as he in reality was when the two started, staggering towards home for their breakfast. When they got to the house they found Mary in one of their filthy beds, sick, she said, of a headache, but if one could have seen that poor, broken heart!

Peacock knew his own baseness and well knew the cause of Mary's illness. It was not kindness, nor any humane feeling which prompted him to offer to do anything to relieve her pain. There was that three thousand dollars he had not yet clutched and she must not die yet, so he began to bathe her head and expressing words of sympathy, but she knew too well now the base hypocrisy in his soul. She complained no more nor said ought of the reeking fumes of tobacco or the stench of whiskey that poisoned the air of the den she was in. When he proposed for her to walk out with him, she gladly accepted his invitation.

"To be murdered outright would be better than what I see and feel here;" she resolved as a means of safety not to let him have the remotest idea of her thoughts and intentions, she only asked him,

"How could you treat me in this way? Why did you have the heart to deceive me thus? Only look at the creatures you have placed me with! Will you tell me what you intend by being here! I hope you have not intended giving up civilization to live among brutes?" [Page 12 End]

"I will tell you, Mary, I will go to a little house I have built near here, for the purpose of spending the summer and will try to do my best while I am here, but where we will go hereafter I don't know."

"Then, Mr. Peacock, if it is poverty that brings you here, why did you hesitate to tell me. You must have a poor opinion of an honorable woman if you think she would place obstacles in your way. If you had spoken outright and honestly you would have saved me and perhaps yourself from some disquieting thoughts and feelings. If you have a house ready or not ready, let us go immediately to it. I had rather lay on the bare ground, with the trees for a covering, than to see or hear those monsters in human shape; those caricatures of humanity; besides, their everlasting questioning distracts me, and the girl talks as if she expected to be your wife. At any rate, she does not know our relationship. She thinks I am your sister and I said nothing to the contrary."

"Well, now Mary, you have told me something. Let them think that and we can get a servant in her if we only keep up the delusion. So you mind, now I tell you, don't tell them any better. Remember now, I am in earnest. We can save money by it and she will help you."

Mary remembered too well the brutal words hurled at her on the mountain and knew he was capable of any brutality. She did not doubt now that he was the originator of all the troubles those creatures had caused her, and that "remember" she knew full well what it meant. She knew while in his power, helpless and unprotected, she had but one course to follow, and that was to be very prudent in words, looks and action.

When they returned to the house, the creatures were glad to see Peacock, but Mary was nobody with them. They insisted on his coming in, but he had promised Mary he would only bid them good-bye. He got two of the men to go with him to get the smashed up trunks.

It was a relief to Mary to get into the log house. While Peacock was gone the privacy for the time was what she needed to recall her excited and shattered thoughts. His worse than demoniacal eyes upon her would have turned her brain. Now she found relief for her burning brain and broken heart in tears, such tears she never dreamed of shedding. Her thoughts reverted to home; her quiet, peaceful home. They may have had trouble and sorrow at times, but the trouble and sorrow were visitations from On high, not the work of a fiend in human shape. She felt now there was no hope. "I can never distress those at home by letting them know the depth of my degradation, and it will distress them if I do not write, and oh! how can I write lies?"

As she sat with clasped hands and streaming eyes she did not notice the lapse of time until roused by the scream of an owl and lest Peacock should come and find her in her misery, she rose up in great terror and began fixing up the few things the mountaineer had placed there, but Peacock and the men with the trunks came late, and he saw nothing more than her pale face and quiet manner, never dreaming of the storm of agony that had passed over her. He on his way to the mountain, concluded his best way would be to acknowledge Mary to be his wife to them. Fiend as he was, he thought that it would be best not to go too far.

It was like another leave-taking, so heartbreaking was it to Mary to open the trunks and look upon those tokens of affection from the loved ones so far away. But the honorable Mr. Peacock only considered them as conducing to his comfort, wished there had been more. "The handsome rug was just the thing for him to rest on: the pretty curtains would keep the sun from shining too bright through that semblance of a window where he liked to sit." Mary soon had a pretty and comfortable room and she thought it always looked lighter whenever Peacock left it and darker when he came in. After the old mountaineer and his boys had put the trunks in the house, the old fellow took Peacock off a little distance and wanted to know what kin that woman was to him?

Peacock tried to evade answering, but the yahoo was resolute, and at last he had to tell him she was his wife.

The old man was furious.

"And you had the dog in you to go and marry another wife and fool my datter, did you?

Peacock said: "Now, look here, old man, there is no use in your taking on in such a way. I am going to get a divorce from this one. I have got it, but I want to get some money first from her, then I will marry your daughter."

"Peacock, I know you are telling a lie. I have got sense enough to know that. You haint going to do no sich thing."

"Now, let me tell you, old man, I will make it all right with your daughter, and I will tell you some plans how we can make lots of money?"

"Well Peacock if you can do that ar thing, likely we can agree yit, go on and let me hear you."

"Well old man it is simply this, I understand counterfeiting to perfection, and I understand the art of making whiskey, and we will go in partnership in both, and equally divide the profits."

"Well Mr. Peacock I understand making whiskey. I don't understand making money, how do you go about hit?"

"Well old man I can take this soft clay and make an impression of a silver dollar, I can make silver that could not be detected only by an expert." They shook hands on it and returned to the house good friends. If Mr. Peacock could have found Mary exhausted by hard work he would have had a more complacent feeling. It made him mad to see, how easily she had succeeded in the arrangement of the house, the supper that was being cooked from the lately purchased cooking utensils, had a savory smell, the biscuit looked white and crisp. Peacock of course invited his friend to partake with them, and this was Mary's company and the first meal in her bridal home. Soon after, Peacock and yahoo left; Mary felt it was a release. What her future was to be was not hard to guess, "so young and to be thus wrecked. No hope, nothing but a wretched future."

Mr. Peacock did not return home until late in the night, or rather early in the morning. He had been with a set of roughs plotting how they could manage to make their fortunes. When he returned Mary did not care to ask him any questions, she thought it likely he was a worse man than any of his associates, she knew he was after no good. After breakfast he left, saying it would be late before he returned. So suspicious had she grown of him, she feared he was endeavouring [*sic*] in some way to entrap her.

During the morning she took a walk to see something of the locality, and hoping to see a better specimen of people than she had seen, she found a pretty creek lined with pretty moss-covered rocks and beautiful evergreens and sat down by the side of the creek and gathered up little stones and pretty flowers. At some distance she saw several little girls playing. She went to them and her kind tone and gentle manner soon won their confidence; she interested herself in their little plays and they asked her where she came from. Mary answered all their childish questions patiently and kindly. One said, "oh you are the new woman that has come here to live." And Mary knew now she had been spoken of, "but in what way" she could not tell. Then she said, "you see so few strangers here no wonder you heard of our arrival." They were an uncouth set, but she was glad to meet them. One of the children was worse dressed than the others, but her face evinced more intelligence, and she would have been beautiful had she received the benefits of a cultured mind and manners. Mary asked her where she lived.

"Only a little way down the creek ma'm." she said.

"What business does your mother and father follow?"

"They don't do much, but work about the house."

"Are they crippled or sick?"

"Oh no ma'm, they are deaf and dumb, they have some land and a cow. I milk the cow."

"What is your name?" "Sallie ma'm. I get mighty lonesome at home, there is no child but me, and I get tired talking on my fingers."

"Did you ever go to school?" "No ma'm, but I hope some day I will get to go."

"Would you like to have some nice clothes and learn to read?"

"Oh yes ma'm I would real like that."

Mary said she would go and see her mother, and they walked on when the others scampered off feeling aggravated that they were not more noticed too. They gave vent to their ill nature in shouts of derision.

Mary walked with Sallie to her father's cabin, and told the child to tell them who she was and how they met; this was soon done and the mother told Sallie to ask her in the house. Mary went in and was glad to see everything looking neat and cleanly. She attributed it to the fact they had few visitors because they could not gossip. After a little time she rose to leave, but first got the parents consent to let Sallie come to see her. She gave them some change that she had in her pocket. She had been at home but a little while when Sallie came in. The two soon sat down to a book, and Mary was pleased to see how well her little protege comprehended. She enquired of the child if she could get a good little girl to help her in house work. Sallie knew, she said, a mighty good little girl she knew would be glad to come. And Mary said:

"Then if she is good and sensible I will take her and teach her too." She dreaded the girl from the house she had been staying in, she thought the whole family were deceitful and cunning, and the male members, she thought were capable of committing any diabolical crime.

[TO BE CONTINUED]

[Page 13 End]

Figure 17 - The Dumb Alphabet, A woman using sign language. Coloured aquatint by W.T. Annis, 1819, after a painting by J. Northcote. (Wellcome Collection. Public Domain)

CHAPTER XVII.

After dinner Mary went to the store which was a miserable concern, and took Sallie and gave her as nice an outfit as she could and it made a wonderful improvement; the fashion of the cheap goods were tastefully made, the little white apron and collar with the pinkish dress, with the nice combed hair, almost made Sallie a little beauty. The girl she got to help in house duties was also neatly clothed. Mary commenced teaching them their spelling lessons from the book, but told or read to them the history of the United States, describing the war of the colonies against England; at first it was missionary work, but after a time they would ask each other and give their own ideas about what they had heard read to them. The day after Mary first met them, all were engaged sewing—making up the new clothes—but of a sudden the needles lay idle on the work, the laugh was hushed and Mary's heart beat as if it would burst its bonds. Peacock and his gang were heard coming, screaming and yelling in their drunken fury. Peacock, as he came on began yelling.

"Mary we are tired and hungry, get us something to eat, quick, I say. Coming into the house, he asked, who have you here?"

She told him how they helped her, and she taught them."

Well never mind, you get on and get us something to eat."

Mary and the children soon got the meal ready, and when over they prepared to go, but said in their rough and savage manner they would be back that night. Peacock had sneered at the dinner; at her attempt to teach the children. Her danger was too great to allow the slightest shadow of displeasure to be seen. It was his wish to make her resent his brutal abuse, she did not do that, and then he began in a snappish way to ridicule her, still she was silent, he took revenge on chairs, doors or whatever else stood in his way, by pitching them over, slamming doors and so forth, at last the ruffians were gone. Mary could not hide her fear of being murdered one day by Peacock, or one of his gang. Those men had built a rough shed close to the distillery—and under this shed they intended to use the moulds freely. Peacock thought he could make money that would pass in that country, then he would buy up stock and make money enough to assist him to accomplish a devilish plan he had in view; no one but the old yahoo, knew of this plan. The counterfeiters began work making dollars and half dollars that would take an expert to detect. Time went on, and Peacock bought up all the cattle he could, at first he spread his money out with those living somewhere hid in the mountains, he gave to the store, in return for provisions and golds, some of the cattle he had bought. And as time went on, Mary set up a little school, where she taught the young yahoos in warm weather, under a large tree in front of the cabin. A feeling of danger prompted her in this; a school, and a woman teaching, was a new sight, a crowd would gather round and listen to what was going on; they laughed and would say,

"I wonder what is the usen theyern has got fur sich stuff," then they would laugh louder,"at that ar kink of book larning." Mary had to listen in her helplessness, to all their rude and low sayings. Many of their remarks she could not understand, and began to think a master fiend, in the shape of Peacock, was the spirit that brought them there and made this horrid annoyance for her; but she controlled her feelings enough not to let them suspect her fears, and went on quietly with her teaching.

Sallie now staid with her at night, going home for a little while in the morning. Often during the night they would be aroused at late hours by Peacock and his gang—who would occupy the bed Mary had prepared for herself. One evening while she was attending to her school as usual, Peacock came running up in breathless haste and told, her his friend—the yahoo—had been arrested for distilling, and he was afraid he would be arrested too, as his accomplice.

"I must hide. Take good care of yourself, I will see you again, so soon as all is quiet. Get me some bread and meat to take with me, get it quick, you[.]"

He left right away to find a hiding place for himself. Mary doubted his story and could not help thinking it a trick of some sort; but it was not long before she saw some men, she took to be revenue officers, with two prisoners whom they had captured counterfeiting and distilling, and enquired—with an oath—if such a man as Peacock was in the house?

Mary very quietly replied he was not.

"Then where is he, woman?"

"I cannot tell you, sir, for I have no idea where he is."

"Well," says a rough-looking fellow, "we had just as soon have you as him, you are his wife, I believe."

"Yes sir, but I know nothing of what Mr. Peacock has been doing."

"Well, now I know that is not so, you are bound to know what he has been doing; and you say, you don't know, and he has been running a counterfeit concern here on a pretty large scale."

Mary's blood ran cold as she said to herself, "oh, what shall I do! heavens! to be connected with a counterfeiter, oh my God!"

The men were searching the house and every conceivable hiding place. One of the men came out of the house in a rage, because he thought they would be baffled in their search. In a rough manner he caught Mary by the arm and said:

"Now, old gal, you have either to go as prisoner or else produce that villain [sic] Peacock."

"Oh, sir, how can you treat me thus, I am nothing but a poor unfortunate girl, just married and brought here from my family and friends, to this desolate place which is nothing more than a prison, I was trying to be contented and do the best I could; the only company I have had has been these poor little children. I have been teaching, them, trying to do what good I could." One of the officers had said not a word, but saw that Mary did not belong to the class around her and when she had finished talking to the ruffian, he walked up to him and said:

"Let go the woman, she is innocent, and while I have strength no one shall molest her; I know the poor girl's situation, she did not know whom she was marrying; furthermore, I believe every word she has said to be the truth."

The man let go her arm, and she returned heartfelt thanks to the officer for his kindness, he offered her any assistance she needed, would do whatever was in his power for her. She needed assistance, but did not dare to ask for any, she feared Peacock too much to complain and knew his gang would repeat all she said, besides, she knew the full extent of Peacock's cunning, and did not know but what he was listening. After while the officers rode off with their prisoners.

Mary watched them until they were out of sight, and being too horrified to teach more, that day, sent all the children away except Sallie. She threw herself upon her bed and burying her head in the clothes, let her mind run full length upon all the wretchedness that encompassed her.

"Oh! how sweet death would be to me."

She had long since known Peacock was a vagabond, but never dreamed he was a felon. How can I bear this disgrace? Tied to a vagabond of the worst description, and a felon too, the most cruel. I will never let my parents know what has been my doom. I can no longer hope, even that is denied me. May be God will look in mercy upon me. He alone is now all to whom I have to look for protection."
[Page 14 End]

She felt a hand laid lightly on her aching head; it was little Sallie's, who was frightened at all she had seen. She said:

"Oh Miss Mary, what is the matter, won't you let me help you— you won't be taken, will you?"

"Oh, no, Sallie, we will stay here, we can be happy together, can't we?"

"Oh, yes, Miss Mary, and I had rather stay with you than any one else in the world, you have been so good to me."

At this Mary kissed her and thought, "this is one comfort I ought to be thankful for, and it makes me think God has not altogether deserted me."

The whole community was surprised to hear of the news and how nearly Peacock had come being arrested, and that he was in connection with counterfeiters; and while a good many of these people were down on him for deceiving them, he had many desperadoes who were warm friends of his, who were perfectly reckless, and he knew he could depend on them in time of trouble. This gang called themselves the ku klux, and were a large band and had released several persons arrested for violations of law; they had at times put up notices not to arrest or confine them again, and nobody dared to disobey them.[48] Peacock knew they were powerful in that part of the country, and consequently he joined them when he first came among them. He left his hiding place and went to see some of the most influential members of this organization. Although the youngest his education made him a leader. On a consultation among them they agreed to a plan for all to meet at a certain place and hour the next night, and then go to the town of B., and there by force, if necessary, release the prisoners as agreed upon. They sent messengers out for all the members to be present promptly at the crossing of Tooxy creek. Peacock did not go home, nor did he care to see Mary, but went to a miserable den to await the hour for the

---

[48] See Appendix VIII for more information and primary source material regarding the Ku Klux Klan in Tennessee during the 1870s, including a confidential "Letter of Advice" sent out by the first Grand Wizard, Nathan Bedford Forrest in 1872.

band to meet. When the time drew near, he borrowed a horse and left at full speed, armed with a large knife and pistol. After riding for some distance he came to the creek where the party were to meet him, and found he was the first to arrive. He secreted himself under a large tree which went by the name of Juno's tree. A negro by that name had been hung on it some time before. Peacock did not have long to wait before he heard horse's feet in the distance, and looking up saw men coming from every direction. When they arrived a salute was given—the leader rode in front and fired his pistol twice in the air; then all started at full speed. The people they met were much frightened, for they knew that gang too well. They kept at full speed into the town, right up to the jail yard through the gate and stopped right in front of the jail door. The jailer was ordered to turn the keys over to them, and he was only too glad to obey. A roll was called, beginning with the names of the officers who arrested the prisoners the day before, the roll including a great many persons living in town—this as a warning. When this was done they entered the cell and took charge of the prisoners, and then posted a notice on the jail door, warning the authorities never to trouble these men again—naming not only the prisoners but Peacock also. The key was returned to the jailer, and the masked party left.

When Peacock returned home the next morning he found Mary and Sallie cooking breakfast. He went up to Mary and kissed her, thinking at the time he had better get her good will, for some time in the future he hoped to get the money that he knew would become hers. Mary returned the kiss, but it was a terrible dose to her. She even then smelled the whisky he had been drinking the night before, but knew not who had been his associates. If she asked him if he was in serious trouble his reply would be, "I have my troubles, but they are not serious; it is true my acts are indictable, but I don't intend to let such as that trouble me much, for I have good backers. The men who were arrested yesterday are now released, and if my name is connected any longer in this matter those who connect it shall suffer the effects of a cow-hide, and if that is not severe enough they will have the experience of swinging in the air."

Mary did not know who all this was meant for, but had a strong suspicion that it was meant for herself. She asked no further questions, but went on with her work.

Peacock was not no sure of his safety. He knew he had committed a grave crime against the United States. Thinking he was risking too much to be at home, concluded he would go down and see his partner and make arrangements to move their machines to another hiding-place. He told Mary it would be late before he returned. She made no reply ; nor did she tell him a word about how the officers had treated her. It was a relief when he was gone. Clasping her hands over her aching heart, she exclaimed, "Oh, how can all this end! if I was only with dear papa and mama! Dear mama never gave me one unkind word, but always taught one what was right in the kindest manner; and when I was with dear Eva and Kate, we all lived in such happiness together. Now to look back on those dear times. Oh! it is enough to break my heart;

"For past pleasures
Doubles present pain,
And sorrow adds regret,
Oh, memory, torture me no more,
I ask but to forget."[49]

____

[49] This poem, most often attributed to Lord Byron (1788-1824), reads:
"Oh Memory, torture me no more,
   The present's all o'ercast;
My hopes of future bliss are o'er,
   In mercy veil the past.
Why bring those images to view I henceforth must resign ?
   Ah ! why those happy hours renew,
That never can be mine?
   Past pleasure doubles present pain,
To sorrow adds regret,
   Regret and hope are both in vain, I ask but to — forget."

While she was repeating these lines her heart was all pain, but she had resolved to die rather than let her parents know of her suffering and misery, and add to their present troubles on account of their uncertainty concerning her. She loved them too well to ever give them a single pang; and she resolved to remain where she was and try to live the life of a hermit, let it end as it would; and said she: "I fear it will be an awful ending." [TO BE CONTINUED]

Figure 18 - "The Ride for Life." 1880. Albion W. Tourgée, 1838-1905. Published by Fords, Howard & Hulbert. "Violent moonlit pursuit on horseback involving a hooded Ku Klux Klan member and a caped young woman firing a gun. Albion Winegar Tourgée championed the civil rights of blacks in the Reconstruction South. He used his position as judge and his training as a writer to advance radical Reconstruction policy and Negro rights. He supported political, legal and economic reform in the face of racial conflict and Ku Klux Klan violence. His crowning literary achievements were his two Reconstruction novels of social criticism, A Fool's Errand and Bricks Without Straw." See Appendix VIII for expanded discussion about Klan activity in Tennessee during the 18780s/1880s. (Courtesy Tennessee State Library and Archives)

Figure 19 – "Raiding a Counterfeiter's Coin Den," Frank Leslie's Illustrated, 1879, "By the end of the Civil War, nearly one-third of all currency in circulation was counterfeit. As a result, the country's financial stability was in jeopardy. To address this concern, the Secret Service was established in 1865 as a bureau in the Treasury Department to suppress widespread counterfeiting." (Courtesy of the US Secret Service), "This engraving from Leslie's Illustrated in 1879, a weekly newspaper, depicts a raid by 'operatives' of the US Secret Service. On the left, two men use a screw press, whereas a third man is putting the freshly minted coins in bags. In the background, two men appear to be preparing the metal for coining. The Secret Service agents in their characteristic bowler hats climb from above into the counterfeiter's den." (Courtesy of American Numismatic Society, http://numismatics.org/the-beginnings-of-the-secret-service/, accessed 1 Sep 2021)

CHAPTER XVIII

Two years had passed and John Hill was no longer a clerk, having inherited a large sum from an almost unknown uncle. On the receipt of the letter, he resolved to ask for the place of his uncle in the banking house, and his request was granted. Now he was no more just John Hill, but Col. Hill. One day looking over a newspaper he saw the death of Mr. Laurette announced; can it be Bessie's father? yes it is; here are his initials and it says the gentleman was from Mississippi. The notice spoke of his wealth and also said he had no children to grieve his loss. "Can Bessie[50] be dead?" and the very thought made Col. Hill very sad. He forgot the bitter pangs her thoughtless unkindness had given him; now he only remembered her loveliness and the many times that she was kind and friendly, how he, as a poor unknown man, had received every attention from her. Now it would have been, in his eyes, profanity to have coupled her name with any fault whatever. Col. Hill never, in his poorest and shabbiest days was as miserable as he was now, seated in his charming breakfast room, surrounded by all the appliances of luxury that wealth and taste could give.

---

[50] Original says "Annie," but "Bessie" makes sense in the context.

"Poor Bessie! my dear Bessie, now an angel, and my hopes are shattered. I had pictured the day of our meeting again, but alas! even that boon is denied me!"

The distressed banker, if he had known more about the Laurettes, he would have known that Mr. Laurette had taken Bessie from and orphan's asylum when she was almost an infant; he was a widower and was not fond of society, but still he was not satisfied to be entirely alone: he had no children, and seeing this lovely little prattler, asked for her and promised to rear and educate her as his own, and no expense was spared for her happiness and improvement. He had died without making the least provision for her maintainance [*sic*]—a singular occurrence, indeed. A few hours before his death, his only brother arrived from his poor home in the country. He attended the funeral with a woeful face but not a broken heart; his family now were provided for and he was a rich man. He knew Bessie was not his niece, and no will was found, so she could not claim the wealthy estate. All the necessary forms had been passed through, and he thought it best, to let Bessie know at once who she was. He entered her elegant private parlor and found the poor girl almost heart broken at her loss of so dear and kind a papa. Her supposed uncle shocked her by asking:

"What is the matter?"

"Oh, dear uncle how can you ask me that? oh, my father, my dear father, I miss your [Page 15 End] protection now already;" and she sobbed as if her heart would burst. The unfeeling man said:

"Bessie, my brother was not your father. He took you out of an asylum and you ought to be very thankful to him for all his kindness to you. If it had not been for him you might have been to-day an outcast. But don't cry so, Bessie, you can stay here. I am going to send for my family and will live in this house and you can be as one of my children." Then he left her alone in her wretchedness. But his cruel words and manner recalled her shattered senses. She knew full well that a man who could use such language would not for a moment hesitate to act the part of an unfeeling villain [*sic*]. She ran off as it were for protection, to her old nurse.

"Oh, nurse what is this I hear from my uncle? What does it mean? Am I dreaming? Have I been deceived! You and all have made me believe my mother was dead and that my own dear adopted father was really my own papa. Oh, dear, nurse what is to become of me now?"

"Baby don't cry, it will all come right one of these days."

And nurse took her in her arms and smoothed her hair, and soothed her with words of encouragement, and told her she would watch over her; told her of the family that were coming to take possession, they knew little of the kind of society her Bessie had mixed with.

"Be careful honey, for they will envy you, but I will see that they will do you no harm; put up with their affectation of good manners, and all the nonsense they will put on, for they are ignorant people. Your dear papa could not bear to have them about him, but I will see that they treat you well. Now go honey, and take a little walk on the lawn."

The nurse was an English woman and had been much trusted by the late Mr. Laurette. She had had charge of Bessie ever since Mr. Laurette had brought her from the Asylum. Bessie walked out on the lawn and gazed upon every shrub and flower as if she was looking her last, and turned to look upon the house where she had spent so many happy years. "Likely I shall be driven forth as a beggar, thought she, no one to care for me, none but my nurse to give me a kind word. Dear papa would not let me make many acquaintances, and now I am alone and know not one to ask assistance from or to ask what I must do. Oh, never did I think such a fate would be mine, and I am so helpless! Oh, how I dread the coming of uncle's wife and daughters; they did not like me when they came here once. I understand now, the rude things they then said to me; then I only laughed at them, but now they will make me cry bitter tears; oh, I wish I knew where to go; nurse will show me how to work and I will help her; if I stay here they will ill treat me and that will kill me."

The nurse came out to her child as she called her, and tried to console her, but her grief seemed too deep; she was at last prevailed on to go into the house. She saw no one but her nurse.

The new proprietor came and took possession. Several gentleman [*sic*] called upon him, for the respect they had for his dead brother, but suspected the new master would prove a failure. He telegraphed to his family to come to their new home.

Bessie dreaded their coming and feared they would only come too soon.

They came at last; a hack and baggage wagon [*sic*] deposited the living freight and old trunks at the door of the late Mr. Laurette. Poor Bessie watched them from a window—they were five in number—the mother and father, the two sisters and the gawky awkward son of eighteen. By their appearance they had fixed up for the occasion, and no doubt, their new clothes would have been thought very fine in the country where they came from, but in the city they looked shab by genteel, and did not correspond with the mansion they entered.

Bessie met them with all the fortitude she could command, thinking, possibly, "This is the last time I will have a chance to act as mistress."

They were all seated in state in the fine drawing-room. The father asked about the friends and neighbors up in the country. The daughters began asking Bessie about the fashions and what was the most fashionable dress goods. The lout[51] of a son began a display of his ignorance by talking of city amusements. The father and mother were anxious to go through the house "and give it a good inspection." The daughters and son said: "We must see all the pretties too."

---

[51] Lout = an awkward brutish person

To chaperone these yahoos was more than Bessie could do—her fortitude would break down there. She called her nurse to show them the house and to let them select their rooms. She made a feint as if she were going, too, and as she was totally unnoticed, it was no difficult matter for her to escape to her own room, and there alone in her wretchedness she gave free vent to her pent up feelings. The nurse came in with a frightened face, but it looked worse on seeing the distress of her young charge, and she dared not add to it by telling her that the daughters had concluded, that they would take her rooms.

The family had now gone to inspect the outside surroundings. Both mother and daughters suggested the moving of shrubs and flowers into this or that place and then they would look more like Squire R's and Miss Jones'. The boy, fancying himself a perfect Apollo—not that I know if he had ever heard of Apollo—was standing back with his hands in his pockets, looking as if hung together on pivots; now and then he would put in a word and tell something about his "hoss." Returning to the house, they held a long and whispered talk about Bessie.

"I don't like that stuck-up thing. She ain't a bit like Susan Jones. Now if she was here I would be mighty glad," said one of the girls.

"By jingo! wouldn't we have a fine time" said Apollo.

"Girls," said the father, "you must watch these city people and see how they do. I am rich now and don't want to be outdone. You must dress fine, and I wouldn't talk about the folks where we come from."

Bessie mustered up courage to come down and go in with them to supper. She stood her usual place at the head of the table, and, controlling her voice as well as she could, asked:

"Madam, I suppose you will take this place now?"

"Deed will I. I have always poured out my own coffee, and my old man thinks I fix up hisen better than anybody else can." And down she sat, she and all her family looking a strange and strong contrast to Bessie and to the finished appearance of the room. Their mode of handling knife and fork was awkward; their ravenous eating was disgusting. Their total ignorance of table etiquette was astonishing. Bessie thought, locking at them, that instinct should tell them better. The servants would hastily leave the room to prevent their seeing them laugh.

When gentlemen called their attention and conversation were very naturally directed to Miss Laurette and this exasperated the family exceedingly and one day one of the girls in a fit of desperation said to her:

"That if she didn't quit trying to draw the men to notice her and quit her fool talk about books and telling men, yes, men, how she liked a fellow she called Walter Scott[52], yes, you ought to be ashamed of yourself, you brazen-faced thing, you ought to be shut up!"

"Yes," says the mother, "she not only tells how she likes that man Scott, but she talks of ever so many more fellers. There's one she calls Thacry[53], something like that. Some outlandish name. Why, husband, she calls dozens of them fellers' names and she says she likes them all. I'll tell you, you 'Jeze-bell!' my darters have been living among the first in the land. They have always been in good society and I will not let them know sich as you."

On one occasion Miss Laurette was in her room. The girls had gone shopping; the father and Apollo had gone to see if they could not get their roasts and steaks cheaper. Bessie did not know of the family dispersion, but supposed they were all in the drawing room and went down as usual to see the gentleman. When she saw he was alone, she

---

[52] Sir Walter Scott, 1st Baronet (15 Aug 1771 Edinburg, Scotland – 21 Sep 1832) = Scottish novelist, poet, historian, and biographer who is often considered both the inventor and the greatest practitioner of the historical novel. Famous titles include *Ivanhoe*, *Rob Roy*, *Waverley*, *The Heart of Mid-Lothian*, and narrative poems *The Lady of the Lake* and *Marmion*. Charley references his novel *Guy Mannering* in Chapter XXIX.
[53] William Makepeace Thackeray (18 Jul 1811 – 24 Dec 1863) = British novelist, author, and illustrator. He is known for his satirical works, especially his 1848 novel *Vanity Fair*, and the 1844 novel *The Luck of Barry Lyndon*. (Source: Wikipedia)

asked "if he did not wish to see the young ladies?" "No, Miss Bessie, as heaven is my judge, I do not." [Page 16 End]

The time passed very pleasantly with the two. How long he had been there neither had taken notice. But how Bessie regretted to hear the rustling of the silks and the coarse voices of the young ladies. One asked the servant in the hall:

"If any one had called?"

"Yes, Miss, a gentleman."

"Where is his card?"

"He sent it to Miss Bessie."

The girls made a rush for the company to stop further mischief. They met the gentleman at the door coming out. No entreaties of theirs could induce him to return. He knew all conversation with Bessie would be at an end in their presence. The speech to Bessie was,

"Just wait till pa comes, then you will catch it, Miss Impudence!"

"Why, you were not here to receive the company and besides, he asked for me. I suppose your father will tell me what to do the next time."

There was a spice of mischief in Bessie's nature and she could not help enjoying the discomfiture[54] of the two sisters who were mad with envy. The gentleman who had called was a "bone of contention" between the sisters. Both were fighting for him, and to think he had been listening to the hated Bessie; it was too bad. They could not deny to themselves she had beauty, that she was a splendid performer and was greatly admired. So many good reasons why she must be gotten rid of. The friends she had made all told her to have patience. Those who had known her but slightly in the days of her prosperity knew enough to make them suppose a will in her favor had been suppressed, for her supposed father appeared devoted to her and it was not a supposable case that he would have left her in this forlorn condition,

---

[54] Discomfiture = a feeling of slight embarrassment or confusion.

and she was told that morning by the lawyer friend that he was confident from what he knew of her father some bad act had been perpetrated. He asked her if she had examined the hidden corners in his desk—examined recesses in his room. She never had, besides she believed her uncle was too big a fool ever to have thought of taking that advantage.

"Now I can't go in dear papa's room for they occupy it."

Still she was told to keep a look out for a will they were sure had been made, and it was impressed upon her not to leave the house: "be blind and deaf to them." So she gave up her cherished idea of working her fingers "to the bone" before she would stand their ignorance, meanness and taunts. She would try—sometimes only—to conciliate them.

One day the man and his wife were having a talk, the old man says:

"Look here, wife, I am owner here and I am thinking that gal, Bessie, is trying to run the hog over our gals and that's something I am not going to stand, not going to put up with. We are rich and she is nobody and I am not going to stand her much longer. Our gals are as proud as peacocks and knows a sight more then she does."

"And, husband, our darters don't set up and tell how they like that man, Dickens[55], and that feller Scott. Just to think on it, and I wonder if them fellers air rich. If you say put her outen the house I will soon do it, and she won't carry any silks and jewelry with her either."

"Put her out. Yes I will and that soon too. Any feller that I want to notice our gals she goes and hauls over to her side. Yes, she will go soon. Then see who will notice her when I give her up."

---

[55] Charles John Huffam Dickens (7 Feb 1812 – 9 Jun 1870) = English writer and social critic. He wrote 15 novels, five novellas, hundreds of short stories and non-fiction articles, lectured, and performed readings extensively. Published *The Pickwick Papers* (1836) as a serial, the novella *A Christmas Carol* (1843), but also *Oliver Twist* (1838), *Great Expectations* (1861), and *The Tale of Two Cities* (1859). https://en.wikipedia.org/wiki/Charles_Dickens, accessed 4 Sep 2021.

The nurse who had from the first kept a watchful eye upon the man in particular, overheard this dialogue. She did not tell Bessie any of it, but told her not to go out of her room no matter who called and if possible not to see any of the family while she was gone.

"And, nurse, where are you going?"

"Only a few streets from here. I must attend to a bit of business of mine. I will not be gone long, but I will feel easier if you will remain entirely alone while I am gone."

Bessie promised to lock her door and pretend to be asleep. The nurse was seen to go to the house of an old lawyer who had been on intimate terms with the late Mr. Laurette.

(TO BE CONTINUED.)

[Page 17 End]

CHAPTER XIX.

Near two years had passed and poor Mary was still a prisoner in that miserable hut, with mountains around her as prison walls, but she was not all alone with Sallie. There sat on her lap a pretty baby boy, his sweet face was his mother's miniature as she was in happier days, he was laughing and cooing to Salle as she played bopeep with him. The hut looked even worse than usual; from time to time Peacock had carried off what books she had and all the little articles she had accumulated to make the place look comfortable. Now there was but little to eat, and Mary looked paler and thinner than she ever did before; she strove to keep up for the sake of baby, and must try to live now to protect him. She had of late thought of writing to her father, but knew if it was discovered by Peacock her life would be taken, and if he got the letter and came for her, his life would be taken, and none of his family would ever hear what his fate had been. She knew the lawlessness of Peacock's life; now, and of his associates. One day while Sallie was playing with the baby, and Mary was reading the only book she had, Peacock came home alone, for the first time in a long while, his habit now was to bring his gang of ruffians with him to eat, to play cards and drink whiskey. But, Mary feared him more alone than with his gang. He walked up to her and said:

"I have a proposition to make to you, and it will be to our advantage. I would not think of making it if it was not for our boy. I could not realize our awful condition before, it is all for our child's sake. I will tell you. I want you to give me an order to your father for the amount he said was due you. I promise not to let him know our condition, but will tell him we have been to Europe and I will make it all right with hum. With that money we will go to some pleasant place on the railroad and put up a store and we will invite your parents to come and visit too. What do you say, Mary?"

"Oh, Mr. Peacock, it sounds nice, but you have deceived me so often, how can you want me to ruin my father?"

He began to get frightened for he thought she would have jumped at any proposal to get away from there. He said:

"Now, Mary don't you want to get away from here?"

"Certainly I do, but you brought me here through deceit and wrecked my life by your unkindness, and now you would ruin my father."

"Then, am I to understand you say you will not give me that order?"

"Yes, Mr. Peacock, I feel it would be wrong to do so, to injure my father, perhaps ruin him in his old age."

Peacock got into a violent rage, took the child from her arms, and exclaimed.

"If I can't get the order and the money to live decent, I will take the child and leave, and you may stay here and rot if you desire."

He knew this was the way to accomplish his purpose, he knew Mary would die before she would give up her child.

She exclaimed, "for God's sake don't take my child, I will trust you once more." She wrote the order at his dictation and a lying letter about having been in Europe, and that the money would be returned in a few days. He was now satisfied, but he told her if she dared to betray him, she would do it at the risk of her life, and that he would kill her child.

He was tired living there, he wanted to be more comfortable, he wanted his wine and turtle soup[56], he wanted to hear music and see flowers, and see rich people, and so forth.

He hastened to the railroad where he took a train, and as he rolled along on his mission of ruin, he digested in his mind which would be the best course to pursue to accomplish his devilish designs. At last he was in the town of A— and was soon surrounded by his old friends and acquaintances, he inquired directly for John Hill. When told he was now a rich banker in a distant city, it made old Satan rise in him, and he thought instantly how he could blackmail him; but he also remembered Hill was brave to the heart's core and would stand no fooling, "And," thought he, "Hill believed I was a better man than I am, or he never would have helped to ruin an innocent girl. I can say he is a true man, true as steel. Now look at me—a wreck—while he is a prosperous man." Then he almost exclaimed aloud, "Death to this thing called conscience! It will sometimes throw a fellow off his guard anyhow.

He soon got a horse and rode out to Mr. Anderson's. He rode rapidly to drive away thought. Arriving at the gate, he jumped down gaily and almost ran into the house, taking the family by surprise; but they all met him kindly, and with the question, "Where is Mary?"

"We have all this time been in Europe. Didn't you get our letters?"

"No; not a line."

Well, that is the reason we didn't hear from you, Mary wanted to come here now with me, but the physicians said she and the baby were too weak to come so far. She is now with my mother. You see I had

---

[56] Turtle Soup = Between the mid-1800s and the 1920s, the diamondback terrapin [turtle] was firmly lodged in the hearts and stomachs of the wealthy and powerful in America. During the Civil War, Confederate soldiers supplemented their meager rations with the abundant terrapin. During the early-1800s, turtles [and turtle soup] became known as a delicacy, and were prepared with a healthy dose of sherry or Madeira wine. https://www.wvpublic.org/2019-07-18/our-taste-for-turtle-soup-nearly-wiped-out-terrapins-then-prohibition-saved-them, accessed 4 Sep 2021.

to come on to Washington in great haste on important, very important business." He had a pleasant and plausible answer for every question. Told the girls Mary was just loaded down with the rarest and prettiest things for them, they ever saw.

"A letter from my child, I would rather see than anything else in the world but herself."

"Now just see my carelessness. All from being so glad to see you all. Here, Mrs. Anderson, is a letter from Mary."

All gathered around and read in silence the lying letter.

"God grant my child is well and happy."

Peacock was eyed with suspicion by those unhappy parents. His appearance was against him. There was the air of a vagrant about him. His face showed the effects of low dissipation; his manner of being respectable was forced; he was unnatural in his desire to be agreeable; overdid everything he attempted. Eva and Kate thought his presence hateful, Mr. and Mrs. Anderson thought he was a liar, and perhaps, shuddering thought, a murderer.

Peacock thought he might be suspected of falsehood, and felt frightened from the looks of Mr. and Mrs. Anderson, and he began with a bold face and a glib tongue to tell of their long journey's sightseeing in Europe, and of the wealth he would reap by entering in partnership with this big firm. Then he talked incessantly of his baby and of Mary, and by the wish of both himself and Mary they had named it for Mr. Anderson. He could talk well, his voice was good and he could tell the most plausible stories where he was concerned. During the evening he saw a change for the better in the manner and faces of all."

"My elegant conversation has made this change beyond a doubt," he thought. So early in the morning he took Mr. Anderson aside and had a long talk with him in regard to this large business in New York. "To complete it," he said, "I need a little more money," and he banded the note from Mary which read as follows:

"DEAR FATHER:—You will please let my dear husband have my portion of the money which you said would become mine. We need it very badly at present in our speculating business, and I will say further we will be able to return it in two months if you will need it. Your affectionate daughter.

"MARY ANDERSON."

The old man looked at it, and says to himself, "There is nothing wrong in this: here is her handwriting beyond a doubt." Peacock talked with all his might, and said, "it would be all right, just as Mary said, and he could return it in a very short time," and, he said he "wanted Kate to go on to New York with him now, and in a short time they would all return together."

This pleased old Anderson. He knew his children never had many advantages, and none in traveling. He told Peacock he did not have the money on hand, but he thought he could soon raise it, but he must say nothing about it to his wife. Peacock assured him he would not for anything, as he did not wish to create any bad feelings among those he had such high esteem and love for. Anderson said he would go and see what arrangements he could make. Told Peacock to speak to his wife in regard to Kate's going to New York. Peacock said he would do his best, for he wished Kate to see the king city of the United States. Anderson got on his horse and went to see his friend Col. Rollins and told him his business, and Rollins consented to let him have it, provided he would give a mortgage on his land as security, which Andersen agreed to do. The papers were fixed, and he said Mrs. Anderson would sign soon as she was able to be out. Anderson started home with the three thousand dollars safe in his pocket. At home he found Peacock in lively conversation with his wife and daughters. Kate was anxious to go, but her mother was somewhat afraid, although Peacock had now regained her good opinion. Still, she said she was not exactly willing to let Kate go. Peacock and Anderson begged she should go. Peacock's flattery of Mr. Anderson's great business talents and every other good talent had turned the old man's head. At last it was agreed that Kate could go, and preparations were made to leave the next day. Mr. Anderson was so pleased that he started right off to let the Agen family know all the good news Peacock had brought, and the fine trip Kate was to have to New York.

CHAPTER XX.

Peacock and Kate were off early the next morning, and as the train went rapidly on, he was exulting in his villainy and consequently very happy and talkative. He and Kate were talking with all their might, but at the same time he was thinking deep, while poor Kate was as thoughtless as a kitten. His plan was made out; he was to have some of his mountain pets—as be called them—to assist him in his devilish design, and that was to horrify Kate at Mary's condition; then take the child and force Kate to go with him. He was satisfied he could dispose of the child some way, and now he thought that an excellent plan. He turned suddenly to Kate and told her the same story he had before told Mary; that he had a little business to attend to, and would be forced to stop and get a buggy and go a little distance in the country, and it would rest her before starting on their grand tour. Kate thought her dear brother-in-law all right, and cheerfully agreed to go.

They were soon on the road. Peacock was very assiduous[57] attending to Kate's comfort and amusing her with his conversation. Determined not to stay all night at any place, but would go on if it took him all night, or till midnight. He pointed out the mountains in the

---

[57] Assiduous = showing great care, attention, and effort : marked by careful unremitting attention or persistent application

distance, spoke of their grandeur and was, or imagined he was very eloquent. Night was fast coming on, and he asked her "if she had not rather go on than stop at any of those country cabins." [Page 18 End]

"Go on by, all means," she said. He told her they were going to a little village where she could be comfortable. He drove at a rapid pace but night overtook them when he came to the precipice, over which the poor driver fell, he checked his horse. He thought his life was precious now and would run no risks. It was beginning to be quite late. He told Kate they were almost there now, but he checked up the horse under the pretence [*sic*] to look out the best road, but in reality to study out which would be the best plan to pursue.

"Had I better take her right on and let her see the fix Mary is in, at once? Or had I better take her to some other house and leave her there until I get the child, and then leave again to night? Yes, that will be better, then there will be no disturbance." Turning to Kate, at the forks of the road, he said:

"Kate, by jingo I have lost my road. I don't know where we are."

"Well, what do you say we are to do, Mr. Peacock?"

"Well, the only thing I know is to stop at the first house end stay all night."

He knew exactly where they were and then exclaimed:

"Good luck! yonder is a house of some sort, but any kind is better than none, and we are running a risk of our lives here to be driving through these roads."

In a few moments they were in front of the house, which belonged to his old partner in crime. He told Kate to hold the reins until he would go and see if they could stay all night. He went to the back door to keep Kate from seeing or hearing anything; he gave a hard rap on the door and the old man called out:

"Who's there?"

"A friend," said Peacock.

The old man knew in an instant who it was. He opened the door and Peacock touched him to be quiet, then handed him five dollars, and explained that he wanted him to talk very rough so Kate could hear him—that he couldn't stay, but the lady could, while he had to go a short distance to another house.

Peacock only wanted to stay until he could go and get the child, and then leave these parts in post haste. The old fellow was to assist him after Kate was in the house; then the scoundrels would leave together. On arriving at Peacock's house[,] they knocked at the door. The plan they laid was for Peacock to take the child and the other brute was to hold Mary until he escaped. When Mary heard Peacock's voice she jumped up and opened the door. Yahoo had hid in a corner waiting his turn. Mary shook hands with Peacock and asked how were all at home.

"All well and happy," replied Peacock; and continued, "How is baby and Sallie?"

She replied: "Oh, baby is as gay and bright as ever," picking up the child as she spoke.

Peacock stooped over as if to kiss the child, and snatching it from her, started off as fast as his legs could carry him. She screamed and jumped out of the door after him; but, poor thing, there was no chance for her, for their stood the ruffian who had been lying in wait, and who caught her in his vile clutches, choking her to prevent her screams being heard. He carried her back in the cabin. In the meantime[,] Peacock ran with all his might until he came to a house on the road near by. He ran in and gave the old woman a dollar to take charge of the child until he came back, which would be in a few minutes, and told her how to act when he drove up. Going back to where Kate was, he saw her sitting before a blazing pine knot fire, and said to her, "I have found a place where we can stay."

As they drove to the house where the baby was, the old woman ran out and cried: "Oh, kind sir, will you please take charge of this child, for there are some men drunk here, and they will kill if it is left in my possession."

Peacock said: "Certainly, madam, I would do anything to save the life of an innocent child." He placed it in Kate's arms and drove off as fast as possible.

(TO BE CONTINUED.)

CHAPTER XXI.

When the ruffian felt satisfied that Peacock had made good his escape, be released Mary. She had exhausted all her strength struggling with him and had now fainted and lay lifeless. When she revived, the full realization of her horrible state flashed full upon her mind. Now she had lost all she cared to live for and in her burst of agony screamed wildly:

"Oh! my child, oh! my dear child. May God have mercy upon you. Oh, what a fool I was! I am to blame for all this. Why did I not make an effort to escape, or to write the truth of my condition home and ask for help? Oh! I can see now what my fear and my lying letter has done. Too late now! Probably he has ruined my dear father to raise that money."

Sallie was frightened and crying, and daylight found the two in the deepest agony. No sound inside of the house but the deep sobbing of the two; outside, the sun shone as bright as if all were joy and gladness; nothing was heard but the gurgling stream as it flowed on; the slight rustling of the leaves and the cow bells in the distance. How calm and quiet was all nature around them! But in that hut, oh heavens! what misery! Mary could not stay in it, she went to the creek and laved her brow in its cooling waters, she then took Sallie and went to that den of a store and found that the men were just up. They were a rough looking set. She told them her sad story and her wretched looking face and weeping eyes made them almost shudder. One of them had often shown Mary little kindnesses; he looked pained and said:

"Peacock made us believe he was kind to you, and now this is a case so bad, he ought to be arrested and brought to justice."

"Is there such a law here?" Mary asked.

"Oh, yes. I am a justice of the peace and I will issue a warrant and make him suffer for this."

An officer was dispatched with the warrant on a fast horse. He soon got on the track of Peacock and was satisfied he would soon overtake him. He inquired of him at every house he passed and asked of every person he met, whether man, woman or child. He rode rapidly on and knew Peacock was making for a near cut to get into North Carolina and if he did then he could have no further jurisdiction, but riding nearly all day as fast as was prudent for the safety of his horse, he came to a small postoffice and inquired how far it was to the North Carolina line, and describing Peacock, asked if they had seen such a man with a young child.

"Yes, he passed here an hour ago, going on at a rapid rate in that direction and must be there now."

The man, hearing this, gave up all hopes of catching him and turned his horse's head homeward.

Peacock was satisfied he was now safe and stopped at a small inn for supper. They had not stopped for their dinner. He called for a room and was determined to tell Kate his intentions. Kate, as when going to the room, knew there was something wrong and was very much frightened. She was fatigued and nervous too. When inside the room he locked the door and sat down beside Kate and said he had news for her. She turned deadly pale and asked what it was.

"Well, my dear child, your poor sister, Mary, is dead. This is my child and her dying request was that, you should be my wife and be his mother. I did not wish to distress your parents said managed it in this way. I came to that mountainous country and left her child and took you there to see it."

Kate listened in dumb horror. Peacock saw she was about to faint and lifted her to the bed where she lay lifeless. He did everything to restore consciousness, but getting frightened, ran down and asked for a physician, but was told there was none nearer than five miles. He was sent for in hot haste by the landlord, and on his arrival was very much frightened at her condition. All the ladies in the house rendered every assistance. The doctor said she was dead and had died from some very sudden shock.

When the officer returned and told Mary he was unsuccessful and that Peacock had made his escape into another State, she then asked the merchant if he would purchase the few things she had which was some trunks and a few clothes. He said he could not do much with them, but would be willing to give her half of what she asked for them. Getting the money, she got up what she could carry, and bidding Sallie an affectionate good-bye and cautioning her with regard to those she associated with, she told her never to forget baby or herself and if ever the time came when she could assist her she would. [Page 19 End]

She was now going to try to find her child. She would try to get some work to support life while she made the effort to find her darling babe. She started in the direction Peacock went and had to carry her little bundle herself. Sallie grieved exceedingly at parting and went to her parents' hut and begged she might go with her, but they could not be prevailed on to consent and began her woful [*sic*] journey alone and on foot. Her intention was to walk to a small village which was sixty miles distant. She made her way the best she could, going nearly all day without eating and without stopping, and would eat her bread as she trudged along. One evening, more tired than usual, she seated herself on a rock beside a spring, and was holding the hard crust bread in her hand when quite an old man came along; seeing her and thinking she was sick, he came and asked if he could assist her. This kindness from a rough old stranger cheered her. She said she would like to find some place to stay all night, that she was tired and sick.

"My house, miss, is humble and poor, but it is always open to the weary and sick and you are welcome to the best I have."

"I do truly appreciate your kindness, for if ever a poor mortal needed rest, I do."

The old man took up her little bundle and said:

"Come with me."

They went slowly along until they reached the spot where his cabin stood. When in the house she asked how far it was to the town of Vale[58] as she was going there.

"Miss, it is forty miles, and you don't expect to walk there, do you?"

"That is my only chance to get there. I see no other way."

"Well, miss, if I had a horse, you wouldn't go there on foot, and I would go with you, but you see I am a poor old man trying to make an honest living on very poor land."

Mary thanked him for his well meant kindness. She knew she had a long and weary trip before her, but to find her baby was the mainspring. She could forget hunger and fatigue in her exertions.

When morning came[,] she was a little rested and wanted to pay something for their kindness, but they refused to take anything. She thanked them kindly and began again her weary journey.

One evening she stopped in a pretty grove and sat down to rest; a while after she saw a gang of rough looking men coming towards her and prayed that they might not see her, but they soon bawled out to her:

---

[58] Vale = Possibly Vale, West Virginia, an unincorporated community in Greenbrier County, WV. It was called Vale because it was "situated in a small valley almost surrounded in every direction by hills." *West Virginia place names, their origin and meaning, including the nomenclature of the streams and mountains.* H. Thomas Kenny,. (1945). Piedmont, W.Va.: The Place name press. Pg 642.

"Old gal, come take a drink with us."

She did not answer, but was greatly frightened. They came up to her and one said:

"By jingo! she was out late last night. Look at her eyes how red they are."

Tremblingly she said:

"Oh! please, gentlemen, do not trouble me. I am a poor, defenceless [*sic*] woman, trying to make my way to some house."

One of the gang said:

"Well, how would you like a handsome fellow like me to take a trip with you through this country," and at the same time started towards her.

She screamed aloud in her terror. Providence protects the innocent, and just then a carriage came dashing up the road. A gentleman in it, hearing the screams, stopped and came running to her. When the scamps ran off, she soon told her pitiable tale of wrong and how weary and tired she was. He said:

"You must go to town with me in my carriage and not run these risks." He told her he had been taking his wife to see her sick father. She told the gentleman as they went on that she must find some employment to get money to proceed on her journey. He saw she was an educated woman and despite her poor appearance, could see she was a lady who had seen better days. He told her he would assist her and would do anything in his power to help her. She thanked him so much for his kindness.

They arrived in town. She got a plain, quiet, nice place to stay at and after looking for a day or two, with the assistance of the gentleman, secured a good situation in a millinery establishment where she got a good salary and lived comfortably and easy and had hopes she would yet find her baby. Her unuttered prayer was, "Oh. God! protect my child." This was her thought, day and night.

CHAPTER XXII.

Months had passed since Peacock and Kate had left for New York, and no word was heard from them. The family could not imagine what was the matter. Mrs. Anderson saw that Mr. Anderson was in great trouble and first thought it was at not hearing from Kate; "But then," she said, "there is some other trouble beside that."

He had been acting differently from his usual custom. He had been riding over the country to see men he had not been in the habit of visiting. She would ask what troubled him, but in a gruff and surly man[ner] he would answer, "Fools, let me alone!"

But ah! there was something wrong and it was very serious. The money mortgage had become due. Rollins had been to see him and said he would be bound to have the money right away and must close the mortgage. Mr. Anderson asked for time. He said Peacock was a very reliable man and would send the money very soon. He had not yet heard from him, but he knew he was all right and Kate and Mary who were in New York now, he knew would write soon and it wouldn't be long before they would all come with plenty of money.

"When did you last hear from Peacock?" asked the pompous Rollins.

"Not a word since he left here."

Rollins had set Peacock down as an impostor and now he knew it and said old Anderson had not only lost one daughter but two. The Colonel was not a man who would listen to excuses, especially where a dollar was at stake, and determined to close out if he did not get the money the next week. Anderson had written to New York to find Peacock and gave the name of the street he said he lived on; but when an answer came saying no such man was living in New York, then the old man was frightened in earnest; he knew he could not get out of paying that debt without losing his valuable land. He went home in a terrible rage; went into his room[,] threw his hat on the floor and raved in such a manner that his wife ran in to see what had happened, but all she could get out of him was:

"Oh, you cursed fools, you have ruined me! Yes, I will leave, I will leave and never return! Oh, you cursed fools!" He got out the letter from New York and said: "Look at that! look at that! Oh, where can that man be with my daughters."

"Mr. Anderson, maybe it will all turn out right yet."

"Yes, it will turn us all out of doors where we will perish."

"How can that be!"

"You know you all meddled with my business so much—you are always meddling, curse you; I never can do anything, but you are meddling with—I will leave and never [Page 20 Ends] see one of you again; then see whom you will meddle with. See what I have tried to do for that lying scoundrel Peacock. He has lied to me, he has lied to me! He brought me a note from Mary, requesting me to send her some money; they would only need it for a short time. To accommodate them I gave Rollins a mortgage on my farm for the three thousand dollars"—here he yelled—"and tomorrow we will be sold out and God only knows what will become of us."

Mrs. Anderson and Eva left the room nearly distracted, not knowing what to think.

"Mamma, can this be possible?"

"I am afraid it is too true," sobbed the heart-broken woman. Mr. Anderson, left to himself, threw over chairs and tables, upset everything in his way as he stamped through the room swearing and cursing everybody but himself.

"Oh, what will Mary and Kate think when they return and find we have no home."

"Oh, Eva, I am afraid they will never be permitted to come to us. I care less about the loss of land. I am in deep dread for my children's safety."

Poor woman! she disparaged no one to save herself, but all knew she did not approve of Mary's hasty marriage or Kate's going with Peacock. She now knew some deep and dreadful villainy was going on through Peacock. She as usual blamed herself to spare that old fool husband of hers. She was suffering untold agony for those two poor lost children: she groaned in distress at the thought of what might be their fate; every thought brought pain worse than death. Her husband cursed and raved at her about the loss of his land, but she would answer very meekly and try to console him, which only made him worse.

One morning men began to gather in from all parts, and some rode into the pretty yard and hitched their horses to the shrubs and shade trees. Anderson knew now all he had was to he sold and his old friends were eager to buy at as good a bargain as possible. At last the sale began and as it was bid off, Colonel Rollins would ride back and forth in front of the house to show his authority and that he was the big man of the day. Agen wanted to be there mighty bad to buy some thing he had wanted very much; but such is the force of habit; he had always stood in a sort of fear of Anderson's mighty magnificence, and it was nothing but a sheepish fear that kept him away. Ninthy said:

"Go, White; they are nobody now, and hit's just what I always said they would come to, the poor stuck ups. Hit does me real good to see sich come down," and she shook her fat sides laughing. She got all the news from the distressed household by hailing every passer-by, white or black.

The sale was over. It brought a few hundred dollars more than the mortgage. Mr. Anderson got notice to vacate in a short time the home his wife and daughters had beautified. No kind and friendly word was spoken to these distressed ones. Envy had hardened the hearts of some, and self-interest had made enemies of others.

Anderson resolved to leave the country and go where he was not known and try to make a living at something. It is almost useless to try to describe such wretchedness as theirs. With the mother this loss of property was not like the loss of or uncertainty about her poor children. In the depth of misery she and Eva bade a weeping adieu to their once happy home. Old Anderson feared the fatigue he would have to undergo, thought it mighty hard that he had to go to work in his old age and thought Mary was very mean to have asked for that money, to ruin him in order to pamper up herself and Peacock.

As they traveled on for days—days of misery—he still cursed and grumbled. At last they reached the village where they expected to make their future home. It was a small place, but only ten miles from a large city. The money they had left forced them to use the strictest economy. They rented a small house with a few acres of land and went to raising chickens for market. Eva got up a little school where she made something to help along. Mrs. Anderson took in sewing and helped take care of the chickens. Soon they were quite comfortable as to physical comforts but the poor mother still mourned her lost children and the deep marks of unutterable misery were too deeply marked on her face to deceive.

Old Anderson got the "chickenry" started by every one but himself doing the work. He would spend most of his time up town where, as he said, he was very much distinguished for his elegant conversation and had got to be immensely popular." While he was idling away his time his poor wife was writing to all parts of the country trying to hear of her children, receiving no answers. She had to work with a broken heart, trying to keep up, hoping that God would some day take pity on her and help her to find those loved ones.

CHAPTER XXIII

The old uncle's family continued to treat Bessie worse and worse the longer they were together. Mrs. Mitchel, the nurse who had had charge of her since her infancy loved her as a mother. Colonel Laurette in his affection for the little waif[59] would never allow her to be neglected; he saw that Mrs. Mitchel's watchful care of her and it caused him to make a confidant of his plans. He made her promise him upon honor and her love for Bessie, never to cease that watchful care. Truly and faithfully she obeyed him, and watched with ceaseless love and care the beautiful and witching girl who was left to her. The new family were never from under her surveillance, not a moment except when they slept. She even watched them to their sleeping apartments. As all their sleeping rooms were contiguous, they as would very often meet there to discuss the time and process of driving Bessie into the street.

"Just let her do agin what she did to-day and out she goes"

"What on arth has she been doing agin. She is aggravating. I do say, but I 'low I will fetch her down."

"Why, pa, when Mr. Smith came expressedly to see me she wouldn't leave the drawing room, as she calls it, but there she set and

---

[59] Waif = a stray person or animal; especially : a homeless child.

set. She made him talk to her and she wouldn't let him say a word to me."

Each had some similar complaint except Apollo, who said: "If she was rich I would marry her, for she is dead in love with me, and I believe I am a sick duck too. I do think she is real purty, and I feel kinder sorry she loves me so, as I can't marry a poor body."

There was one listening—as all advantages are fair in war times—who with this knowledge could ward off the evil time of being thrown "on the street," as the enemies termed it. But Bessie herself was now growing weary and heart-sick at the rudeness and almost brutality of the father, mother and sisters. As for Apollo, he followed her continually to tell her of the love he had for her. He would intrude on the privacy of her room. At that she ordered him out in a jesting, good humored way; but she was not obeyed, and to get rid of him would run down stairs, he following and bawling: [Page 21 Ends]

"When I ketch you I will kiss you."

Mrs. Mitchel, the nurse, was never far from Bessie and saved her from his polluting touch. There was no rest for her here; this last scene made Bessie say: "I shall leave; they are always saying in company, 'That gall no such can stay in my house,' and that wretched fool sot[60], that boy, why, he alone will prevent my staying. I will not remain among such bad people. To be with bad people chokes me. I cannot feel natural among them, and nurse, if these persons were good, as the term goes, why their ignorance would disgust me beyond measure. Nurse! dear nurse! do invent some plan to let us get off and live somewhere quietly; I shall choke to death if I stay here much longer. I cannot stay with bad people."

Bessie burst into a passionate fit of crying, and throwing her arms around her nurse's neck, plead with her to carry her off somewhere. The nurse said:

____

[60] Sot = a habitual drunkard

"Well, I will go and get the little money I have and we will get ready to leave. I will save your jewels for you, they were given you by your dear papa."

"Oh nurse, how can you save them?"

"My dear child, I will give them to lawyer Ford and he will put them in the bank and these creatures will never be the wiser."

Mrs. Mitchel had charge of Bessie's wardrobe, diamonds and other very valuable jewels. Bessie never had been troubled to take charge of anything. Her clothes had always been laid out for her, every suit to fit the occasion, as though she were some princess. So nurse selected the jewels that were to be put in the bank and left the remainder for Bessie's use.

"Must I, dear nurse, lock myself in?"

"No, dear, but go to the library, they never go there; go and select what books you will want and what we can carry."

"No, they never go there, but I will lock the door I am so afraid of that sot. And nursie, don't be gone long, please, I am always so nervous when you leave me."

Mrs. Mitchel saw Bessie safely in the library, and then she went out, walking very fast until she came to lawyer Ford's. She went up the steps and rang the bell. The old gentleman was standing by a window and saw her—one would think he had been waiting for her. He eagerly and softly opened the door himself and conducted her into a private parlor. After they were seated, rubbing his hands together, he quickly asked:

"Well, Mitchel, how is my pet? and are the vipers still snapping at her?"

"Oh, sir, they grow worse day by day; she says it will kill her to stay there."

"Does that young devil still worry and torment her with his love?"

"Oh, sir, it is that she says she can bear with less patience than the others' abuse. She is begging me to go somewhere with her and says she will work"—here a grim smile wrinkled about the lawyer's lips—"some place where she will be safe from insults. Oh, the poor child begs so hard to get away."

"Mitchel, you know about the will Laurette made. It has been recorded in the place where he formerly lived, as he wanted no one here so suspect she would have anything; he wanted to try the friendship of relatives, lovers and friends; you know he was a peculiar man and he wanted no man to marry Bessie for her money. Now that will says the property was to be left to Bessie and his brother who, by the way, he always had a contempt for, and the brother was to have charge of it until Bessie married, and that she must live with his brother and his family for one year, and if they treated her kindly they were to have two-thirds interest and Bessie one-third. But if they were malicious and unkind to her, or made threats of driving her away, or used abuse toward her, then they were not to have one cent's worth of that property and Bessie would inherit all and every portion of it. He tried to prevent her being a prey to fortune hunters or dissimulating friends. If left as his heiress he was afraid she might be the victim of designing people. In her innocence she suspected no one, but I think she has been made to learn a severe lesson in experience by this time, poor child! Now I will give you some directions how to proceed and I will hand over to you the necessary funds to take you to the city you will see named in the directions. Your means will be ample but I don't think it prudent to take Bessie to a large hotel. You will find here a letter of introduction and a check for a thousand dollars. Now keep Bessie in ignorance of these things. Let her believe you must economize, it will do her no harm to think she must depend on herself, and she will not be thinking every man and woman she meets is perfection itself, let her know that everything that glitters is not gold."

After a few more directions about the route and so forth, the nurse left and walked home very fast, as she had staid longer than she anticipated. Arriving at home she found the household in an uproar.

The uncle and aunt were in a terrible rage because Bessie had struck their boy in the face, drawing blood, "Oh, she has knocked my tooth almost out with that book," he yelled.

The father screamed; "Leave my house this instant, you vile pauper, I will not let you stay here to murder us all."

Nurse took Bessie's hand and asked how all this came about.

"Git outen my house, you old sarpent, don't stand there axin' that pauper how it came about," screamed the mother.

Nurse paid no attention to the master's and mistress's commands but listened to Bessie, who said:

"That fellow saw me in the library through a window, and slipping in caught me round the waist and attempted to kiss me. With the book in my hand I began beating him to make him release me. At last I got away, but to do so I had to hurt him," and in her excitement she fairly tiptoed, and looking bravely up she said:

"We are allowed to kill foul reptiles that attempt to bite us."

"Oh, husband, call in a policeman to put her outen our house, for you see she glories in trying to kill our poor Moses. Oh, husband be quick."

"Oh, Pa why don't you, for she told me only this morning that she would go in the parlor to see just as much company as she pleased."

The old man yelled at the nurse and Bessie and asked what they were standing there for? and if they didn't make haste and get outen his house he would have them up before a Justice as vagrants."

Mitchel said, "When my young Mistress is ready to go, I will go; when she is ready to leave her house, we both will go." It was a comparative calm until this answer was given, now the storm of rage was awful, father, mother and children joined in, one and all, in the most vituperative [61]manner. Bessie in her clear musical voice added fuel to the flame by saying:

"Why, I had no idea the English language, bad as you use it, was so copious in low down abuse." Turning contemptuously away, she continued, "I not only set you all down as ignorant fools, but as poor lunatics, too."

She and nurse went to her room where they began preparing to depart. Bessie crying slow, out of sight of her enemies, she was a poor distressed child, before them, she was in spirit and haughtiness old Queen Bess herself. The nurse told her the train they would have to go on would not leave before four o'clock."

"Oh dear nursie, what will become of me if I have to wait so long, let us start off on foot, don't let me stay here to choke to death. And this was once my dear sweet home, and now like a criminal I am driven out of it; oh I never thought to experience such degradation. On how often of late has despair swept over my heart; oh what is to become of me?"

Mitchel consoled her as well as she could. She dared not tell her of the will or whatever else Mr. Ford had told her for that was an inviolable secret.

At last the hour came for them to go to the railroad station; the hack and baggage wagon had come, Mr. Ford had attended to that. Mitchel had made him a hasty visit and apprised him of all that had happened during her visit to him in the morning. At meal time Mitchel did not hesitate one moment to go down and select for her mistress a nice dinner, and tell the servants of their intended departure, and when the time came every servant met their dear young mistress in the hall or on the portico to shower blessing upon her and to wish her speedy return, then humbly giving their hands bid her good bye. She bid a

---

[61] Vituperative = uttering or given to censure : containing or characterized by verbal abuse. Synonyms = abusive, invective

solemn farewell to the hustle that had cherished her in helpless infancy, and in happy childhood, and bursting into passionate weeping she cried, "And in my unprotected and helpless girlhood I am driven forth like an outcast."

Mitchel told her mean and prying eyes would be on her and to compose herself.

"Oh, dear nurse I will try, but this is so hard."

Leaving her room she said, "I have papa's portrait, but I kissed the one I left, and I kissed the pretty furniture he gave me."

Every piece of furniture had a little romance of her own weaving, She knew her enemies were watching her and she tried to retain her self-possession, but came near breaking down when she came to bid farewell to the servants, they followed her to the gate and said farewell again. They drove rapidly to the depot, and were soon on the cars. The rapid speed, the change of scene, the many acts of courtesies shown, revived Bessie in some measure, and Mitchel's comforting promises of better days in store for her, and telling her to forget what was so bitter to remember, and that they could get along. Now and then a smile or a laugh would illumine Bessie's sweet face.

When they arrived in the city directed by Mr. Ford, the gentlemanly conductor with other gentlemen offered their services. They were escorted to a fine carriage, their baggage was taken charge of, with no trouble to Bessie or her attendant. They drove to the gentleman's house—again nurse following the directions of Mr. Ford—the letter of introduction was presented, requesting the gentleman to take Bessie in charge, to let her enjoy herself and to draw upon him for funds whenever necessary. She was his ward and it was his wish that she should pay visit to his city.

The gentlemen and his family received Bessie with open arms; she was made soon to feel perfectly at home among those hightoned and cultivated persons, a strong contrast to the ignorant horde she had left or fled from. All this was a mystery to Bessie, but Mitchel told her an old friend of her papa had given her the letter to this gentlemen, and all she had to do was to enjoy herself, you will soon be valued for your own and all the kindness will not be owing to the letter. Bessie had no inclination to quarrel with her good fortune, but only felt too thankful she was out of the atmosphere of ignorance and brutality.

[TO BE CONTINUED.]

[Page 22 Ends]

CHAPTER XXIV.

Kate lay in this swoon for several hours. For some time all but the doctor thought that she was dead; at last there were signs of returning life. Tonics and stimulants were given her and every care was taken by the doctor to prevent a relapse.

"Whatever caused this prostration, it surely must have been some terrible and sudden shock, I beseech you not to recur to it," said the doctor.

Peacock watched her and seemed very anxious for her to get well. He said:

"If she was strong enough to start it would be the best thing for her to travel and have a change of scene."

At last the doctor said,

"Yes, perhaps it is best, as pure air is a great restorative."

Kate was so stunned she was scarcely a responsible person. They started, and Peacock argued with all his might that his reasons were best why he did not tell them at home of Mary's death.

"It would have distressed your poor parents so much, and it was Mary's last wish for you to become my wife and be a mother to this dear little child," at the same time holding it in his arms and kissing it passionately.

"Oh, Kate! Can you desert this darling child, your dead sister's idol? She knew you would be kind to it, and it's all that remains to us of her dear self on this earth. You will not, you cannot leave us all alone! And if you will not consent to be my wife, you will have to return to your father, and will it not be dreadful for you to tell them the sad news?

Peacock pretended to be much distressed, and had recourse very often to his handkerchief to wipe his eyes. The sad news, the heart broken man and the poor, wailing helpless infant and the thought of taking this sad news home made Kate shudder. She finally consented for the sake of the dear child that she would marry him. So they were married and were soon off on their journey. They travelled several weeks, stopping at different fashionable places, for Peacock had plenty of money and spent it freely. He was drunk most of the time. He began now to treat Kate as he had treated Mary, but got Kate subdued much sooner. He stopped and abused her until her self-confidence deserted her. She dared not ask a question or be seen talking with any one. She did not even know what part of the State she was in. It appeared to be a very fashionable and intelligent community, but Kate was ignorant of her surroundings. Whether the people were good or bad, she did not know. She knew she was afraid to open her mouth. Peacock was in the habit of taking the child out riding, one day he came back without bringing him. Kate asked without hesitating now:

"Where is the child?"

"Shut your foolish mouth and don't dare to speak to me on that subject again."

They now left that place and went to quite a large city a long distance away. Peacock had sold his buggy and now they took the train. They got board in the suburbs of the city. One day Peacock heard to his great astonishment that his old friend, John Hill, was in the same city. But now instead of being a comparative nobody, Mr. Hill was a wealthy and respected banker. It made Peacock shudder. Here he was a ruined man, with only a few hundred dollars of Anderson's left. He thought at first he would go and tell Hill about his want of money, then he reflected that this would not do, for he would be sure to ask all sorts of questions about Mary and the Anderson family and he knew smart John Hill would catch him lying. He then began gambling at the lowest gambling dens that surrounded his boarding house. Kate nearly distracted at the uncertain fate of her sister's child, and cowed and frightened at Peacock's cruelty, kept herself in almost total seclusion. But in the frail and shabby house she was in, she could hear the oaths of coarse and drunken men, the songs and laughter of women, and fiddling and dancing. Kate was different from Mary. She was easily tempted. She lacked Mary's fine sense of right and the brave fortitude that made her endure much without being contaminated. Kate in her loneliness felt tempted to join in these frolics and spend the rest of her life in reckless dissipation. But a better feeling came over her, she remembered the teachings of her dear mother and purer counsel prevailed.

Mr. Anderson's home was ten miles from this city. One day he accidentally met Col. John Hill while on a little business to the city. He had heard Hill spoken of in such high terms, he felt awkward when they first met, but Hill was so kind and seemed so glad to see him that he soon warmed into confidence and told of the misfortune of his family through Peacock's villainy and that he feared the worst as to the fate of his daughters.

Hill sent word to Mrs. Anderson he would go to see her daughter and would assist and help Mr. Anderson to the utmost in his power to catch Peacock. John Hill had never felt right after his connection with Peacock; it was his only fault and it cost him many a painful thought. His boyish freak, impelled by the desperate wish to get some business, made him shudder. In his luxurious mansion he would walk back and forth and call himself the murderer of the Anderson family. Remorse filled his heart. No prompt luxury could still it. He felt he deserved to suffer.

"I thought the loss of dear Bessie was a life long punishment and now added to this is the heart broken misery of an innocent family."

Hill appeared before men affable and sprightly, but his keenly sensitive nature suffered in secret. Some men would have said "The whole batch of them were fools to be so easily duped, and Anderson the greatest fool of all. I am not responsible for Anderson giving the three thousand dollars to Peacock or sending that child Kate off with the scoundrel. They themselves are to blame," but John Hill's sense of honor would not let him reason in that way.

One day while Col. Hill was sitting in his office in his banking house[,] he heard the name of Miss Bessie Laurette mentioned. Hill quit writing and listened. A gentleman said:

"Miss Bessie Laurette is without doubt one of the most beautiful and accomplished young ladies I ever met."

Hill now went in the next room and asked the friend where he met that young lady.

He was answered:

"Miss Laurette is visiting the family of Mr. Valley here in the city. Hill, I propose we go round now and call on her. Will you promise not to make yourself to agreeable, but let a poor fellow like me have a chance?"

Hill excused himself then on a business plea, but he went right home and wrote a note, asking permission to call on Miss Laurette. Bessie was surprised and wondered if it was her dear old beau. She went to the library and asked her host who this Mr. Hill was. She was told enough to know he was her old friend. Permission was instantly given. Col. Hill's handsome turnout[62] soon stopped at the house where his heart's treasure was staying. Bessie was not prepared to see such an

---

[62] Turnout = a coach or carriage together with the horses, harness, and attendants

elegant man. He had greatly improved and now was a man of imposing appearance. She was taken by surprise. He approached her with an easy dignity of manner. After the usual salutations, he expressed his joy at meeting her, regretted the death of her father for the sorrow it had given her, told her how he had become impressed with the idea of her death and taking her little hand in his, he said:

"And have you thought of me in all these long years?"

Impulsive, affectionate Bessie not only told him she had, but informed him that she was now left penniless and had been turned out of the home of her childhood with no one to protect her but her old nurse. Hill listened to all in indignant amazement. They talked long and seriously and would have still continued to talk but the lady of the house came in to pay her respects to Col. Hill whom she greatly admired and to ask him to take a family dinner with them and she was glad he and dear Bess were old friends. Col. Hill gladly accepted the kind invitation. His equipage[63] was sent home and he remained to spend one of the sweetest days of his life. That evening before leaving he got Bessie's consent to visit her daily if he wished.

The next day Anderson called on Col. Hill and told him his wife was dying of grief for the loss of her children. Hill sympathized and advised and gave him money to pay his expenses; told him to spare no expense to secure that rascal and bring him to justice. Hill would be often with Bessie. They walked and drove out together and Bess was so happy and so was Mr. Hill. Mitchel, the nurse, met the kindest treatment and so many thanks for the care she took of her young lady. Nurse had no limit to her praises of Col. Hill for faithful love to Bessie. Hill had an elegant watch prepared for her with her name engraved on it and presented it to her.

---

[63] Equipage = a horse-drawn carriage with its servants

CHAPTER XXV.

Peacock had about run through with what money he had and was determined, as he said, to make a raise. He succeeded actually in drawing a forged draft on the Express Company for five hundred dollars. He thought himself safe in this as he did not give his own name. Staying in the portion of the town he was in, he supposed he would not be detected. He was disguised in a false beard, a red wig and spectacles when he received the money. But the guilty cannot prosper long. Peacock's time had come. He was found out and arrested. He at first denied it and defied the officers; said he was a gentleman and would not be guilty of such a thing and furthermore, he would not be called a forger and would prosecute any one who attached that epithet to a name as honorable as his. The officers paid little attention to his bombast, told him he either had to go to jail or give bond to await his trial.

"Well," he said, "will you take Mr. John Hill as security?"

The men astonished, asked:

"Do you mean the rich banker?"

"Yes, sir. He is a friend of mine, he is the man I mean. Take me to his office and I will show you."

The officers consented. When they reached the bank, Peacock saw Hill in the room and he called out as he used to do.

"Hello! old boy, how are times with you now?"

Hill hastily left his chair and went up to Peacock and said:

"What have you been doing that you are under arrest?"

[Page 23 Ends]

"These fellows are accusing me of a piece of forgery I had nothing to do with. I have come to ask you to assist me as I am a stranger here."

"Mr. Peacock, if you are, as you say, innocent, they cannot convict you, and I will see that you get full justice."

Hill was determined he should have a justice he was not dreaming of. He wanted to have a talk with him to find out about Mary and Kate.

"Mr. Peacock, where is your wife?"

"She is in town, sir."

"Is it possible! And why didn't you come to see me?"

Peacock made an excuse. Hill said:

"I would like to see your wife."

Peacock objected on the ground that he would not like for her to see him in that condition. Hill replied:

"Oh! That makes no difference. We will see that you get justice."

He having faith in Hill gave his consent for her to be brought. An officer was sent for her. The man found her in the wretched den in a miserable condition. When she was told she was wanted at Col. Hill's bank, she could not imagine what he wanted with her. She thought, "any place but here," and they started. When they arrived at the bank, Hill in an instant saw what had been Peacock's motive in carrying Kate off. He knew at a glance and she knew him and remembered he had asked her to marry him. The poor creature felt humiliated to the very earth, but she ran and threw herself at his feet and exclaimed:

"Oh, for God's sake! Mr. Hill, protect and save me from that vile man?

Peacock had been so used to beating her that he started forward now to strike her, but was prevented by the clutch of the officer who pushed him up in a corner and set a guard over him. Hill said:

"Dear lady, do not kneel to me." At the same time he lifted her up, told her to tell her story and no one would dare to molest her, she now would have his protection and the protection of the courts. She went on and told the miserable story of how she had been treated and she supposed the same treatment had killed her sister Mary, but she had not seen her dear sister, but was forced to marry that bad man. Hill turned to Peacock and said:

"I am, sir, partly to blame in this. I ask God to forgive me for that part, but then, I thought her were human; now, I find you are a fiend, worse than a fiend in your usage of these poor girls. Now I hope, sir, the law will award the punishment due to your crimes if it is possible."

Peacock said: "Let me explain. That girl has told nothing but lies," He was instantly silenced.

Hill said, "I know the lady, and I know every word she spoke is true, the whole truth and nothing but the truth: and as for you sir, you get no assistance from me."

The officers took Peacock in charge and carried him off to jail to await his trial.

Hill and Kate were now in a more private room. He expressed his regret and sorrow for her and told her all the trouble her father and mother had on her own and Mary's account and how Peacock had broke up the old man, and told her where they were now living.

"Oh, Mr. Hill, can I go there?"

"Yes, I will take you there myself. Have you anything of value at your lodging?"

"Nothing whatever."

Col. Hill took Kate to a neat and quiet boarding house to rest while he was getting through a little business. He told her to be ready by the time the carriage came. She took her bath in the pretty bathroom adjoining her bed-room; dressed herself in a neat black dress and felt relieved as far as personal comfort was concerned and the thought of being released from Peacock. But oh, the degredation [*sic*] of her own situation! No words could tell half her agony. The breaking up of her parents in their old age, their distress for the loss of Mary—it was almost too much for her to live through. The carriage with Mr. Hill in it drove up and he assisted her in. On the way, he gleaned every particular of the way Peacock tolled her into that mountainous country, and of their wanderings. He told her of whatever she had not heard in regard to her father's family. On arriving in the village, he told the driver to stop a bit from the Anderson House. He told Kate her mother was sick and persuaded her to stay in the carriage until he could prepare the mother to see her. A sudden surprise might be fatal. He went to the house and Eva conducted him to the sick room. There he cautiously informed Mrs. Anderson that Kate would soon be there. But mother and sister wept tears of joy. As soon as Mrs. Anderson was over the excitement[,] she thanked God for restoring her child to her. Col. Hill went out and the carriage was brought to the door. He assisted Kate out; she ran into the house where Eva met her and took her to her mother's room. Kate threw herself on her knees beside her mother's bed and mother and daughter were wrapt in each other[']s arms. For some time no questions could be asked. Sometimes a wailing cry would come.

"Oh! Where is Mary, my dear child?"

Hill had told Kate not to tell her sick mother anything of Peacock's vile conduct, that her father might be at home, and he, himself, would also be there to advise and console them.

Hill said that "when Mr. Anderson returned all would be right, and told Mrs. Anderson she must not now grieve; he had no doubt but she would yet see happy days. If I can find that child, and Mary," he thought "with those two given to their mother's arms and what I can yet do for her, all will yet be contented. But after such a violent slam of misfortune, happiness is doubtful."

Kate had told Hill that after knowing Peacock's true character, she did not believe Mary was dead. Hill, when he left the house, was sure

Mrs. Anderson would soon be up. His consoling words did ample good in making her believe she would be again happy with all her little household around her. When he was about to leave she gave her hand, saying:

"May God ever bless you; for you have been an angel of mercy to me and mine, in rescuing us out of the power of a foul fiend."

He drove on rapidly home, as he had not seen Bessie in the last twenty-four hours. He rested awhile at home, changed his dress and jumped in a street car. In a little while he was seated by the side of Bessie in Mrs. Valley's splendid dressing-room; and there he gave her a truthful account of how he had been employed in rescuing the Anderson family from Peacock.

No man ever rose, in either public or private esteem, whose habit was to lie!

Hill felt keenly what guilt he had incurred, merely by insinuating that Peacock was what he represented him to be. Hill was too brave a man to let even the shade of a lie pass his lips now. He dared to be truthful. His ideas of honor demanded it. He told Bessie where and how he got connected with that plausible scoundrel, Peacock. He was too good and honorable even to try to palliate his fault. He did not lug in his inexperienced youth; but now looked on his part as infamous, accepted no excuse, but considered, to make what reparation he could, was all that was left to atone for the hideous fault.

Bessie said comforting words to her intended husband, and he felt the strongest desire in his heart to do what was right in the unfortunate matter. With this high minded honorable woman by his side for life, he might yet command his own self-esteem. Guilty conscience had often made him exclaim; as he passed up and down his splendid rooms. This evening he asked Bessie if she was now willing to marry a guilty wretch like himself. She replied:

"Col. Hill, you made a sad mistake by your insinuations in favor of a bad man, but I think if you had known him, millions would not have tempted you to assist him. In thoughtlessness you did this wrong, and you have suffered but with your innate integrity and your wish to atone, you have the right to hope for happiness."

"But, Bessie, I could never have known happiness if I had lost you. You first awakened in me my sense of guilt. Thinking of it, I felt I had no right to be in the presence of one so pure. Oh, Bessie! There is no load so heavy to bear as self-condemnation."

Bessie again cheered him with words of encouragement. His was a mind that could "grow pure by being purely acted upon."

Dissipation had not blurred and stultified his nature.

Mr. Anderson had said hard things of Mary as being the cause of breaking him up, and had threatened if she and Kate came again he would drive both of them out of his house. It was his habit when in his rage, to threaten, always, to drive his children out of his house. Now Mrs. Anderson feared his return on account of Kate. She knew if he thought it would cause talk about her staying at home, and make him unpopular among a certain set, her poor afflicted child would be driven off and no one to protect her unless Mr. Hill would. He was her only hope that her child would not be an outcast, dependent upon the cold charities of the world.

[TO BE CONTINUED.]

[Page 24 End]

CHAPTER XXVI.

Mr. Anderson had a long and round-about trip in search for Mary and Kate, but had no success, and a bad feeling began to show itself. He was tired both in mind and body and began to think on the loss of his old home and to curse Mary as the cause. He would tell those he happened to be with that his children had been a curse to him; that they had ruined him by causing him to lose his property in his old age and they had disgraced him; he "himself" was a born gentleman and inherited his property; had never worked and now in his old age he had to work and go about looking for that rascally Peacock gang to try and make them disgorge the money they had swindled him out of. No doubt they are shining in silks and satins every day while I am in rags and almost begging my bread. Yes, he continued, "a man of my importance to have such children. I have always thought only of gratifying their own wishes. Oh! I might have known what they would bring down to. I might have known they would put me in the power of some adventurer, and they have done it. Oh! What a fatal gift my kindness of heart has been. Why, I feel for everything! The poor, downtrodden negroes in Africa even make me weep when I think of them. These poor convicts that purse-proud rich men take out of the penitentiary to work for them, why it distresses me. I can't help thinking they once had mothers who were proud of them when they were children; and I even feel sorry for the poor cattle that have to be left out to pick up what they can in the open fields. It distresses me to see a bug hurt. I am kind to everything. There never was a man with as much feeling, I am easily imposed upon, because I had always thought everybody was noble-minded like myself. My children are not like me. I only know what the nobility of the soul is. I like to see people noble and generous, but in all my troubles I have not met one generous man, and I have always, even against the wishes of my wife and those ungrateful children, been giving to the distressed; but in my troubles not a man has come and said, 'I will assist you.' Now there are men I have helped, and there is one Hill in particular. Why that fellow to day would be in jail if it had not been for me. I assisted him with my advice, I gave him money to go into business. Why, sirs, I was making of him, and by rights, what he now calls his is my own rightful property. He has swindled me shamefully. I was honorable to the last degree. When he told me a pitiful story about his distress, I told him, like a kind-hearted and honorable man as I am, to go on and use my money, and now, sirs, not a cent can I get from him. If he were not so low down in public opinion I would try for it, as you say, but a man like myself cannot stoop to get mixed up with such men as that Hill; and a man of my kind feelings can't bear to distress such a bad man as he is."

The idle crowd around him were more amused than sympathetic. He saw no further into their feelings that the listening attention paid him. Some half idiots believed him, but others with more sense laughed at him. He was a new subject with them.

But the next time he began this harangue, it was at a cheap dinner he had stopped to get. Some women were present and he enlisted the sympathy of one or two of them, but the others did not mince matters in replying to him. After his usual way he began to abuse his family, and to persist in the idea that he was an ill-used man.

"My kind feelings," he said, "have always been an injury to me." But he was suddenly interrupted by a woman who said:

"Yes, the kind of feelings you have ought to be an injury, and the same kind will injure every one you have anything to do with."

Mr. Sanders, in the nobility of his soul, gave her a glowering stare out of his furious eyes, and walked off thinking, "I fixed her. She will know how to talk to a gentleman;" and the woman said, "Why, what is this world coming to? What a shame an old idiot is allowed to go about talking in such a manner!"

The rebuke to Mr. Anderson had a bad effect upon his temper. When the next opportunity to talk came, he cursed and abused his family worse than ever.

He seemed to have a wonderful amount of hate and spite for Hill. He never once remembered his earnest request to Mary and to his wife to treat Peacock with distinguished consideration, and Mary must marry him to get money to improve their land. Not once did he think of the faithful and true kindness of his wife and daughters—no; nothing but his utterly selfish feelings filled his mind.

When he got to the station on his return home he did not ask after his family, but the depot agent called him aside and told him of Kate's return and of Peacock's being in jail for forgery. Hearing this he became furious and said, it was a pity they hadn't put the whole crowd of fools in who had ruined him.

He hardly spoke to Eva when he got home. She was in the kitchen, and there he first went. He had not had his dinner and was now very hungry. His poor wife did not know what to do. She dreaded the worst for poor Kate. She thought it best they should all be together in her sick rom.

After eating his dinner, Mr. Anderson went to his wife's room. She was afraid to ask any questions, but thought, "He surely will not raise a difficulty here?"

He came in in a violent manner, slammed the door, gave Kate a long and diabolical stare, but did not speak to her or to anyone else.

Kate cried out: "Oh, dear papa, wont' you speak to me?"

He flew into a range, and said:

"Speak to you, you vile hypocrite! You have brought me to starvation and disgrace. Why do you expect of man of my eminence and popularity to associate with such cattle as you, oh, you infamous low-down wretch!"

He threw her hat at her and struck her in the face. She dropped on her knees and said:

"Oh, dear papa, have mercy on me! will you not have mercy on me? My dear mother is sick, do please have mercy on her!"

Just then a rap at the door made the kind Mr. Anderson pick up his hat and the chairs he had kicked over. Eva opened the door and Mr. Hill and General T—came in.

The General was a big man with Mr. Anderson. The two men saw the distress and confusion. The noble Anderson cleared his face, held out his hand and gave the men a hearty shake. His voice was gentle and soft; he enquired so kindly after the General's family; was so sorry to hear the baby was sick.

During his palaver[64] Hill was by the bedside of poor Mrs. Anderson. She only shook her head when he pressed her hand. He saw what it all meant. He turned to Mr. Anderson and said:

"We have had better success here at home than you in your long wanderings. I suppose you heard nothing."

Anderson still wanted to complain of the ingratitude of his family, but the General said:

"Kate has shown a great deal of prudence and forbearance during her sufferings, and I am glad to see that she was successful in getting out of the clutches of that wretch, Peacock. She is a brave woman.

---

[64] Palaver = idle talk

Every one sympathizes with her distress and all are willing to use every means in their power to search for that little child and for the daughter. A great many think Peacock ran off from her and that she is alive."

These words consoled Mr. Anderson. He held the gentleman in high esteem because he was a rich man, and he looked kindly at Kate and said:

"Yes, sir. If none of my other children come out all right, Kate will. I always said so, and what I say I know."

The poor women were glad to see this trouble was to pass so smoothly. The mother spoke to Colonel Hill alone of the agony she had endured on Mary's account. Hill said he had interviewed Peacock, but he would tell nothing in regard to the child, and said Mary was dead, but he thought he was telling a falsehood and believed she was still alive. He encouraged the distressed mother to live in hope that Mary would come home, and when rid of Peacock all would be right. He told her he would be married in a few days to Miss Bessie Laurette.

"You heard of her at the Springs, did you not?" he asked.

They all remembered hearing her spoken of.

"And is she as lovely as she was then?" asked Eva.

"More lovely now, I think, and her fine sense and good qualities exceed, if possible, her lovely personal perfections."

The poor mother prayed that Heaven's choicest blessings might be showered upon them.

He bade them good-bye and said he would always be ready to assist them whenever called upon. The poor family thought there was a time when Colonel Hill or Miss Laurette would not have been ashamed to have had them at their wedding, but now what a change! From independence to poverty! from respectability to disgrace and degradation! Connected with a man who fills a felon's cell! No words could tell all the horrors that filled the minds of these unfortunate women! As for that old imbecile Anderson, he started off up town to tell of Col. Hill's and General T—'s visit to himself.

"Colonel Hill and Bessie wished their wedding to be private but Mrs. Vally said: "Not too private. Let me show my appreciation of the two friends I most admire by doing them every honor in my power."

They permitted her to have her own way and a grand wedding was the result. The daughters of Mrs. Vally had minature [*sic*] horse-shoes entwined with the wreaths of evergreen for good luck's sake. The wedding was not only a grand affair but it also was a gathering of social, genial hearted friends. The old nurse was rejoiced beyond measure. Colonel Hill was everything grand and good in her eyes. The bridal party were going on a grand tour to New York and then to Cuba, but a telegram came soon after the ceremony, also a letter from Mr. Ford congratulating Bessie and Hill. The telegram was handed to Colonel Hill and read:

"COLONEL HILL;--Yours' and Bessie's presence is required here immediately.

J. FORD, Attorney.

[Page 25 End]

Now the trip had to be postponed until they went to see what the telegram meant. They started next day. Arriving in the city they drove to Mr. Ford's residence. He met them cordially and gave them his hearty congratulations. The old uncle and his son had been sent for; they came with their man of business; two of Mr. Laurette's old friends came in and gave Hill and Bessie their best wishes for a long and happy life. The old uncle had not heard of Bessie's marriage, neither did he know fully why he and his son were there. They came according to the order of Mr. Ford and to bring their lawyer. There the three sat, looking dazed and confused. The will was produced and read by Mr. Ford. The old uncle was the first to speak, and said it was a forgery.

"Be careful old man, I have witnesses present to prove its genuineness. Will you contend with Colonel Hill for the property of his wife?"

The man said no; his lawyer said yes.

Hill said: "I am able to give you a small share if you will vacate, for you see by this will you have no chance. If you had been kind to my wife you would still have been a rich man, but as it is either give up or I will institute suit against you."

The old fellow considered discretion the better part of valor and gave possession. Bessie was rejoiced to go back to her old home, but it had to be renovated and refurnished, for it looked like a deserted place. But while all this was going on she and her husband returned to his home, where dinings and parties were given by their many friends. After awhile they made their trip to New York, Newport, and then to Cuba. The world was bright to Bessie.

CHAPTER XXVII.

Mary had become a great favorite with the owner of the large millinery establishment. She had after a stay of a month, told him of all her troubles and the distress she was in about her child. He was confident from her education and appearance she had been well brought up. He knew from his own knowledge of her that she was reliable and truthful. He gave her a good salary and she was living comfortably. She had the confidence of the patrons of the establishment. When a large bill had to be filled Miss Mary was usually called on to do it. Some of her new friends, as well as her employer, had written letters and inserted notices in the papers in the endeavor to discover Peacock and her child. At every fresh disappointment Mary's brain almost gave way and her heart was nearly broken; she was at times almost wild with agony and life or reason must soon yield to such a weight of misery. It occurred to her that Peacock after getting tired or the child, would take it to her mother, and likely had destroyed the letters that had been sent. She knew he would assume control of all her father's business if ever he got a foot-hold there. When she was preparing to depart for her old and dear home she was told that if she was unsuccessful, to return to her old establishment again and she would find all ready to assist her. She said, after bringing trouble on her parents she did not wish to be a further drag on them, and would earn her own support. She got on a train and traveled to within half a day's journey of her father's house. She intended to keep out of the way of any acquaintance, as she did not wish to be recognized. She felt that Peacock would kill her before he would let her father hear of his rascally treatment of her. She stopped at a small house which entertained travelers, kept by a woman, and fortunately for Mary there were no men about, only some half-grown boys who worked in the field. She knew the place, though the little public house had been put up since she left. It was only a mile or two from her old home. She got into conversation with the woman and asked if a man named Anderson was living near.

"No miss, no sich man is living here now."

An observing person would have noticed the pained expression of Mary's face, and off her guard she exclaimed: Oh, is it possible!" She saw her mistake and tried to ask as composedly as she could, "What had become of him?"

"Wal, Miss, I can tell yer, there come along here a man, his name was Peacock, (the name made Mary shudder,) so the folks tells me, and goten in with old men Anderson and married a daughter of hisen, and money too arterwards, and the old man couldn't pay back to Mr. Rollins, you see, Miss he borrows that air money for his gal and Peacock, so Rollins sells him outen house and land, and he and his folks left thar."

"Can you tell me where they have gone to madame?"

"No, indeed I can't exactly, but some think he has gone where he usen to live."

Mary now thought she knew where he had gone to. But to know she had been the cause of his ruin, by allowing herself to be ruled by that black hearted wretch, with difficulty she repressed the scream that rose to her lips. "Oh! if money can make any reparation, I will work day and night," she exclaimed

It seemed to her that each fresh blow upon her heart was worse than the last; ruin seemed to follow her as its own particular object.

She said she needed some out door exercise and would take a walk. She must be alone now or die, she could not repress her tears much longer, and went on until she came within sight of her childhood's home. She recalled the happy days when all was so happy. Now she saw strange children playing in the yard, "Oh dear old home, oh, dear little yard, where my sisters and I were so happy and joyous once together. Oh if this dreadful degradation and wretchedness had been foretold us, we might have been on our guard against that stranger who has caused all this."

She stood in a thick grove on a hillside, and leaning against a large old oak tree, breathed many a wish and prayer for the safety of those dear ones who were outcasts from that home. "Now I must again begin my weary pilgrimage to find those whom I have ruined. Farewell! farewell, dear old home; farewell dear and deserted home! farewell forever! Sobbing as if her heart would break, she murmured, I found no home! no mother or sisters! no child that my weary heart aches so to see! nothing but blank misery I found, and it holds me a tight prisoner."

Often she had to sit down to rest—for misery is such a load to carry—she got at last somehow to the little Inn, the woman was going to the spring, Mary went with her and laved her aching head in its cold waters. As they went on together the woman who was talkative, told Mary the gossip of the country; she said one of the big lawyers of the country had at last got his just dues, and every body was so surprised for he was a rich man and lived in such a fine house.

"Who was he? and what was his name?" Mary asked.

"Hit was Squire Ol, Miss, and the way he comes to git in dat fix, he took hit in his head to blackmail one old gentleman some years ago and got money outen him, and he had no right to, and dis old man swore he did on his death bed, but then Ol was sich a big man, nobody took any notice of hit until lately, what youens call the grand jury tuck hit up and saunt him to the pinetintiary fur ten years."

Mary said it was bad that he had acted so, but thought he had got his just dues, for he had swindled her father out of his mountain lands.

"Madam, do you know how Col. James Rollins comes on?"

"Wal, Miss, they tells me he has been tuck up for swindling when he was something, youens call District Attorney here, and they do talk mighty hard about him, they do talk of his wearing the stripes too, but I would hate to see hit on account of his darter Ada, for she is a mighty fine little gal."

Then all come fresh to Mary's mind what Ada had told her at the pic nic [*sic*].

She thanked the woman for all her well meant kindness, paid her bill and went to the station to take the cars and go back to her place of business, and determine there what course to pursue. Now, there were father and mother, as well as the dear child to search for. Her disappointment had filled her mind with terrible forebodings of further evils.

Figure 20 – The Millinery Shop, Edgar Degas (1834-1917), 1879/86, Oil on Canvas. The Art Institute of Chicago, Mr. and Mrs. Lewis Larned Coburn Memorial Collection, 1933.428.

CHAPTER XXVIII

Mary had returned to her place of business, and her friends who felt for her in her many troubles, advised her to get a divorce and resume her family name. She agreed to do so. "Oh," she said, "If I could dissolve all memory as well as connection with that fiendish man, how thankful I would be!"

A report was out that her rich employer would likely offer her his heart and hand when the divorce was gained. He was a rich old bachelor who had never been known to pay any special attention to ladies. He was charitable, and would place worthy men and women in his business houses as chief directors; he increased his capital by their abilities, and they would become independent through the advantages he gave them—The report had truth in it; the old batchelor [*sic*] had fallen in love with Mary. He would frequently say to her, "You are attending too closely to business; you need a little outdoor exercise and you must take a drive with me. Now be ready by the time I come with my landau[65]."

She would occasionally ride with him, but no word of suspicion was ever breathed against her. All knew the misery and woe she had undergone, and they took pleasure in cheering and aiding her to forget

---

[65] Laundau = a four-wheel carriage with a top divided into two sections that can be folded away or removed and with a raised seat outside for the driver

the fearful past. Her friends hoped she would marry the kind, good gentleman who had shown so much respect for her. Marriage with him had never entered Mary's mind. She had regarded his attentions as being prompted by a kindly nature sympathizing with her of the troubles she had passed through.

Rest, with good, nutritious food, had greatly benefitted Mary's health. Her face had lost the pallid look of fear; her cheeks had a slight roseate tinge, her glossy hair was still glossy, and her dark-blue eyes with their long dark lashes were still bright, and with that sad, subdued expression she interested all who met her. Her form and size were faultless. Always dressed in deep black that suited best her melancholy thoughts, she was one with whom no person could long be with without loving. The gentleman who rescued her from the ruffians would frequently call and take her to his house, especially if his wife or children were sick. Her name became a household word with them. The poor and distressed generally always found a true friend in Mary. If she saw a little street-arab[66] she would find a place for it where its condition was bettered, saying the while, "May others do likewise for my poor little lost one."

She never gave up the hope of again seeing her child. One evening she was out walking on a retired street and came face to face with the most hideous-looking old hag that she had ever seen, who asked her if she did not want her fortune told. The creature looked so repulsive that Mary's first impulse was to run, but overcoming it she said,
[Page 26 End]

"Yes, I believe I do. And now I remember," she added, "an old gentleman told me of you." "

Told youen uv me! Who the devil has been er mixin' up my name in any way?"

---

[66] Street arab = a raggedly dressed homeless child wandering the streets.

"He didn't mean any harm, or say anything against you. But will you tell me my fortune? I want you to tell me in regard to what——"

"Now, white woman, stop right thar. That is the way they do—always go and tell thar life before they git it from me; so, woman, don't tell me nothin',—let me do the telling, and if I don't tell it mighty correct you may pulp[67] off my old head; for many has gone to a better home than I have got and lived in. I have exhausted the world at large."

Mary did not understand that foolish sentence, but listened on as the old woman continued:

"Woe has it been ter me that I ever left my native country and roamed round with another; but I am strong now and all ye powerless around me, and I have never let youens know what my business is. I sit under my own fig tree and chaw my own terbaceer and never swaller any ambier. Now woman, put yer foot on this pack of kerds, make yer wish—do it quick but say nothing. Thar, that's enough. Here—yes, here, this kerd shows disappintment [*sic*]. Yes, and look at that man—yes, a man and a child too! You may be married and you may not; that I don't know. Here—seven for luck. Oh, ye air proud, sure; love high associates—'um, here is disappintments—great loss; but ye'll see much, much success yit."

Mary was too much frightened to say anything to the old hag, but she paid her and hurried off to her own room. She thought if witches were burnt in these days the old creature she had just left would surely go to the faggot and flame.

Troubles make some people superstitious. Mary caught at dreams and omens. She now had a fresh hope although coming from such a repugnant source. She had written to every postmaster she could think of, but no information had she gained. This was the first day she had been encouraged in the hope of again seeing her child. The day after

---

[67] This word is unclear from the original. The only letters visible are "lp" at the end. There is room for 2 letters prior to "lp." What word do you think it might be?

seeing the old woman a letter was handed her. She quickly opened it, and read as follows:

"Dear Madam—Your letter received, and I would have answered earlier, but I have been making enquiries for the man and child you described. I have ascertained that about a year ago a man came through here by the name of Peacock, and hired a woman who kept a very low house to take charge of a child, and I understand she has it still. I will be glad to render you any assistance in my power.

Yours very respectfully,
ASHBY REDWINE."[68]

Mary hastened to her employer and gave him the letter, saying:

"I must go immediately."

He read the letter and said: "I will go with you, for I think this is a clue, and I hope you may find your boy.

It was needless for him to go, she said.

"But you may be running into danger."

"I am not afraid; I know Mr. Ashby Redwine and he is brave and the soul of honor."

Mary's preparations were made in time for leaving on the first train. Her friend kind and true, took her in his carriage to the depot and saw her start on her journey. She was placed particularly under the conductor's care. Her friend and employer hoped for her success but he missed her and dreaded when she found her child she might refuse to be his wife. She had told him she wished never to marry again, but he hoped he could induce her to change her mind and accept him, for he really loved her.

---

[68] Charley's brother, **Ashby** Peck, was 5 years younger than him. In addition, there is a **Redwine** family that lived in Cocke Co., and a **Redwine**, TN, located 10 miles southeast of Morristown, on the way to Wolf Creek, TN (where Charley's family lived in the 1870/1880s). Both Wolf Creek and Redwine are in Cocke County, TN.

On her journey Mary took time to think of his parting words. "If I marry him," she thought, "he will be a protection to me and my child against Peacock; he will assist me in finding and caring for my poor parents. When I told him how I had been instrumental in ruining them and driving them from their home, how quick his noble generosity made him propose plans for their benefit." But almost every moment of her time was passed in thinking of her child. She was told by the conductor that she could not get to Marshal[69] on the train, but he would put her off at the nearest point and she could get a conveyance.

It was now evening. She got off at the little station, but found that no conveyance was to be had. She got a horse and resolved to go on if it took all night. She traveled as fast as she could and did not stop until she arrived at the little burg. It was now past ten o'clock and the place was in almost total darkness. Seeing one light at a window she stopped there and enquired where the postmaster lived. She was directed where to find him but the woman said: "You can't get him up this time of night." Mary was determined to try. Going to his house she dismounted, and holding her horse by the bridle rapped at the door. It was some time before anyone answered, but on hearing a woman's voice Mr. Redwine rose and dressed quickly and came to the door and asked her in. She told him she was the mother of the child she had written him about. He asked how she came. When she told him he looked astonished and said: "Why, were you not afraid to come that lonely way by yourself? You don't know the danger you ran." She replied that her mind was absorbed in her child. At times she feared he might be dead, then her speed slackened, then again came the idea that she would soon see him, which caused her to press forward with redoubled energy. "Oh, sir!" she said, "I hardly know how I got here."

---

[69] Marshall, North Carolina is the county seat for Madison County. It is located approx. 10 miles down the French Broad River from Hot Springs, NC.

"Madam, you are surely no stranger to me. I have certainly seen you before; your voice strongly reminds me of a lady I once knew— Miss Mary Anderson."

"Mr. Redwine, I am that Mary, or, at least, the wreck of her."

He sprang forward and cried: "Oh, Miss Mary! Is this you? My God! What troubles have been yours."

They grasped each others' hands, while Mr. Redwine was pained to see the ravages cruelty had made on that fine face.

"You do not think of going for the child tonight?" he said.

"Oh, yes, Mr. Redwine, let us start immediately."

"But do you think you will recognize it in all this time? There must be a great change in its appearance from want of proper food and care. People say the old hag lives in squalid poverty."

Mary shuddered at the thought of the little fellow's sufferings and began to dread again lest it was dead. She said she was very sure she would know him for the last time Peacock was at home before he stole it, either accidentally or purposefully he chopped off the child's great toe on the left foot; by which means it could easily be identified.

By this time the boy whom Mr. Redwine had told to catch his horse and to get one for the lady, came to say they were ready. Mr. Redwine used every argument to induce Mary to remain and let him go alone. He said there was danger if any of the men were about, but he had heard they had gone on a tramping expedition, still he prepared himself for the worst, insisting that she should let him go alone.

"Oh, sir, I cannot! I would go wild with fear and apprehension of further evils. Oh! Mr. Redwine, I might be some help to you in case of resistance. With your determination and bravery I know you are host in yourself, still I might be able to help you and I will share the danger with you."

"Miss Mary, I think we are bound to succeed. Our cause is right and just before God and man and we have the nerve to do what is right, so I will help you to mount your horse."

He could not bear to call her by the name of Peacock. They had agreed to ride on in silence; it was too dark to see far ahead and they rode as fast as the darkness and the road would permit. When they could ride abreast they held a whispered conversation. She asked again for everything he could tell her of her child. He asked about her parents; she only told him they had moved away from their old home. He judged from the melancholy tone of her voice that there was something wrong in that quarter too, and decided that Peacock must be at the bottom of it. How he detested the wretch who had brought all this ruin on an innocent and too confiding family.

At last they came up to the hut. Redwine had taken the pains to go and get a good look at it and all its surroundings. He made it a rule after writing to Mary to ride out there frequently. He would fill his pockets with candy and cakes to toll the three starved looking children the hag had charge of, to get them to come to him. To the old hag herself he would give a little flask of whisky, pretending he called to get some water to put in his toddy. He would be extremely friendly with "granny," as the children called her, and whenever he came granny would wipe off the chair she gave him with her apron or her rag of a sun bonnet. He would praise her grandchildren. One, she said, was not "hern, but that ar thing that's always lookin' like he saw somethin' way off. I don't like that, sir. He looks like he was seein' speerits, or maybe youens call 'em spooks, and I don't like the creetur nohow, fur its taking the bread outen my own children's mouths; but Ike says it has to be kept here, for he knew the daddy in the mountains and they were counterfeiters together and mighty great friends."

Redwine feared when he was made the depository of that piece of news, so he in an adroit manner questioned the hag to find out if she was aware of the importance of the secret. She was not; had hardly an idea in regard to the penalty attached to it; rather thought it was a splendid business and the government paid them well.

Redwine replied, "Hardly paid them enough."

The children were kept so dirty he could scarcely tell one from another, for the two youngest were near the same size and with faces so begrimed with dirt, he thought their mothers could not know them.

He listened attentively at the hut door to try and discover if Ike and the other men were there, but he heard nothing but the snores of the hag. He went back where had left Mary still on horseback, in case they would have to beat a hasty retreat. He lifted her down lightly, fastened the horses and returned to the house.

The snoring still went on. He rapped loudly once, twice. Her gruff voice called out:

"Who in thunder is thar making that noise?"

Redwine asked permission to come in.

"And whaten in the thunderen air you coming back here this time o'night for? Ye git back where ye come from!" [Page 27 End]

"But, granny, I have a lady here who wants to rest."

"Let her sot on the ground, fur its not so very cold."

"Well, granny, I'll knock your door down if you don't open it."

"I shan't open my house this time o' night! Ike says I shan't and I shan't!"

Redwine repeated: "Open it now or I will burst it open."

He was confident big, burly Ike, the worst ruffian in the gang was not there and another blow at the door would open it.

The hag called, "Will you hurt me if I let you in my house?"

"No; of course not, Why should I hurt you, granny?"

Then an immense bolt was drawn and a prop taken from the door, and they were admitted.

"Sure enough, youens has got a gal with you."

"Well, here, you must now make us toddy."

While the hag was making it and sipping it, Redwine lighted his lantern that reflected a light through the filthy place. The hag lighted a pine torch that threw its bright glare everywhere, and poor Mary, with her heart in her throat hastened to a pile of filthy straw in the corner.

She came first to a child five or six years old. She took the dirty rag covering from off the smallest child, and scarcely looked at its faced but took hold of its feet.

"Oh, the Lord be praised!" she almost screamed.

The old woman said, "Hey wha herns mean?"

"Just as I have been telling you, how fond she is of little children. See, she has gone to the door to let in the moonlight."

To prevent an alarm Redwine had been pouring into her the strongest whisky with a speck of opium[70] in it, all the time he had been in the house. He knew as Mary was out of sight that all was right and said:

"Granny, make that foolish girl a good toddy, while I go and make her come in."

As he went out he heard the hag say:

"And hern is a fool, for I don't see no moon."

Mary was on her horse. Redwine took the child out of her arms almost by force, but talking softly and kindly to her.

"I am afraid you may have to use your pistols yet," said Mary.

"Well, give me the child, and you take one pair and I will keep the other safe, and you can shoot as well as I can."

It was but a few minutes before they were safely on their road. It was now lighter and they could ride faster. Every now and then Mary would ask about her poor ill-used child.

"Sleeping like a top," was Redwine's cheerful answer.

"Oh, thank you a thousand times." The tears of joy and gratitude flowed freely down Mary's cheeks.

---

[70] Opium, in pill and powder form, was widely available in the 19th century. It was used extensively to treat Civil War soldiers, and many returned home addicted after the war. Opiates made up 15% of all prescriptions dispensed in Boston in 1888. For more info see: https://www.smithsonianmag.com/history/inside-story-americas-19th-century-opiate-addiction-180967673/.

They did not draw rein until they halted before Mr. Redwine's house just at daybreak.

He said, "We will leave our horses here and walk to my boarding-house and then no one will be the wiser for our ride, for before we left I sent my boy to a friend with a note to have the stage stop here for me. It is not a mail stage and sometimes it takes a near cut and does not come by here."

He took Mary and her precious child to his boarding house where she soon had a nice room. In there to herself she hugged and kissed the little lost one.

"And don't you know it is your own mother who has got you now?"

Redwine tapped at her door to give her some clothes for the child until she could make some. He seemed to know and think of everything. She washed, combed, and dressed the haggard, half-starved child, talking, kissing and petting it all the while. Her breakfast was sent in to her, and very carefully she fed the famished little one. She sent for Redwine after he had eaten his breakfast. Holding the boy up to him, she asked:

"Would you have recognized him as the dirt and rags we picked up and brought here?"

He took the little fellow up in his arms and fondled him. The child knew him and gabbled his childish talk. Mr. Redwine said:

"Miss Mary, I now see a strong resemblance to yourself."

The foot was carefully examined. It had healed badly, and the scar was there. Mary told Redwine he ought to leave this place now; "from what you told me of that mountaineer, Ike, I am afraid he is daring enough to waylay you. Resign this office and come home with me, and I know you will be joyfully received some warm friends I have. Besides such a man as you are has no business to remain here in obscurity. You are doing yourself an injustice, but I thank God you were here when I wrote to this office."

Redwine replied:

"If I can find a deputy before the stage comes[,] I will go with you as far as the depot to protect you against any unforeseen danger.

"Go, Mr. Redwine; hurry and find one, and make your arrangements to go home with me, do get ready!" said happy Mary.

She never let the child from her arms, but held fast to him as if she feared again to lose him. Redwine found a suitable deputy and all were ready the time the stage came in. In the stage were some good but ignorant old farmers whom Redwine knew. As they talked on their own affairs without cessation they were no hindrance to the confidential conversations of Mary and Redwine. She gave him an outline of all that had passed in regard to her father's affairs. No names were called, but each knew the allusion the other made. Mr. Redwine said:

"The place you saw was my refuge after that unfortunate duel."

Mary interrupted him with,

"Never give that circumstance a thought. I said at the time he was a bad man and without any sense of honor, and perhaps, by doing as you did, you have saved some poor, confiding family from his clutches. I only look on it in this way, that you were only an instrument in God's hands. From what I know of bad men I think the world was well rid of him."

At last the old farmers got tired talking of their crops and got to telling news. One said: "What do you 'spose made that old woman yell so this morning as we were passing her hut?"

"And squalling and screeching for Ike? Who is Ike? Do you know[?]"

One answered:

"Ike is a bully that ought to be in the penitentiary for life, according to my belief and from what I know of him."

Mary exchanged glances with Redwine and he asked in a careless way,

"Have any of you seen Ike this morning?"

One said,

"I saw a fellow who was going down the red mill for him as one of the children was dead or lost, but I was riding so fast I could not hear exactly."

Mary hugged and pressed her child closer to her bosom and breathed many prayers for its safety. Redwine did not doubt but that Ike was fast following on, but he knew the penniless scamp could not get further than the depot. But he was not visible when Redwine helped Mary on the train, and keenly Redwine looked in every direction. Mary now would not let him leave her. She said:

"Never mind business. What is that paltry office, or any other office, compared with the value of your life? Come with me for the sake of the child you saved."

He said:

"On no account now would I let you go alone. There is no mistake but that is a daring scamp, and he has the cunning of the fox."

Mary said;

"And remember always, he is a scholar of Peacock's and for that reason to be doubly feared, and Peacock no doubt taught him—if he did not already know—many underhand villainies; for he was always threatening violence against any one who interfered with him."

"But, Miss Mary, threats are only a coward's fortitude," said Redwine, cheerfully.

"But, oh! Mr. Redwine, a coward you know, is merciless where he gets the advantage over you. How distressed I shall be to see you return to that town. You will be in danger. I want you to live to allow me, if I ever can, to pay this blessed debt I owe you."

"Miss Mary, I do not feel afraid of such scamps. They dare not molest me; besides, my intentions are all good. I have not an evil principle in my constitution, and I will do all the good I can, at least I shall try."

"I know, Mr. Redwine, they will not molest you openly, and you have always been called brave and good and you have proved to me you are good. But, yet, wise and just principles sometimes can be ill applied. To return there will be doing yourself injustice. It is true, your being there will benefit the few who told me they relied so much upon you to keep that obscure little town in order and safe from desperadoes, still there is something due to yourself. Your talents are too bright to be buried there; your power to do good ought to have a wider scope."

"Well, Miss Mary, your arguments are very flattering indeed, and more I am afraid than I deserve, but if I thought I could be successful in my profession—"

Mary here exclaimed:

"Successful! why of course you will be. A man of your talents, honor and energy, is bound to be successful! Mr. Belmont[71], the gentleman who owns the store I am in, complained to me of the young lawyer he has employed as being too careless and indolent, and he would be obliged to employ some one else. Do please allow me to try and show my gratitude to you for rescuing that poor child that you are now playing with. Let me introduce you to Mr. Belmont? I am convinced your own worthiness will be your strongest ally; but then, I must be allowed to serve you as far as my poor influence can go."

"Miss Mary, with your advocacy in my cause, I am sure I will succeed. You are too good for it to be otherwise. Do you remember in the happier days we both have had how much good you did; how you soothed the distressed and stimulated and cheered up the vacillating and doubting ones? We were all benefited by the advice and

---

[71] Belmont is a French word meaning "beautiful mountain." The famous Belmont Mansion was built in Nashville, Tennessee in 1853, with its final phase completed in 1860. During the decisive Battle of Nashville, December 1864, Belmont Mansion was the headquarters for the 4th Corps of the U. S. Army of the Cumberland and witness to the unfolding of the battle that effectively ended the Civil War in the Western Theater. (Source: www.belmontmansion.com)

encouragement of your good lessons, and now, thanks to you I am going to begin a new life and try to rise out of the mean position an unfortunate incident threw me into."

Mary spoke cheering words of his probable—more than probable success. He now proposed that he should telegraph in her name to Mr. Belmont of her success and what time she would arrive.

Her little boy improved, she said, every hour and she did believe he knew her to be his own mother. The principles of affection [Page 28 End] had not been taught him in the squallid hut of the old hag, still he showed they were inherent in his nature. He would throw his poor, little arms around his mother's neck and kiss her and say:

"Where you been you leave me so long?"

No doubt he had some remembrance of poor Kate's kindness. He would dive down into Mr. Redwine's pockets and if he got a piece of candy, he would laugh gleefully, and Mary said:

"I will make my boy a good man with God's help; and I hope he may be both good and great enough to be of service to both friend and country."

After it was settled that Redwine would not return to that dangerous locality, Mary was better satisfied and so was he. They chatted pleasantly as they travelled on. When they arrived at the city Mr. Belmont came aboard the train and was introduced to Mr. Redwine, and took the child and offered Mary his arm, but the observing Redwine relieved him of the child and all were soon seated in his elegant landau. Mary was driven to her quiet lodgings and now she was happy, sitting there telling Mr. Belmont and a few other friends how she had obtained success in her hunt for her child.

Redwine says, "Mr. Belmont, she attributed too much to me, she did a great deal herself."

Mr. Belmont laughingly said: "You shall not quarrel over each other's good qualities, for I see the very act required nerve and daring and only the brave could have succeeded as you did."

It was evening and they all took supper together. At a later hour Mr. Belmont left, taking Mr. Redwine home with him and told him,

"Now, this is your home until you get tired."

Through Redwine he learned more particularly about Mary's former life and the more he heard the more in love he grew.

(TO BE CONTINUED.)

Figure 21 - Belmont Mansion Estate Portrait, Artist Unknown, 1860-1861, Oil on Canvas, https://www.belmontmansion.com/copy-of-baccante-carrying-baby-bacc.

Historical Note: The owner of Belmont was Adelicia Hayes Franklin Acklen Cheatham (born 1817). "At the age of 22, Adelicia married Isaac Franklin, a plantation owner whose previous company traded slaves from the Upper to the Lower South. Franklin was 28 years her senior and their marriage produced four children, all of whom died by the age of 11. At his death in 1846 his estate included: 8,700 acres of cotton plantations in Louisiana; a 2,000-acre farm in Tennessee; more than 50,000 acres of undeveloped land in Texas; stocks and bonds; and 750 enslaved people. The young widow, Adelicia Franklin, was left independently wealthy at age 29."
https://www.belmontmansion.com/belmontstory, accessed 5 Sep 2021.

Relevance: Charley's dad, Dr. Isham Peck, and his family, also owned cotton plantations in Louisiana and Mississippi, and a large farm in Oakland, Tennessee.

CHAPTER XXIX.

(CONCLUDED.)

Mary, through the laws of her country was now free from Peacock. The divorce was obtained without any trouble. She was not called Mrs. Peacock, as none knew that hated name but Mr. Belmont. She was in the store always called Miss Mary.

One bright, lovely morning, a small bridal party entered a fashionable church two weeks after Mary's return, and the principals in this transaction were Mr. Belmont and Mrs. Mary Anderson. After the ceremony, hearty and true were the congratulations spoken to the bride and groom. Mr. Redwine had charge of little Harry, who wanted to know what that tall man in his night gown was saying to mamma. Redwine told him to listen and then he would know.

From the church they drove home to Mr. Belmont's palatial mansion and there, for the first time, Mary entered to be introduced to new friends and to take her place at the head of the sumptuous and elegantly set table. This was no trial. She was only returning back to her old accustomed life before she had the misfortune to marry Peacock. Mary was thankful to God for His protecting care. She now no longer felt herself forgotten by Him. But even in this waking dream we call life there is something still wanting.

"If I could only know where my parents and sisters are, then my cup of happiness would be but overflowing."

Months passed on. Mr. Belmont had engaged Mr. Redwine as his attorney and he lived with them, and he and little Harry were as inseparable as old Dominie Sampson and little Harry Betram.[72] One day Mr. Redwine had to go some distance to a large town. He was on business for Mr. Belmont, and he had always been told by both Belmont and Mary, whenever he went to make enquiries for her parents, as they had not returned to the place reported to her. Redwine replied that he had set enquiries afloat in every direction and had left nothing undone to find them. He left for H--. The next day after his arrival, walking along one of its principal streets, he met Col. Hill with the very gentleman he was in quest of. He was introduced to Col. Hill and was struck with his improved likeness to his old and staunch friend, John Hill, and in a little time asked if they were related. How hands were grasped when John said:

"I did not hear distinctly your name, but I was thinking you must be a relation of my old chum."

Col. Hill said to the gentleman,

"We will see you to-morrow," and took Redwine immediately home with him. They went to the library, Hill saying,

"My wife is out visiting and we will remain in here until her return."

Old news began to be talke[d] over. Soon the Anderson name was called up by Mr. Redwine. He told all about how he had again met with Mary. Hill listened with breathless attention, making exclamations of pity, astonishment and joy on hearing at last of her happy and prosperous state.

---

[72] Reference to *Guy Mannering; or The Astrologer*, a novel by Sir Walter Scott (1771-1832). The novel was first published in Edinburgh in 1815. In the novel, the main character is Mr. Harry Bertram, and his tutor is Dominie Sampson.

"Perfectly happy she would be if she could only find her parents and sisters," said Mr. Redwine.

"I could not interrupt you, so great was my interest in poor Mary's case, but now I will tell you, Anderson and his family are living about ten miles from here."

"Let us go right away," said Mr. Redwine.

Hill ordered his buggy and as they drove on he told of all their troubles and told how Peacock had been convicted of forgery and would be sent to the penitentiary in a few days. Hill said:

"We will drive up to the gate," and he jumped out, followed by Redwine.

Mr. Anderson was sitting in his little gallery alone, but Eva saw the gentlemen stop and told her mother who came out, hoping there was some news from her dear child.

"Mrs. Anderson, I have brought an old friend to see you. Don't you remember Mr. Redwine?" asked Hill in his cheery, clear tone.

After the meeting of the family with Redwine and much talk, he said to Mrs. Anderson:

"I have some good news for you. Now listen and make up your mind to tell me what I must telegraph to Mr. and Mrs. Belmont, your Mary."

"My Mary! my child!" screamed Mrs. Anderson, in the fullness of her heart.

"Yes, she is now the wealthy Mrs. Belmont and would be happy indeed, if she only had you with her."

Tears flowed fast from the mother's eyes, but they were the tears of joy and thanksgiving. The whole family were deeply affected. Mr. Redwine did not tell all of Mary's sufferings with Peacock, but they knew they were terrible. He told of her present style and state, of her charming boy, her noble and kind husband.

"And now," he says, "let me hurry to telegraph them and you will see for yourselves I have not exaggerated. I have not told half."

"Now, all fix up to be supremely happy, for she will be here as quickly as steam can bring them."

"And now," he said again, "my wife will be wondering about me. I only left a little note for her. Come, Redwine, let us be going; and will we not leave a happy mother?" he said as he took Mrs. Anderson's hand.

They drove back rapidly to town. Mr. Redwine was presented to Mrs. Hill and he thought, what a picture of loveliness!

He had telegraphed and soon as possible an answer was flashed back, "We are starting."

Hill said:

"I will meet them with my carriage and take them right out, but I do not think I have the fortitude to see the meeting of the mother and daughter."

Mr. and Mrs. Belmont arrived one bright day in the early forenoon.

Mr. Hill and his wife were both at the depot waiting for them. But there was another class there, hardly belonging to the same species of humanity; a class of the vilest and blackest character; but there was one, head and shoulders above all the rest in cruelty and crime. Col. Hill could not see these criminals, for he had told his driver to move up a short distance from their view, but when the train approached, he went on foot to meet Mary, her husband, and child. The convicts were put in motion, guards guarding them on the train, and suddenly the cruelly treated wife came face to face with the fiendish husband. As she came out of the car she saw Peacock with his wrists in steel cuffs and he was looking so horribly. She was thankful that her thick veil prevented his seeing her face. Col. Hill met her and knew she had recognized the villain for her manner was nervous and frightened. After the most friendly and kindest salutations, he conducted the party to his carriage and introduced his wife. She insisted that Mary must drive home with them and take some refreshment before driving out to the village, but she said:

"Many thanks for your kindness, but I could not rest until I see my parents."

Hill took a chance moment to whisper to her that it was impossible for that villain, Peacock, to live long, he was in a manner dying of consumption.

The Belmonts drove off in Col. Hill's carriage while he and his wife returned home in his buggy. He moralized on the danger of forming an intimacy with persons we know nothing of, and taking his wife's little hand between his own, he said:

"I am speaking my own experience, for the first time I met Peacock he was to me the most repulsive person I ever saw, but I let that feeling wear off. I endeavored to do so, for I began to think it must be meanness in myself to have such a dislike to a stranger without a cause. He amused me and I forgot the warning, but even worked the harder to make amends for the dislike that at first I had for him."

Mr. Redwine was at Mr. Anderson's. He and all the family were in nervous excitement to meet again after all the dreadful trials and after this long separation.

Mrs. Anderson exclaimed:

"Oh! I am afraid it is a dream and all this happiness is not for my poor weary heart to feel."

"Oh! Mrs. Anderson, it is all true and you will realize it," said Redwine cheerfully.

The meeting soon took place between those long afflicted and separated ones, but it was beyond description. It was Mr. Anderson who first recovered his equanimity and played to his son-in-law, as far as his means would go, the elegant host, but Mr. Belmont's attention was mostly given to his wife and her mother. He was unremitting in his endeavors to make them forget the dark past and look on the bright future that loomed upon auspiciously before them.

"Oh! I am happy, but I am afraid I can't be sufficiently thankful to Heaven for the restoration of my dear child and her boy," Mrs. Anderson exclaimed.

The first day was passed in a sober, melancholy happiness. The heavy hand of affliction had been too strong for them to emerge immediately from its influences. But the next day Col. Hill and his charming wife drove to see them, and during the day plans were made. Mr. Belmont proposed that the whole family should get ready to go home with him. Col. Hill and his wife said no, that Mary and all of them must come and spend some time with them, but Mary—a model of grace—thanked them so very kindly and asked them to wait until her nervous system had quieted down to its usual tone.

Mr. Belmont seconded his wife's true request. Then a time was specified and if they [Page 29 End] did not come, Col. Hill and his wife would visit Mr. and Mrs. Belmont. After the Colonel and his wife left, Eva with Mr. Redwine went to bid good-by to the poor neighbors who had been kind to them. Her little scholars wept tears of sorrow as they bade farewell to their kind teacher. Mary told her mother to give the few things they had to the most deserving, and not to take with them anything but their clothes. The next morning they were all ready by the time the conveyances sent by Mr. Belmont's orders arrived, and a last farewell was given to the place that had known them in such sorrow. Col. And Mrs. Hill met them at the depot and there bade them all good-by. As he shook Redwine's hand—who had little Harry in his arms—he said:

"You must come and stay a long time with me."

He closely scanned little Harry's face, fearing he might see a line of Peacock, but was delighted to find there was not in feature of expression one particle of resemblance, but he was Mary in miniature.

The travellers [*sic*] arrived safely home and for a short time all lived together, but Mary saw a hint that her father missed his old home. One day she proposed to her husband—timidly at first, for she thought he had done so much—but he reassured her, and then they said they would go to the old home, without saying a word to anyone, and see what arrangements could be made.

On pretence [*sic*] of business, Mr. Belmont said he would have to leave home for a few days and take Mary with him. They left and in a few days were in the vicinity of Mary's old home, her childhood's happy home. They got carriage and the husband and wife and little Harry started to the old, dear place. On arriving they found it in rather a dilapidated condition. They learned that Col. Rollins owned it but had leased it out. They went to see him about buying it back. They found all the family in the greatest distress. Mary and Ada flew into each other's arms. They found out the trouble. Rollins was under indictment and it was going hard with him. Mr. Belmont made a satisfactory purchase of the homestead and those who had leased it were bought out and left the place to the new purchaser, who retained the hands to work out the crop. Carpenters were employed to build up and renew the house and fences. An order was given to furniture dealers to send in carpets and all required furniture. Mr. Belmont left a supervisor, and he and his family left for home.

CHAPTER XXX.

Mr. and Mrs. Belmont's return was hailed with joy by the loved ones left at home. Little Harry was almost devoured with kisses and Mr. Redwine was rejoiced too, and as demonstrative as a boy in his rejoicing when Mr. Belmont whispered to him what he had been absent for. Some weeks passed in quiet happiness in that happy home.

One day Mr. Belmont got a letter saying all had been finished; the house was now ready, and he read it to Mary. When he finished it he said:

"Now we will tell them we are going on a pleasure trip—Redwine and all—and we must be ready on Thursday."

The announcement was made and Mrs. Anderson said:

"Let me stay?"

"Not a bit of it, dear mamma; we must all go."

"Dear Mary, I will do just as you say."

The day came round, and in a few days the father and the girls recognized their old vicinity. They stopped at the hotel. Old acquaintances—not one of the family called them old friends—their old acquaintances greeted them in the friendliest manner; all returned the meeting, but still they had a memory of former slights. Their memory was not impervious to the unnecessary slights in the day of their deep trouble—the day of the sale. Their stay in town lasted no longer than the waiting for conveyances. The drivers were told where to go, but the Anderson family did not hear Redwine tell them.

As they drove up to the house, Mr. Belmont said:

"We will go in here."

"Oh, no! oh, no!" cried Mrs. Anderson, "not in there. It will kill me to go in there."

Mr. Belmont took her by the hand and said:

"Oh, no! you must come to please me."

That was sufficient. She would have died if it would please him. They all went in and Mr. Anderson exclaimed:

"Why, no one comes to receive us, to do the honors of this new, fine house."

Mrs. Anderson looked around.

"Mary, dear," she said, "this is all finer than when we lived here. No one has come to receive us."

Mary threw her arms about her mother's neck and laughingly said:

"Why, dear mamma, have you forgotten your politeness? Why don't you welcome Mr. Belmont and me to your dear old home?"

Then began a scene. Questions were asked; thanks were returned, and then Mr. Anderson strolled out to look on old familiar objects. Mr. Belmont said:

"My dear Mrs. Anderson, it seems your last days are to be happier than your first. Now you are back in your old home everything will be as it was."

"Mr. Belmont, a life time of gratitude could not repay you. I am more thankful than I can tell, but my friend, where there has been a change, nothing can be as it was before; and, oh, heavens! such a change. This is my old house, but my old home is gone and the same feelings can never return. But I am so thankful, oh! so thankful to you that has been so kind to me and mine."

He replied gaily,

"Well, cheer up and come see and help enjoy the good supper the girls and Redwine—and Harry helping—has got for us."

At the table was real enjoyment. The happy faces around it would have cured an anchorite[73] of his love for solitude. After supper, all strolled about the yard in the bright moonlight. Mary leaning upon her husband's arm, walked up and down the moonlit gallery. She was telling him every moment that her life must be devoted to him in thought and deed. He answering that she had made the world to him an earthly paradise.

One day Col. Hill came home and his wife gave him a letter she had received that morning and asked him what she must do. He read it and said:

"Will you let me do as I please with it?"

"Most certainly, you know your pleasure is the only law I know."

"Well, then, here it goes into the fire," and suiting the action to the word, he continued, "to think of such impertinence! How barefaced! After treating you with abuse and wrong, then to write to you for assistance! Surely that girl must take you to be without sense or memory. No! we will set her new husband up in business. They can forget us, she says, but we will not forget them, my love. But, Bess, here is a letter more to my taste. It is from genial hearted Ashby Redwine. Let me read you the news from Happy Hollow, as he named it."

"And, Colonel, a good name, too. You don't know how much I rejoice in their happiness."

"But, Miss Bess, I want to know why, or how you came to call me Colonel instead of the pet name you gave me. Were you feeling dignified?"

---

[73] Anchorite = a person who lives in seclusion usually for religious reasons

"Yes, I am feeling very matronly just to-day. You know our boy put on his first trousers to-day. I can assure you I think my little John will be handsomer than my big John, handsome as he is."

Hill laughed and gave his wife a hearty kiss. He said:

"And I hear nurse coming with Bessie number two."

And nurse, with a little beauty in her arms, came smiling in.

(THE END.)

[Page 30 End]

APPENDICES

APPENDIX I. FRONT PAGES WITH NOTES

Charley cut, pasted, and wrote the following photos and quotes into his "form book," a journal used by attorneys. Each item has been analyzed for historical significance. These items help us understand him, the Pecks, and the 1870s-1880s in America.

Title: MONTENEGRO AS WE SAW IT ENGRAVED BY R.D. SERVOSS N-Y.

Print: Dark-heaving; boundless, endless, and sublime,

The image of eternity, the throne of the Invisible.

Figure 22 - Scan to read the 1854 edition of Childe Harold's Pilgrimage for free with Google Books

Historical Note: The above quote is from Lord Byron's romaunt, *Childe Harold's Pilgrimage*. "It is a long narrative poem in four parts. "Childe" is a medieval title for a young man who was a candidate for knighthood. The poem was published between 1812 and 1818. Dedicated to "Ianthe", it describes the travels and reflections of a world-weary young man, who is disillusioned with a life of pleasure and revelry and looks for distraction in foreign lands. In a wider sense, it is an expression of the melancholy and disillusionment felt by a generation weary of the wars of the post-Revolutionary and Napoleonic eras.

The poem was widely imitated and contributed to the cult of the wandering Byronic hero who falls into melancholic reverie as he contemplates scenes of natural beauty. Its autobiographical subjectivity was widely influential, not only in literature but in the arts of music and painting as well, and was a powerful ingredient in European Romanticism."[74]

George Gordon Byron, 6th Baron Byron (22 Jan 1788 – 19 Apr 1824) known simply as Lord Byron, was an English peer who was a poet and a politician. One of the leading figures of the Romantic movement, Byron is regarded as one of the greatest English poets. He remains widely read and influential. Among his best-known works are

---

[74] https://en.wikipedia.org/wiki/Childe_Harold%27s_Pilgrimage, accessed 6 Sep 2021

the lengthy narrative poems *Don Juan* and *Childe Harold's Pilgrimage*; many of his shorter lyrics in *Hebrew Melodies* also became popular.[75]

Lord Byron had one daughter, Ada Lovelace (10 Dec 1815 – 27 Nov 1852) by his wife Lady Byron (Anna Isabella Noel Byron). Because the name "Ada" for a girl became important for the Peck family with the birth of Ada Louise Peck, a short bio of Lord Byron's Ada is included here.

"Lord Byron expected his child to be a "glorious boy" and was disappointed when Lady Byron gave birth to a girl. The child was named after Byron's half-sister, Augusta Leigh, and was called "Ada" by Byron himself. On 16 Jan 1816, at Lord Byron's command, Lady Byron left for her parents' home at Kirkby Mallory, taking their five-week-old daughter with her. Although English law at the time granted full custody of children to the father in cases of separation, Lord Byron made no attempt to claim his parental rights, but did request that his sister keep him informed of Ada's welfare.

On 21 April, Lord Byron signed the deed of separation, although very reluctantly, and left England for good a few days later. Aside from an acrimonious separation, Lady Byron continued throughout her life to make allegations about her husband's immoral behaviour. **This set of events made [Ada] Lovelace infamous in Victorian society**. Ada did not have a relationship with her father. He died in 1824 when she was eight years old. Her mother was the only significant parental figure in her life. Lovelace was not shown the family portrait of her father until her 20th birthday."

"As an adult, Ada became an English mathematician and writer, chiefly known for her work on Charles Babbage's proposed mechanical general-purpose computer, the Analytical Engine. She was the first to recognize that the machine had applications beyond pure calculation, and to have published the first algorithm intended to be

---

[75] https://en.wikipedia.org/wiki/Lord_Byron, accessed 6 Sep 2021.

carried out by such a machine. As a result, she is often regarded as the first computer programmer."[76]

Ada Lovelace died 27 Nov 1852 from uterine cancer in London, England. Her death made international news. Charley's oldest sister, and firstborn of his siblings, Ada Louise Peck, was born 8 months later on 25 Jul 1853. According to *Ada's Journal*, kept by their mother Emma, at the age of one she could "sit like Lord Byron and walk like Napoleon."[77] Clearly the family enjoyed reading Lord Byron's poetry, and did so for their little girl Ada. Could this be where Isham and Emma got the name, Ada? What are your thoughts?

Figure 23 - Portrait of Ada Byron, later to be known as Ada Lovelace (1815-1852). Oil on canvas. Artist: Comte d'Orsay (1801-1852). Portrait presently held in the library of Somerville College, Oxford. Circa 1822. Public Domain.

Ada Lovelace was an intriguing young girl and woman. Here are a few facts about her life. She conceptualized a flying machine at the age of 12, even writing a book about her findings. Though she and Lord Byron were not able to have a personal relationship, she maintained a life-long fascination with him and his works, and chose to be buried beside him. She had a gambling

Figure 24 - Ada Byron at age 17. From The Calculating Passion of Ada Byron by Joan Baum. Originally from the Lovelace-Byron Collection. 1832.

---

[76] https://en.wikipedia.org/wiki/Ada_Lovelace, accessed 6 Sep 2021.
[77] Ada's Journal and Emma's Letters, Cross Mountain Books, 2021, Pg 21.

addiction and even used her programming skills to try and predict horse race results. While she lay on her deathbed, Charles Dickens read a well-known scene from his popular 1848 novel *Dombey and Son* in which 6-year-old boy Paul Dombey dies. She died three months later.[78]

Here is the quote pasted by Charley above the image of Montenegro, from Lord Byron's *Childe Harold's Pilgrimage* in context. It is in the final section of his long poem, and is about the ocean. Maybe after his sea voyage to South America, he longed for the adventure of the open seas once again. Charley clipped the image of *Montenegro As We Saw It* from *Scribner's Monthly* Magazine, Dec 1880, Pg 277, from a 17 page article about an epic adventure to the country. Montenegro is a Balkan country with rugged mountains, medieval villages, and a narrow strip of beaches along its Adriatic coastline. I would guess that Charley never made it to Montenegro, but he must have dreamed about it.

Figure 25 - Read "Montenegro As We Saw It" as Charley read it, from the original Dec 1880 issue of Scribner's Monthly, Pgs 276-293

Childe Harold's Pilgrimage [Canto Four, Stanzas 178-186]

CLXXVIII.

> There is a pleasure in the pathless woods,
> There is a rapture on the lonely shore,
> There is society where none intrudes,
> By the deep Sea, and music in its roar:
> I love not Man the less, but Nature more,
> From these our interviews, in which I steal
> From all I may be, or have been before,
> To mingle with the Universe, and feel
What I can ne'er express, yet cannot all conceal.

---

[78] https://www.history.com/news/10-things-you-may-not-know-about-ada-lovelace, accessed 6 Sep 2021.

CLXXIX.

Roll on, thou deep and dark blue Ocean — roll!
Ten thousand fleets sweep over thee in vain;
Man marks the earth with ruin — his control
Stops with the shore; — upon the watery plain
The wrecks are all thy deed, nor doth remain
A shadow of man's ravage, save his own,
When for a moment, like a drop of rain,
He sinks into thy depths with bubbling groan,
Without a grave, unknelled, uncoffined, and unknown.

CLXXX.

His steps are not upon thy paths, — thy fields
Are not a spoil for him, — thou dost arise
And shake him from thee; the vile strength he wields
For earth's destruction thou dost all despise,
Spurning him from thy bosom to the skies,
And send'st him, shivering in thy playful spray
And howling, to his gods, where haply lies
His petty hope in some near port or bay,
And dashest him again to earth: — there let him lay.

CLXXXI.

The armaments which thunderstrike the walls
Of rock-built cities, bidding nations quake,
And monarchs tremble in their capitals.
The oak leviathans, whose huge ribs make
Their clay creator the vain title take
Of lord of thee, and arbiter of war;
These are thy toys, and, as the snowy flake,
They melt into thy yeast of waves, which mar
Alike the Armada's pride, or spoils of Trafalgar.

CLXXXII.

   Thy shores are empires, changed in all save thee —
   Assyria, Greece, Rome, Carthage, what are they?
   Thy waters washed them power while they were free
   And many a tyrant since: their shores obey
   The stranger, slave, or savage; their decay
   Has dried up realms to deserts: not so thou,
   Unchangeable save to thy wild waves' play —
   Time writes no wrinkle on thine azure brow —
Such as creation's dawn beheld, thou rollest now.

CLXXXIII.

   Thou glorious mirror, where the Almighty's form
   Glasses itself in tempests; in all time,
   Calm or convulsed — in breeze, or gale, or storm,
   Icing the pole, or in the torrid clime
   Dark-heaving; — boundless, endless, and sublime —
   The image of Eternity — the throne
   Of the Invisible; even from out thy slime
   The monsters of the deep are made; each zone
Obeys thee: thou goest forth, dread, fathomless, alone.

CLXXXIV.

   And I have loved thee, Ocean! and my joy
   Of youthful sports was on thy breast to be
   Borne like thy bubbles, onward: from a boy
   I wantoned with thy breakers — they to me
   Were a delight; and if the freshening sea
   Made them a terror — 'twas a pleasing fear,
   For I was as it were a child of thee,
   And trusted to thy billows far and near,
And laid my hand upon thy mane — as I do here.

CLXXXV.

My task is done — my song hath ceased — my theme
Has died into an echo; it is fit
The spell should break of this protracted dream.
The torch shall be extinguished which hath lit
My midnight lamp — and what is writ, is writ —
Would it were worthier! but I am not now
That which I have been — and my visions flit
Less palpably before me — and the glow
Which in my spirit dwelt is fluttering, faint, and low.

CLXXXVI.

Farewell! a word that must be, and hath been —
A sound which makes us linger; yet, farewell!
Ye, who have traced the Pilgrim to the scene
Which is his last, if in your memories dwell
A thought which once was his, if on ye swell
A single recollection, not in vain
He wore his sandal-shoon and scallop shell;
Farewell! with him alone may rest the pain,
If such there were — with you, the moral of his strain.

Figure 26 - Childe Harold's Pilgrimage - Italy, J. M. W. Turner (1775-1851), before 1832, oil on canvas, Public Domain.

<u>Chas. T. Peck</u>

<u>Form book</u>

Handwriting: I would not bear it, though I let it bee

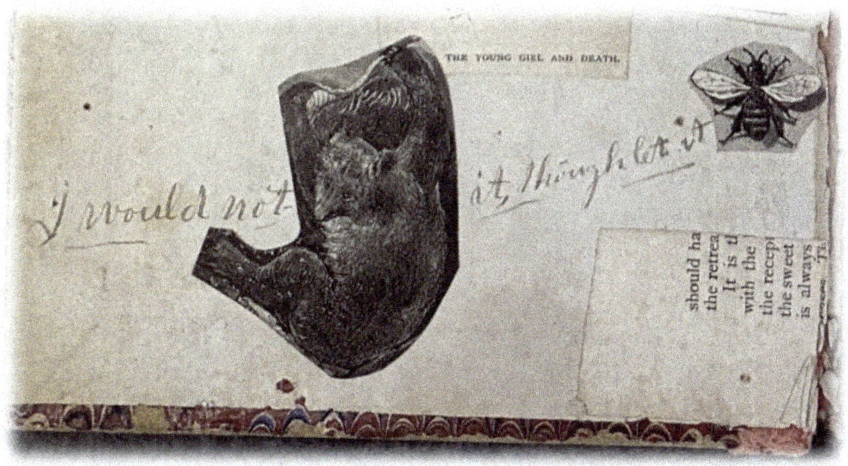

Print: THE YOUNG GIRL AND DEATH.
"I HAVE LOST MY WAY, MISS."

Historical Note on "The Young Girl and Death"

This lithograph of Sarah Bernhardt was published in 1879. See Appendix III notes on Sarah Bernhardt, a famous French stage actress.

Figure 27 - The Young Girl and Death. (Sarah Bernhardt). 1879.
https://catalogue.wellcomelibrary.org/record=b1194634, accessed 6 Sep 2021.

*President James A. Garfield's inauguration - 4 Mar 1881

Historical Note on
The Inauguration of President James Garfield

While I could not locate the source of the lithograph placed in Charley's form book, the inaugural address by President Garfield is extremely informative of the time period regarding a number of topics.

March 4, 1881: Inaugural Address
Transcript (from National Archives)

Fellow-Citizens:

We stand to-day upon an eminence which overlooks a hundred years of national life--a century crowded with perils, but crowned with the triumphs of liberty and law. Before continuing the onward march let us pause on this height for a moment to strengthen our faith and renew our hope by a glance at the pathway along which our people have traveled.

It is now three days more than a hundred years since the adoption of the first written constitution of the United States--the Articles of Confederation and Perpetual Union. The new Republic was then beset with danger on every hand. It had not conquered a place in the family of nations. The decisive battle of the war for independence, whose centennial anniversary will soon be gratefully celebrated at Yorktown, had not yet been fought. The colonists were struggling not only against the armies of a great nation, but against the settled opinions of mankind; for the world did not then believe that the supreme authority of government could be safely entrusted to the guardianship of the people themselves.

We can not overestimate the fervent love of liberty, the intelligent courage, and the sum of common sense with which our fathers made the great experiment of self-government. When they found, after a short trial, that the confederacy of States, was too weak to meet the necessities of a vigorous and expanding republic, they boldly set it aside, and in its stead established a National Union, founded directly upon the will of the people, endowed with full power of self-preservation and ample authority for the accomplishment of its great object.

Under this Constitution the boundaries of freedom have been enlarged, the foundations of order and peace have been strengthened, and the growth of our people in all the better elements of national life has indicated the wisdom of the founders and given new hope to their descendants. Under this Constitution our people long ago made themselves safe against danger from without and secured for their mariners and flag equality of rights on all the seas. Under this Constitution twenty-five States have been added to the Union, with constitutions and laws, framed and enforced by their own citizens, to secure the manifold blessings of local self-government.

The jurisdiction of this Constitution now covers an area fifty times greater than that of the original thirteen States and a population twenty times greater than that of 1780.

The supreme trial of the Constitution came at last under the tremendous pressure of civil war. We ourselves are witnesses that the Union emerged from the blood and fire of that conflict purified and made stronger for all the beneficent purposes of good government.

And now, at the close of this first century of growth, with the inspirations of its history in their hearts, our people have lately reviewed the condition of the nation, passed judgment upon the conduct and opinions of political parties, and have registered their will concerning the future administration of the Government. To interpret and to execute that will in accordance with the Constitution is the paramount duty of the Executive.

Even from this brief review it is manifest that the nation is resolutely facing to the front, resolved to employ its best energies in developing the great possibilities of the future. Sacredly preserving whatever has been gained to liberty and good government during the century, our people are determined to leave behind them all those bitter controversies concerning things which have been irrevocably settled, and the further discussion of which can only stir up strife and delay the onward march.

The supremacy of the nation and its laws should be no longer a subject of debate. That discussion, which for half a century threatened the existence of the Union, was closed at last in the high court of war by a decree from which there is no appeal--that the Constitution and the laws made in pursuance thereof are and shall continue to be the supreme law of the land, binding alike upon the States and the people. This decree does not disturb the autonomy of the States nor interfere with any of their necessary rights of local self-government, but it does fix and establish the permanent supremacy of the Union.

The will of the nation, speaking with the voice of battle and through the amended Constitution, has fulfilled the great promise of 1776 by proclaiming "liberty throughout the land to all the inhabitants thereof."

The elevation of the negro race from slavery to the full rights of citizenship is the most important political change we have known since the adoption of the Constitution of 1787. NO thoughtful man can fail to appreciate its beneficent effect upon our institutions and people. It has freed us from the perpetual danger of war and dissolution. It has added immensely to the moral and industrial forces of our people. It has liberated the master as well as the slave from a relation which wronged and enfeebled both. It has surrendered to their own guardianship the manhood of more than 5,000,000 people, and has opened to each one of them a career of freedom and usefulness. It has given new inspiration to the power of self-help in both races by making labor more honorable to the one and more necessary to the other. The influence of this force will grow greater and bear richer fruit with the coming years.

No doubt this great change has caused serious disturbance to our Southern communities. This is to be deplored, though it was perhaps unavoidable. But those who resisted the change should remember that under our institutions there was no middle ground for the negro race between slavery and equal citizenship. There can be no permanent disfranchised peasantry in the United States. Freedom can never yield its fullness of blessings so long as the law or its administration places the smallest obstacle in the pathway of any virtuous citizen.

The emancipated race has already made remarkable progress. With unquestioning devotion to the Union, with a patience and gentleness not born of fear, they have "followed the light as God gave them to see the light." They are rapidly laying the material foundations of self-support, widening their circle of intelligence, and beginning to enjoy the blessings that gather around the homes of the industrious poor. They deserve the generous encouragement of all good men. So far as my authority can lawfully extend they shall enjoy the full and equal protection of the Constitution and the laws.

The free enjoyment of equal suffrage is still in question, and a frank statement of the issue may aid its solution. It is alleged that in many communities negro citizens are practically denied the freedom of the ballot. In so far as the truth of this allegation is admitted, it is answered that in many places honest local government is impossible if the mass of uneducated negroes are allowed to vote. These are grave allegations. So far as the latter is true, it is the only palliation that can be offered for opposing the freedom of the ballot. Bad local government is certainly a great evil, which ought to be prevented; but to violate the freedom and sanctities of the suffrage is more than an evil. It is a crime which, if persisted in, will destroy the Government itself. Suicide is not a remedy. If in other lands it be high treason to compass the death of the king, it shall be counted no less a crime here to strangle our sovereign power and stifle its voice.

It has been said that unsettled questions have no pity for the repose of nations. It should be said with the utmost emphasis that this question of the suffrage will never give repose or safety to the States or to the nation until each, within its own jurisdiction, makes and keeps the ballot free and pure by the strong sanctions of the law.

But the danger which arises from ignorance in the voter can not be denied. It covers a field far wider than that of negro suffrage and the present condition of the race. It is a danger that lurks and hides in the sources and fountains of power in every state. We have no standard by which to measure the disaster that may be brought upon us by ignorance and vice in the citizens when joined to corruption and fraud in the suffrage.

The voters of the Union, who make and unmake constitutions, and upon whose will hang the destinies of our governments, can transmit their supreme authority to no successors save the coming generation of voters, who are the sole heirs of sovereign power. If that generation comes to its inheritance blinded by ignorance and corrupted by vice, the fall of the Republic will be certain and remediless.

The census has already sounded the alarm in the appalling figures which mark how dangerously high the tide of illiteracy has risen among our voters and their children.

To the South this question is of supreme importance. But the responsibility for the existence of slavery did not rest upon the South alone. The nation itself is responsible for the extension of the suffrage, and is under special obligations to aid in removing the illiteracy which it has added to the voting population. For the North and South alike there is but one remedy. All the constitutional power of the nation and of the States and all the volunteer forces of the people should be surrendered to meet this danger by the savory influence of universal education.

It is the high privilege and sacred duty of those now living to educate their successors and fit them, by intelligence and virtue, for the inheritance which awaits them.

In this beneficent work sections and races should be forgotten and partisanship should be unknown. Let our people find a new meaning in the divine oracle which declares that "a little child shall lead them," for our own little children will soon control the destinies of the Republic.

My countrymen, we do not now differ in our judgment concerning the controversies of past generations, and fifty years hence our children will not be divided in their opinions concerning our controversies. They will surely bless their fathers and their fathers' God that the Union was preserved, that slavery was overthrown, and that both races were made equal before the law. We may hasten or we may retard, but we can not prevent, the final reconciliation. Is it not possible for us now to make a truce with time by anticipating and accepting its inevitable verdict?

Enterprises of the highest importance to our moral and material well-being unite us and offer ample employment of our best powers. Let all our people, leaving behind them the battlefields of dead issues, move forward and in their strength of liberty and the restored Union win the grander victories of peace.

The prosperity which now prevails is without parallel in our history. Fruitful seasons have done much to secure it, but they have not done all. The preservation of the public credit and the resumption of specie payments, so successfully attained by the Administration of my predecessors, have enabled our people to secure the blessings which the seasons brought.

By the experience of commercial nations in all ages it has been found that gold and silver afford the only safe foundation for a monetary system. Confusion has recently been created by variations in the relative value of the two metals, but I confidently believe that arrangements can be made between the leading commercial nations which will secure the general use of both metals. Congress should provide that the compulsory coinage of silver now required by law may not disturb our monetary system by driving either metal out of circulation. If possible, such an adjustment should be made that the purchasing power of every coined dollar will be exactly equal to its debt-paying power in all the markets of the world.

The chief duty of the National Government in connection with the currency of the country is to coin money and declare its value. Grave doubts have been entertained whether Congress is authorized by the Constitution to make any form of paper money legal tender. The present issue of United States notes has been sustained by the necessities of war; but such paper should depend for its value and currency upon its convenience in use and its prompt redemption in coin at the will of the holder, and not upon its compulsory circulation. These notes are not money, but promises to pay money. If the holders demand it, the promise should be kept.

The refunding of the national debt at a lower rate of interest should be accomplished without compelling the withdrawal of the national-banknotes, and thus disturbing the business of the country.

I venture to refer to the position I have occupied on financial questions during a long service in Congress, and to say that time and experience have strengthened the opinions I have so often expressed on these subjects.

The finances of the Government shall suffer no detriment which it maybe possible for my Administration to prevent.

The interests of agriculture deserve more attention from the Government than they have yet received. The farms of the United States afford homes and employment for more than one-half our people, and furnish much the largest part of all our exports. As the Government lights our coasts for the protection of mariners and the benefit of commerce, so it should give to the tillers of the soil the best lights of practical science and experience.

Our manufacturers are rapidly making us industrially independent, and are opening to capital and labor new and profitable fields of employment. Their steady and healthy growth should still be matured. Our facilities for transportation should be promoted by the continued improvement of our harbors and great interior waterways and by the increase of our tonnage on the ocean.

The development of the world's commerce has led to an urgent demand for shortening the great sea voyage around Cape Horn by constructing ship canals or railways across the isthmus which unites the continents. Various plans to this end have been suggested and will need consideration, but none of them has been sufficiently matured to warrant the United States in extending pecuniary aid. The subject, however, is one which will immediately engage the attention of the Government with a view to a thorough protection to American interests. We will urge no narrow policy nor seek peculiar or exclusive privileges in any commercial route; but, in the language of my predecessor, I believe it to be the right "and duty of the United States to assert and maintain such supervision and authority over any interoceanic canal across the isthmus that connects North and South America as will protect our national interest."

The Constitution guarantees absolute religious freedom. Congress is prohibited from making any law respecting an establishment of religion or prohibiting the free exercise thereof. The Territories of the United States are subject to the direct legislative authority of Congress, and hence the General Government is responsible for any violation of the Constitution in any of them. It is therefore a reproach to the Government that in the most populous of the Territories the constitutional guaranty is not enjoyed by the people and the authority of Congress is set at naught. The Mormon Church not only offends the moral sense of manhood by sanctioning polygamy, but prevents the administration of justice through ordinary instrumentalities of law.

In my judgment it is the duty of Congress, while respecting to the uttermost the conscientious convictions and religious scruples of every citizen, to prohibit within its jurisdiction all criminal practices, especially of that class which destroy the family relations and endanger social order. Nor can any ecclesiastical organization be safely permitted to usurp in the smallest degree the functions and powers of the National Government.

The civil service can never be placed on a satisfactory basis until it is regulated by law. For the good of the service itself, for the protection of those who are intrusted with the appointing power against the waste of time and obstruction to the public business caused by the inordinate pressure for place, and for the protection of incumbents against intrigue and wrong, I shall at the proper time ask Congress to fix the tenure of the minor offices of the several Executive Departments and prescribe the grounds upon which removals shall be made during the terms for which incumbents have been appointed.

Finally, acting always within the authority and limitations of the Constitution, invading neither the rights of the States nor the reserved rights of the people, it will be the purpose of my Administration to maintain the authority of the nation in all places within its jurisdiction; to enforce obedience to all the laws of the Union in the interests of the people; to demand rigid economy in all the expenditures of the Government, and to require the honest and faithful service of all executive officers, remembering that the offices were created, not for the benefit of incumbents or their supporters, but for the service of the Government.

And now, fellow-citizens, I am about to assume the great trust which you have committed to my hands. I appeal to you for that earnest and thoughtful support which makes this Government in fact, as it is in law, a government of the people.

I shall greatly rely upon the wisdom and patriotism of Congress and of those who may share with me the responsibilities and duties of administration, and, above all, upon our efforts to promote the welfare of this great people and their Government I reverently invoke the support and blessings of Almighty God.

Historical Note for "A Brazilian Señora."

Charley travelled to South America in February 1880 and must have visited Brazil since he made the note on the following photo, "I have been there."

Print: A BRAZILIAN SENORA.
Handwriting: I have been there.

Handwriting:

There are sadly such dogs

He is all faults, but cannot see theirs__

But finds fault with every pleasure

a young person engages in.

But he followed every pursuit of vice when young.

Print:

Many men become virtuous in their old age, because they are no
longer able to set a bad example, and make of their forced
[unintelligible] a text to lecture the young;

Notice the "him" and the hand pointing at the hypocritical "virtuous" old man above.

Clock is tilted to the right and time reads 5:12

Figure 28 - Scan to read the actual magazine Charley read when he clipped this quote, *Harper's New Monthly Magazine, 1879, see Pg 478.*

Print: A pious old fellow in Lynn
Believed in original sin;
He "was all on't," he said,
"From his heels to his head."
And his neighbors believed it, in Lynn.[79]

---

[79] *Harper's New Monthly Magazine.* United States: Harper, 1879, Pg 478.

Print:

Reproaches, unsupported by evidence, affect only the character of him who utters them.[80]

The beautiful in heart is a million times of more avail, as securing domestic happiness, than the beautiful in person.[81]

The best friend is virtue; the best companions are high endeavors and honorable sentiments.[82]

---

[80] This quote comes from a debate in British Parliament regarding "Seaman," from 10 Mar 1740. The person speaking is Mr. Horace Walpole, the 4th Earl of Oxford. Source: Stockdale, John., Johnson, Samuel., Guthrie, William. *Debates in Parliament.* United Kingdom: John Stockdale, 1787. Pg 306.

[81] Quote by Mary Ries Melindy. See following page for historical note. Book PDF: www.google.com/books/edition/Maiden_Wife_and_Mother/hLBBAQAAMAAJ? hl=en&gbpv=0&kptab=getbook, or scan QR code on opposite page.

[82] This quote can be found as a stand alone in numerous 19th century periodicals, but it also appears here: Wallace, Horace Binney. Stanley: *Or, The Recollections of a Man of the World.* United States: Lea & Blanchard, 1838. Pg 24. (Google Books)

Historical Note on
"The beautiful in heart" quote from opposite page.

This quote comes from an essay by Mary Ries Melindy (1841-1927). It appeared in magazines and periodicals prior, but in 1903 the quote was included in the book *Maiden, Wife and Mother: How to Attain Health - Beauty - Happiness ... a Complete Medical Guide for Women.* by A.B. Kuhlman Company. The text appears in Part II of the book on "Love, Courtship, and Marriage." Here is a portion of the relevant section. Scan QR Code below to access the book for free using Google Books.

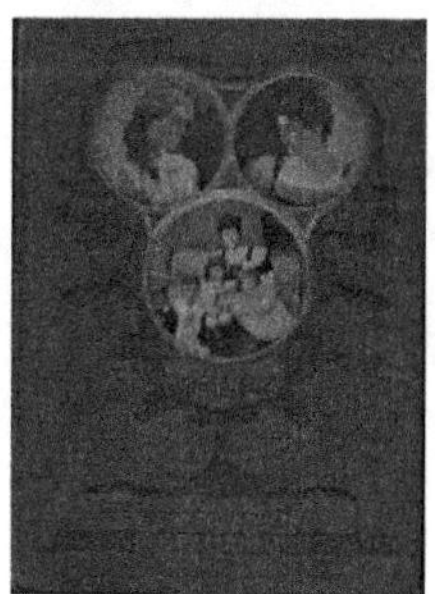  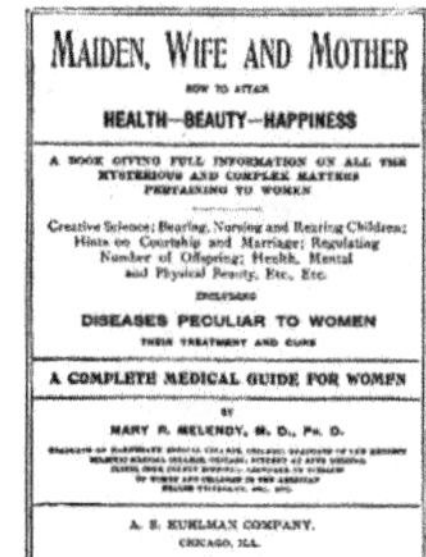

MAKE YOURSELF WORTHY OF A GOOD MATE.

"The place where angels dwell—that is home," reads the old German legend, and the real interpretation of the word is not far different.

Love and intellectual sympathy is one of the conditions of fireside happiness. Let the woman's first requisite be a man who is domestic in his tastes, and the man's first object be a woman who can make his home a place of rest for him. **The beautiful in heart is a million times of more avail, as securing domestic happiness, than the beautiful in person.** They who marry for physical characteristics or external considerations, will fail to find happiness in their homes. As we should say to women who wish for domestic happiness, never marry a pleasure-seeker, an idle man, so we would say to men, never marry any but an intelligent woman, for after purity, quite the next best thing is that good sense which comes with intelligence. It is the best of dowries. There is no burden on earth like a foolish woman tied to a competent man, with the one exception of a false woman. No beauty, no sweetness, can compensate for the absence of clear thought and quick comprehension.

So also studying to make yourself worthy of a good husband, begin now to cultivate all those graces that make a home complete. It is not so much the arts and accomplishments as it is the character that makes home happy. I say in selecting a husband, see to it that you choose a husband with not only the ability to provide a home, but one of honor and principle; see to it that he has a heart—a great, noble, true, self sacrificing heart - one that will love through sickness and adversity as woman. well as prosperity. When you have found such a one then give him all you have to give - love, confidence, good will.

Handwriting:

Friend for thy writing I am grieved

Where still so much is said

One half will never be believed,

The other never read.[83]

[First Inside Page flap]

Individual illustrations expanded…

---

[83] No historical reference found for this quote, possibly original to Charley Peck

Handwriting:

Now behive yourself, Dasy.

Print:

A swarm of bees in May / Is worth a load of hay;

A swarm of bees in June; / Is worth a silver spoon;

But a swarm in July / In not worth a fly."[84]

---

[84] Proverbial bee-keepers' saying, mid-17th century; meaning the later in the year it is, the less time there will be for bees to collect pollen from flowers in blossom.

Print:

Oh, *now* while the sweet Love lingers near,

Grudge not the tender words of cheer:

Leave none unsaid.

For the heart can have no sadder fate

Than some day to awake—too late—

And find Love dead!

Historical Note on
"Sweet Love lingers near" quote from previous page.

The words Charley included here were written by Amelia E. Barr in her poem, "Loved Too Late." The poem appears in a number of publications, including Barr's *Stories of Life and Love*, Christian Herald, 1897, Pg 268 (Scan next QR Code). But it also appears in *The Christian Work Illustrated Family Newspaper* on 17 Sep 1896, Pg 432. Here is the story as shared in that magazine, quoting from the *Ladies Home Journal*.

LOVING TOO LATE.
BY AMELIA E. BARR

Not long ago I met a young lady in poverty whom I had previously known in wealth, and this was, in substance, the story she told me: "Father died suddenly in Washington, and the professional skill through which he had coined money for us died with him. I am not weeping because we are poor. I am brokenhearted because none of us saw that he was dying. Was it not pitiful that he should think it best not to tell any of us that he was sick? And I, his petted daughter, though I knew he was taking opium to soothe his great pain, was so absorbed by my lovers, my games and my dresses, that I just hoped It would all come right. If I could only remember that even once I had pitied his suffering or felt anxious about his life, I might bear his loss better! My dear, dear father! Oh, how terrible it is to love when it is too late!"

The story is common enough. Many a father, year after year, goes in and out of his home carrying the burden and doing the labor of life, while those whom he tenderly loves hold with but careless bands all of honor and gold he wins by toil and pain. Then some day his head and hands can work no more, and the hearts that have not learned the great lesson of unselfish love while love was their teacher, must now begin their sad duty when love has left them alone forever. It is now their place to carry the daily heavy cross that he bore, and under its burden to say with bitter tears, "Would to God that the dear one dead were here once more! Never again would we grieve and cross him! Never again be blind to his manifest weariness and suffering! Oh, for the sound of his voice in our sorrowful house!"

For year after year with glad content
In and out of my home he went
          In and out.
Ever for the skies were clear,
His heart carried the care and fear—
          The care and doubt.
Our hands held with a careless hold
All that he won of honor and gold,
          In toil and pain;
Oh, dear hands that our burdens bore,
Hands that toil for us no more—
          Never again.
But when the love we hold too light
Is gone away from our speech and sight,
          No bitter tears.
No passionate words of fond regret,
No yearning grief can pay the debt
          Of thankless years.
Oh, now while the sweet love lingers near,
Grudge not the tender word of cheer,
          Leave none unsaid;
For the heart can have no sadder fate
Than some day to awake—too late!
          And find love dead.
                              —*Ladies' Home Journal*

Figure 29 - Scan QR Code to read Amelia Barr's 1897 Stories of Life and Love for free on Google Books

Print:

"When patients come to I,
    I physics, bleeds, and meats 'em;
Then—if they choose to die,
    What's that to I?—I lets 'em."

Historical Note on
"If they choose to die" quote from previous page.

This "humorous" quote is attributed to John Coakley Lettsom (1744 – 1 Nov 1815). Lettsom was an English physician and philanthropist born on the island of Little Jost Van Dyke in the British Virgin Islands into an early Quaker settlement. He grew up to be an abolitionist. He founded the Medical Society of London in 1773.[85]

Figure 30 - John Coakley Lettsom, circa 1782, by Johann Zoffany (1733-1810), Public Domain

He was friends with Benjamin Franklin, corresponded with George Washington and Erasmus Darwin (1731-1802). He wrote *Hints Designed to Promote Beneficence, Temperance, and Medical Science.*[86]

Lettsom apparently wrote the poem about himself:

I, John Lettsome,
Blisters, bleeds and sweats 'em.
If, after that, they please to die,
I, John Lettsome.

He also signed his prescriptions, "I Lettsom."

---

[85] https://en.wikipedia.org/wiki/John_Coakley_Lettsom, accessed 6 Sep 2021.
[86] https://blogs.ucl.ac.uk/library-rnid/2014/07/18/lettsoms-hints-designed-to-promote-beneficence-temperence-medical-science/, accessed 6 Sep 2021.

Print:

"I will confess this before God and men, but not to ask forgiveness from either."

Handwriting:

Good Lord Susie. He will come when the twilight falls.

Historical Note on
"I will confess this before God" quote from previous page.

This quote comes from the Russian poet Mikhail Yuryevich Lermontov, Russian: Михаил Юрьевич Лермонтов (15 Oct 1814 – 27 Jul 1841). Lermontov was a "Russian Romantic writer, poet and painter, sometimes called "the poet of the Caucasus", the most important Russian poet after Alexander Pushkin's death in 1837 and the greatest figure in Russian Romanticism."[87] In his famous poem, *The Circassian Boy*, a child who grew up in a monastery escapes to the mountains and says this to monk from the monastery before his death:

"I thank you for your zeal, pious man; you ask me to confess to you what I know. I believe that it may be a relief to men to unburden their hearts by words; but I, during my life, have done harm to none; it is of small avail to learn what has happened to such a one; and of my feelings, how could I tell the story? I have lived but little, and in slavery. Surely two such lives would I have given

Figure 31 - National Review, Pgs 339-340

willingly for one full of liberty and struggles. One single uncontrollable passion has haunted, governed, and tormented me; and consumed by it, my life is coming to an end. It has eaten my heart like a worm; it has led me forth, both when awake and in my dreams, from the dull sufferings in this cell to the noise of battles, to places where the high mountains tower above the clouds, where men live in liberty like the eagles. And to this fire, which has consumed me, I have given yet greater force by nursing my grief and agony. **I will confess this before God and men, but not to ask forgiveness from either.**"[88]

---

[87] https://en.wikipedia.org/wiki/Mikhail_Lermontov, accessed 6 Sep 2021.
[88] The National Review. United Kingdom: Robert Theobald, 1860. Pg 339-340.

APPENDIX II. ANTONY AND CLEOPATRA

On the final pages of Charley's form book, he wrote out the following poem by William Lytle. Lytle wrote the poem in 1858, and was an officer in the Union Army at the time of his death. Like Charley, Lytle had been an attorney. Additionally, Lytle grew up in Cincinnati, Ohio, where Charley settled before his death. Like Charley's father Isham, Lytle fought in the Mexican-American War. Lytle was killed by a Confederate sniper during the Battle of Chickamauga. He was so revered by men on both sides that his body was guarded by Confederate soldiers until the next day, when a truce was called and his body was carried to the Union troops and sent home for burial. As his body was guarded by the Confederate soldiers the night of his death, they read the poem written in Charley's ledger, *Antony and Cleopatra*.[89]

ANTONY AND CLEOPATRA
by William Haines Lytle (1826-1863)

---

[89] https://libapps.libraries.uc.edu/liblog/2018/05/i-am-dying-egypt-dying-a-cincinnati-college-soldier-poets-embrace-of-the-battlefield/, accessed 24 Aug 2021.

I am Dying, Egypt, dying,
  Ebbs the crimson life-tide fast,
And the dark Plutonian shadows
  Gather on the evening blast;
Let thine arms, O Queen, enfold me,
  Hush thy sobs and bow thine ear;
Listen to the great heart-secrets,
  Thou, and thou alone, must hear.

Though my scarr'd and veteran legions
  Bear their eagles high no more,
And my wreck'd and scatter'd galleys
  Strew dark Actuim's fatal shore,
Though no glittering guards surround me,
  Prompt to do their master's will,
I must perish like a Roman,
  Die the great Triumvir still.

Let not Caesar's servile minions
  Mock the lion thus laid low;
'Twas no foeman's arm that fell'd him,
  'Twas his own that struck the blow;
His who, pillow'd on thy bosom,
  Turn'd aside from glory's ray,
His who, drunk with thy caresses,
  Madly threw a world away.

Should the base plebeian rabble
  Dare assail my name at Rome,
Where my noble spouse, Octavia,
  Weeps within her widow'd home,
Seek her; say the gods bear witness -

Altars, augurs, circling wings -
That her blood, with mine commingled,
  Yet shall mount the throne of kings.

As for thee, star-eyed Egyptian,
  Glorious sorceress of the Nile,
Light the path to Stygian horrors
  With the splendors of thy smile.
Give the Caesar crowns and arches,
  Let his brow the laurel twine;
I can scorn the Senate's triumphs,
  Triumphing in love like thine.

I am dying, Egypt, dying;
  Hark! the insulting foeman's cry.
They are coming! quick, my falchion,
  Let me front them ere I die.
Ah! no more amid the battle
  Shall my heart exulting swell;
Isis and Osiris guard thee!
  Cleopatra, Rome, farewell!

APPENDIX III. BACK INSIDE COVER
Image of Sarah Bernhardt. (Georges Clairin) 1879

SARAH BERNHARDT. (GEORGES CLAIRIN.)

Miss Sarah is the most
talented and peculiar woman
I ever saw.
But thirming idea of sence,
beauty, luxury grace, and ease
Combined with refined tastes.
very sweet indeed
Charles Peck.

Print:

> "The folds of her wine-dark violet dress
>> Glow over the sofa, fall on fall,
> As she sits in the air of her loveliness
>> With a smile for each and all."

Handwriting:

Miss Sarah is the most talent and peculiar woman I ever saw.
But this is my idea of sence[*sic*], beauty, luxery [*sic*], grace, and ease
combined with refined tastes.

> Very sweet indeed
>> Charles Peck.

Historical Notes about Sarah Bernhardt

"Sarah Bernhardt, original name Henriette-Rosine Bernard, byname the Divine Sarah, French la Divine Sarah, (born October 22/23, 1844, Paris, France—died March 26, 1923, Paris), the greatest French actress of the later 19th century and one of the best-known figures in the history of the stage. . . . In 1880 Bernhardt formed her own traveling company and soon became an international idol. She spent her time acting with her own company, managing the theatres it used, and going on long international tours. She appeared fairly regularly in England and extended her itinerary to the European continent, the United States, and Canada. New York City saw her for the first time on November 8, 1880, and eight visits to the United States followed.[90]

Wikipedia has an excellent article regarding her life and career, including numerous photographs and paintings of her. A portion of those public domain photos and paintings are included here in honor of Charley's crush: https://en.wikipedia.org/wiki/Sarah_Bernhardt

---

[90] https://www.britannica.com/biography/Sarah-Bernhardt, accessed 24 Aug 2021.

Figure 32 – Portrait of Sarah Bernhardt. Displayed in Salon of 1876, now in the Petit Palais, Paris. Public Domain. Note: The lithograph in Charley's form book was taken from this original painting, and published separately in a newspaper or magazine.

Figure 33 – Bernhardt, 1877

Figure 36 - Bernhardt as Dona Sol in Hernani, 1878.

Figure 35 - Bernhardt in La Dame aux camelias, 1881.

Figure 34 - Bernhardt as Hamlet, 1899.

Figure 37 - Portrait of Sarah Bernhardt (1844-1923), by Jules Bastien-Lepage (1848-1884), 1879, Oil, Legion of Honor Museum, San Francisco, Public Domain.

APPENDIX IV. CHARLEY'S GRAVESTONE

Figure 38 - Charley's Gravestone, Photo by Editor, taken 12 Jul 2017. Located in the Westview Cemetery, Jefferson City, TN. Inscription reads, "In memory of CHARLES PECK. Born Nov. 16, 1857 Died Feb. 22, 1882."

APPENDIX V. WILLIAM COWPER'S POETRY

Charley quoted William Cowper's poem *The Castaway* in Chapter XII. The poem was written in 1799 and describes the hopeless fate of a man who fell overboard into the ocean. He fights and yells for help as long as he can, but in the end, he sinks to his death. It is a poem based on real world events. A crewman on George Anson's 1741 voyage around-the-world was washed overboard, and his crew was unable to save him due to the terrible sea conditions. This poem was the last written by Cowper before his death in 1800.[91]

The Castaway

Obscurest night involv'd the sky,
 Th' Atlantic billows roar'd,
When such a destin'd wretch as I,
 Wash'd headlong from on board,
Of friends, of hope, of all bereft,
His floating home for ever left.

No braver chief could Albion boast
 Than he with whom he went,
Nor ever ship left Albion's coast,
 With warmer wishes sent.
He lov'd them both, but both in vain,
Nor him beheld, nor her again.

---

[91] www.poetryfoundation.org/poems/44027/the-castaway, accessed 28 Aug 2021

Not long beneath the whelming brine,
    Expert to swim, he lay;
Nor soon he felt his strength decline,
    Or courage die away;
But wag'd with death a lasting strife,
Supported by despair of life.

He shouted: nor his friends had fail'd
    To check the vessel's course,
But so the furious blast prevail'd,
    That, pitiless perforce,
They left their outcast mate behind,
And scudded still before the wind.

Some succour yet they could afford;
    And, such as storms allow,
The cask, the coop, the floated cord,
    Delay'd not to bestow.
But he (they knew) nor ship, nor shore,
Whate'er they gave, should visit more.

Nor, cruel as it seem'd, could he
    Their haste himself condemn,
Aware that flight, in such a sea,
    Alone could rescue them;
Yet bitter felt it still to die
Deserted, and his friends so nigh.

He long survives, who lives an hour
    In ocean, self-upheld;
And so long he, with unspent pow'r,
    His destiny repell'd;
And ever, as the minutes flew,

Entreated help, or cried—Adieu!

At length, his transient respite past,
    His comrades, who before
Had heard his voice in ev'ry blast,
    Could catch the sound no more.
For then, by toil subdued, he drank
The stifling wave, and then he sank.

No poet wept him: but the page
    Of narrative sincere;
That tells his name, his worth, his age,
    Is wet with Anson's tear.
And tears by bards or heroes shed
Alike immortalize the dead.

I therefore purpose not, or dream,
    Descanting on his fate,
To give the melancholy theme
    A more enduring date:
But misery still delights to trace
  Its semblance in another's case.

No voice divine the storm allay'd,
    No light propitious shone;
When, snatch'd from all effectual aid,
    We perish'd, each alone:
But I beneath a rougher sea,
And whelm'd in deeper gulfs than he.

Charley then quoted another of Cowper's poems, *On Friendship*. Cowper shared a friendship with John Newton, the famous slave-ship captain turned pastor who wrote *Amazing Grace*. William Cowper struggled with severe depression for much of his life. He attempted suicide multiple times, and spent over a year in a mental asylum. While in the asylum, he had a conversion experience. He wrote in his journal, "Immediately I received the strength to believe it, and the full beams of the Sun of Righteousness shone upon me. I saw the sufficiency of the atonement He had made, my pardon sealed in His blood, and all the fullness and completeness of His justification. In a moment I believed, and received the gospel…my eyes filled with tears, and my voice choked with transport; I could only look up to heaven in silent fear, overwhelmed with love and wonder."[92]

Pastor John Newton was a faithful friend to William. Cowper attended Newton's church, and their friendship was rich and meaningful. In the midst of his years of depression, he wrote 68 Christian hymns including "There is a Fountain Filled with Blood" and "O for a Closer Walk With God." Here is an excerpt of his lengthy poem about friendship:

On Friendship[93]

What virtue can we name, or grace,
But men unqualified and base
    Will boast it their possession?
Profusion apes the noble part
Of liberality of heart;
    And dulness, of discretion.
But as the gem of richest cost

---

[92] https://simsmarc.wordpress.com/2014/11/25/suicide-and-grace-the-life-of-william-cowper/comment-page-1/, accessed 28 Aug 2021.
[93] Hayley, William. The Life and Letters of William Cowper, New Edition, Complete in One Volume. With a Portrait. United Kingdom: Longman, Rees & Company, 1835. Pgs 296-302.

Is ever counterfeited most;
        So always Imitation
Employs the utmost skill she can,
To counterfeit the faithful man,
The friend of long duration.

Some will pronounce me too severe,
But long experience speaks me clear;
        Therefore, that censure scorning,
I will proceed to mark the shelves
On which so many dash themselves,
        And give the simple warning.

Youth, unadmonish'd by a guide,
Will trust to any fair outside:
        An error soon corrected!
For who, but learns, with riper years,
That man, when smoothest he appears,
        Is most to be suspected.

Pursue the theme, and you shall find
A disciplined and furnish'd mind
        To be at least expedient;
And, after summing all the rest,
Religion ruling in the breast
        A principal ingredient.

True friendship has, in short, a grace
More than terrestrial in its face,
        That proves it heav'n-descended:
Man's love of woman not so pure,
Nor when sincerest so secure
        To last till life is ended.

APPENDIX VI. VESUVIUS POEM BY RICHARD TRENCH

In 1877, Henry Wadsworth Longfellow published his *Poems of Places: Italy*. In the section on Mount Vesuvius, he included a poem called *Vesuvius* by Richard Chenevix Trench (1807-1886).[94] Trench was the Dean of Westminster Abbey from 1856-1864 and Archbishop of Dublin (Church of Ireland) from 1864-1884.[95] Charley quoted this an excerpt from this poem in Chapter XIII.

Vesuvius

I.

A WREATH of light-blue vapor, pure and rare,
Mounts, scarcely seen against the bluer sky,
In quiet adoration, silently,
Till the faint currents of the upper air
Dislimn it, and it forms, dissolving there,
The dome, as of a palace, hung on high
Over the mountain; underneath it lie
Vineyards and bays and cities, white and fair.
Might we not think this beauty would engage
All living things unto one pure delight?
O, vain belief! for here, our records tell,
Rome's understanding tyrant from men's sight
Hid, as within a guilty citadel,
The shame of his dishonorable age.

---

[94] Poems of Places Italy Edited by Henry W. Longfellow: Vol. III. United States: Houghton Mifflin, 1877.
[95] www.westminster-abbey.org/abbey-commemorations/commemorations/richard-chenevix-trench, accessed 29 Aug 2021.

II.

AS when unto a mother, having chid
Her child in anger, there have straight ensued
Repentings for her quick and angry mood,
Till she would fain see all its traces hid
Quite out of sight,—even so has Nature bid
Fair flowers, that on the scarred earth she has strewed,
To blossom, and called up the taller wood
To cover what she ruined and undid.
O, and her mood of anger did not last
More than an instant, but her work of peace,
Restoring and repairing, comforting
The Earth, her stricken child, will never cease:
For that was her strange work, and quickly past;
To this her genial toil no end the years shall bring.

III.

THAT her destroying fury was with noise
And sudden uproar; but far otherwise,
With silent and with secret ministries,
Her skill of renovation she employs:
For Nature, only loud when she destroys,
Is silent when she fashions; she will crowd
The work of her destruction, transient, loud,
Into an hour, and then long peace enjoys.
Yea, every power that fashions and upholds
Works silently,—all things, whose life is sure,
Their life is calm; silent the light that moulds
And colors all things; and without debate
The stars, which are forever to endure,
Assume their thrones and their unquestioned state.

APPENDIX VII. PECK FAMILY GEOLOGY

Charley's grandfather, Judge Jacob Franklin Clayton Peck (1779-1869), Tennessee Supreme Court Justice and State Senator from Jefferson and Greene Counties, was an amateur geologist who was fond of the chemistry and physical properties of minerals and mineralized artifacts. He owned thousands of acres of land in the mountains including gold and silver mines. He lived until Charley was eleven years old, and undoubtedly had a large influence on Charley's (and the rest of the family's) interest in mineralogy.

This initial article is a first-hand account by Oliver Caswell King, resident of Mossy Creek, who procured some of the mineral lands amassed by Judge Jacob after his death in 1869.

MINERAL WEALTH OF EAST TENNESSEE.[96]

The Importance of its Iron Mines Commanding the Attention and Securing the Investment of Capital.

We find the following letter which we commend for perusal to our readers, in the Knoxville *Chronicle*, December 27.

EDITORS CHRONICLE: While I do not belong to your school in politics, and consequently do not approve of all you say and do as journalists, still there are some things you do which merit the hearty approval of all sensible East Tennesseeans [*sic*]. I instance your efforts to call the attention of Eastern capitalists to the advantages offered by our country for the investment of capital, and the efforts you are making to induce immigration to our country.

---

[96] *Nashville Union and American*, 29 Dec 1872, Pg 4.

I have lately concluded a transaction which I think will be of interest to you, and possibly to many of your readers. The late Judge Jacob Peck, who was for many years on the Supreme Bench of the State, spent the principal part of the last years of his life in acquiring mineral lands in different portions of East Tennessee. After his death the control of these lands passed into my hands, and I have been quietly at work ever since trying to bring them to the notice of capitalists. The Cincinnati, Cumberland Gap and Charleston Railroad passes through several large bodies of these lands, which are very rich in iron ore of a superior quality.

I last week sold to a wealthy company of Philadelphia about 2,000 acres of these lands, and am negotiating a sale of another large body with another company, also from Philadelphia. These gentlemen expect to erect works on the lands on an extensive scale.

As I have other lands equally as rich as those just sold, and quite as convenient to the railroad, I expect soon to have purchasers for them also, and I think the time will not be long until East Tennessee assumes a prominent position as an iron manufacturing region. I trust you will continue your efforts to make known to the outside world the many advantages of our section, as well in a mining and manufacturing, as in an agricultural point of view, and I trust the entire press of the State will cheerfully and ably second your very commendable endeavors. We have naturally the richest country in the world, but unfortunately the world don't know it.

Why these gentlemen from Philadelphia, of whom I spoke above, were astonished to find here, in the mountains of Cocke county, Tennessee, beds, veins and mountains of iron ore, lying undeveloped and unknown, on a line of railroad in running order, that would rival the great Iron Mountain of Missouri, or the noted iron beds of Lake Superior, both in quality and quantity.

I look to the public journals of our section to inform the capitalists of the North and the East what inviting fields await investment here.

As I remarked before, you have done much as journalists in that direction, and the public spirited citizens of the country recognize the merit of your labors, and feel grateful for them.

I am, very respectfully, your friend,

O. C. KING.

MOSSY CREEK, Tenn., Dec. 23, 1872.

The following excerpt referring to Judge Jacob Peck was a part of a larger article highlighting instances when meteors had fallen in Tennessee. It demonstrates his knowledge of geology, and the fact that educated people from around the state looked at him as credible to speak on the subject:

METEORIC IRON.[97]

Interesting Description of Specimens which Fell in Tennessee.

They are Held by Their Discoverers at an Enormous Value.

If the visitor to the Tennessee State Library has any curiosity on the subject of meteors, upon making inquiry of the Librarian, Mrs. Haskell, there will be shown two odd looking masses of matter, which are supposed to have made their transit from some near relation of the flying fireball seen last Tuesday night. The specimens at the State-house are not positively identified by any records, but they seem to correspond very closely with a description of certain meteoric masses

---

[97] 11 Jul 1874, The Tennessean (Nashville, TN), Pg 4.

in the manuscript of that eminent geologist, the late Dr. Gerard Troost. The Doctor published a treatise on Meteoric Iron, containing an account of certain discoveries in that line which he has made in Tennessee. The manuscript, now in Mrs. Haskell's hands, contains an account of further discoveries made after the publication of his treatise, and is believed not to have been hitherto published. He speaks of one mass of meteoric iron found near Charlotte, in Dickson County, another in DeKalb County, a few miles west of Caney Fork, another in Greene County, twelve miles from Greeneville, and a fourth mass found in Walker County, Alabama. [. . .]

GREEN COUNTY METEORIC IRON.

The Doctor procured this specimen by the assistance of Judge Jacob Peck. He says: Judge Peck wrote me: "The piece of iron I send you from Greene County was plowed up in a field near Babb's Mill, nine or ten miles north of Greeneville. It had been worked for the silver it contained, but the artist could not separate the silver from the other metal, probably because there was none in it." Upon analysis, Dr. Troost found a large per centum of nickel in this mass. Its material structure was coarse granular; its color rather whiter than that of pure iron, and very malleable—equal if not superior in this respect to the softest wrought iron. No traces of pyrites or of any other heterogeneous substances were perceptible in it. Its meteoric origin was, by the analysis, put beyond doubt."

Charley's father, Dr. Isham Talbot Peck, also had an interest in geology, especially with the purpose of drawing people to the area and stimulating investment in the local economy. According to one article, Dr. Isham Peck lived "in the midst of his thirty thousand acres of East Tennessee possessions, embraced in which is a mountain of specular iron that for extent and richness has no rival save the famous Iron Mountain of Missouri."[98] See *Sawbones: The Life and Times of Dr. Isham Talbot Peck* for more details. Here are a few examples of articles pertaining to Charley's father and the subject of geology / mineralogy.

Wolf Creek Granite.[99]

WOLF CREEK, TENN., October 1, '81

MR. EDITOR—In a late number of your paper I see a notice of a piece of granite which I sent to a Knoxville paper. I wonder that more geologists do not come here. There is more geology to the square mile, at what we call the "Bluff," (head of Wolf Creek, six miles from Wolf Creek depot) than any place I know of. I am not a geologist, and I want men to come here who know more on this subject than I do myself. I know that there are several varieties of granite, gold and specular iron, and I think geologists could find other things here. When I came here, twenty-six years ago [*1855*], and built a house as a summer refuge for my family, from the swamps and mosquitoes of Louisiana, at the mouth of Wolf Creek I found a granite boulder in the creek, differing from any granite I had ever seen. I employed an old bear hunter for a pilot, and literally crawled through thick laurel five miles, where I found it in place. I secured specimens, which I have shown to

---

98 25 Dec 1877, *The Tennessean* (Nashville, TN), Pg 4.
99 6 Oct 1881, *Knoxville Daily Chronicle* (Knoxville, TN), Pg 3.

hundreds of persons. I think it was about eight years ago that I met here Professor Bradley. I called his attention to the specimens. He went to the "bluff," and when he returned he said, "I have named your granite 'unakite.'" I asked him why he called it "unakite." He said, "because it is not found anywhere else in the world." Dr. Safford, State geologist, in his recent work on the geology of Tennessee, says Prof. Bradley called it "unakite" because it is found in the Unaka Mountain, Prof. Bradley said nothing about "Unaka Mountain" to me. Burr's Map, 1839, is before me. He was geographer, U.S. House of Representatives. He calls this mountain "Unaka" to the Tennessee River. This side of the Tennessee River he calls it the Smoky or Great Iron Mountain.

Professor Bradley told me that the top of the bluff is 4300 feet above the sea level. From where you strike the granite going up to Wolf Creek to top of the bluff is about 1000 feet, perpendicular height. Mr. Tom Huff, who lives at the foot of the bluff, at an elevation of about 3000 feet, says he will be able to accommodate about ten boarders next summer (mountain fashion); ice cold springs everywhere, and the purest atmosphere on earth.

Respectfully,

DR. PECK.

WOLF CREEK.[100]

PROSPECT FOR THE EARLY DEVELOPMENT OF THAT REGION.

Prof. Colton, geologist to the Bureau of Agriculture, Statistics, Mines and Immigration, who has been on an extended tour through

---

[100] 14 Jun 1882, *The Morristown Gazette*, Pg 2.

East Tennessee, in a conversation with a reporter of the Nashville *American*, gives these interesting facts in regard to Wolf Creek, Cocke county:

"Wolf Creek is the centre of a mineral region containing immense resources, entirely undeveloped. There are vast bodies of iron ore running up into high mountains, where boulders of every size are thickly scattered over the ground. I traced this lead of ore for many miles through the lands of 'Squire Johnson, Mr. Chism, 'Squire Wells, Green Allen and Dr. [Isham] Peck. The English company which owns South Pittsburg owns a large quantity of it. This immense body is limonite, but near by, and in a vein known to extend for many miles, is a compact red hematite ore, in many places approaching specular in appearance. It will answer for making Bessemer pig. The vein is not wide, probably but little over two or three feet wide, but in its length the quantity contained is very large. In the northern part of the county some lead ore has been found, but the great wealth of this region is its iron ore. The English company named erected works on the railroad at Whitwell for the purpose of grinding baryta, but they did not pay and were abandoned. Some adventurous Yankees, however, have leased the works, and now propose to try their hands at it. The beautiful white lumps of this article of deceit and fraud were being rolled down to the railroad side from far up in the Chilhowee mountains.

In a pamphlet entitled *Iron and Coal of Tennessee* published in 1881, J. B. Killebrew, A.M., Ph. D, refers to "Peck's Iron mountain" in Cocke County. He says that Peck mountain covers about 50 acres and 400 yards of its slope is covered with blocks of red hematite iron ore (Pgs 29-31). The mountain is "near the termination of the railroad at Riverside Station", "near the northwestern base of the Unaka chain."

APPENDIX VIII. KU KLUX KLAN IN TENNESSEE

Charley mentions the "Ku Klux" Klan in Chapter XVII. Mr. Peacock, the antagonist in the novel, joins the group after being on the run from the police for his counterfeiting operation. He meets up with them by "Juno's tree" where a Black person had been lynched, and he rides with them into town. They storm the town jail wearing masks, hold up the jailer at gun point, break their "officers" out, and post a notice to leave their officers and Peacock alone.

What was Charley's experience with the Klan? Were they active in East Tennessee where he lived? What follows are some primary source materials for your research and learning regarding the Ku Klux Klan. Ephesians 5:11 says, "Do not participate in the unfruitful deeds of darkness, but instead even expose them." (NASB) It is with this purpose that the following is shared, to expose the **deeds of darkness**.

According to the Tennessee State Library and Archives and the Tennessee Virtual Archive, "The first Ku Klux Klan was founded in 1865 [in Pulaski, Tennessee] by veterans of the Confederate Army. At its inception, the Klan was initially a social club for young men seeking amusement and entertainment in the aftermath of the American Civil War. The Klan resisted the process of Reconstruction by intimidating "carpetbaggers," "scalawags," and freedmen. The Klan quickly adopted violent methods and the increase in murders finally resulted in a backlash among Southern elites who viewed the Klan's excesses as an excuse for federal troops to continue occupation. The organization declined from 1868 to 1870."

Figure 39 - "John B. Kennedy with his Third Regiment flag," undated, 2294, Tennessee State Library and Archives, Tennessee Virtual Archive, https://teva.contentdm.oclc.org/digital/collection/p15138coll4/id/27, accessed 1 Sep 2021. Confederate veteran John B. Kennedy is seated outdoors in Pulaski, Tennessee, surrounded by his saber, his canteen, his cane, and a small dog. The flag of his regiment, the 3rd Tennessee Infantry, hangs on a pole behind him.

The photograph on the previous page is of John B. Kennedy. "John Booker Kennedy served the Confederacy as a private with Company A of the 3rd Tennessee Infantry Regiment. He was wounded at Chickamauga and at Jonesboro, Georgia. A native of Giles County, Kennedy pursued the mercantile business after the war there and in Lawrence County. Kennedy was one of the six original organizers of the Ku Klux Klan on December 24, 1865, in the law office of Major Thomas M. Jones in Pulaski and proved to be the last survivor of the six."[101]

"Dam Your Soul. The Horrible *Sepulchre* and Bloody Moon has at last arrived. Some live to-day to-morrow "*Die.*" We the undersigned understand through our Grand "*Cyclops*" that you have recommended a big Black Nigger for Male agent on our nu rode; wel, sir, Jest you understand in time if he gets on the rode you can make up your mind to pull roape. If you have anything to say in regard to the Matter, meet the Grand Cyclops and Conclave at Den No. 4 at 12 o'clock mid-night, Oct. 1st, 1871. When you were in Calera we warned you to hold your tounge and not speak so much with your mouth or otherwise you will be taken on supprise and led out by the Klan and learnt to stretch hemp. Beware. Beware. Beware.   (Signed)

"Phillip Isenbaum, *Grand Cyclops*.
"John Bankstown.
"Esau Daves.
"Marcus Thomas.
"Bloody Bones.

"You know who. And all others of the Klan."

SPECIMEN OF A KU-KLUX NOTICE.

Figure 40 - An example of a threatening note authored by KKK members, "Specimen of a Ku-Klux Klan notice," Tourgée, Albion W., 1838-1905, 1880, A Fool's Errand and The Invisible Empire, 34016, Tennessee State Library and Archives, Tennessee Virtual Archive, https://teva.contentdm.oclc.org/digital/collection/reconaa/id/216.

It reads, "Dam Your Soul. The Horrible Sepulchre and Bloody Moon has at last arrived. Some live to-day to-morrow "Die." We the undersigned understand through our Grand "Cyclops" that you have recommended a big Black Nigger for Male agent on our nu rode; wel, sir, Jest you understand in time if he gets on the rode you can make up your mind to pull roape. If you have anything to say in regard to the Matter, meet the Grand Cyclops and Conclave at Den No. 4 at 12 o'clock midnight, Oct. 1st, 1871. When you were in Calera we warned you to hold your tounge and not speak so much with your mouth or otherwise you will be taken on supprise and led out by the Klan and learnt to stretch hemp. Beware. Beware. Beware. "You Know who. And all others of the Klan."

---

[101] Courtesy Tennessee State Library and Archives

Another one of the founders, R. J. Brunson of Pulaski, Tennessee, was photographed in 1924 at the age of 82 wearing his original robe. Charley may have had this image in his mind when he wrote about the Klan.

Figure 41 - Caption below photo reads, "R. J. Brunson of Pulaski, Tennessee, aged 82. He was part of the original Klan and is wearing an original robe."
(Courtesy Tennessee State Library and Archives)

The following two articles from The Senior Editor of *Brownlow's Knoxville Whig* on 25 Mar 1868[102] "argue that the Ku Klux Klan does exist in Tennessee, despite attempts by others to "ridicule and denounce" the idea. It goes on to discuss the group beginning to organize in East Tennessee, the types of people who make up the organization, and their objectives." Significantly, this article refers to them as the "Kuklux" as opposed to the "Ku Klux Klan," which is similar to the phraseology that Charley used in his novel. The Senior Editor for the paper was none other than William G. "Parson" Brownlow (1805-1877), Governor of Tennessee from 1865-1869.

The Kuklux.

The Nashville correspondent of the Cincinnati Gazette, shows up as follows the characters of the Kuklux as far as developed:

The people of the North have some knowledge of an order known as the Knights of the Golden Circle. The Kuklux is a rebel organization of a similar spirit and design. The rebels in their madness and blindness want more United States troops in the State. They want the Governor to call out the militia. They do not want the Franchise law modified. Hence they encourage the organization and operations of this secret rebel society. They have been induced to think that Johnson was going to play the deuce with Congress, and that in a few months they would be able to drive white Union men out of the States, and frighten the negroes into complete subordination to their old masters. The rebel newspapers throughout the State give the Kuklux prowlers all possible encouragement, and laugh at the outrages committed by them.

---

[102] "KnoxvilleWhig03251868b," Tennessee Virtual Archive, https://teva.contentdm.oclc.org/digital/collection/p15138coll18/id/628, accessed 1 Sep 2021. (Courtesy of the Tennessee State Library and Archives)

A gang of these villains surround a poor negro man's house in the still hours of the night, break down his door, take him out and whip him, and the rebel papers laugh. It is a good joke! They rob the colored people of their arms, and, if they resist, shoot them, and all the rebel papers laugh again.

Attacking houses at night, ordering people out of their beds, carrying them into the woods and whipping or killing them, is funny! All this is evidence that the rebels are peaceable and law-abiding, and that they should not be disfranchised.

**The Knoxville Whig
BROWNLOW AND HAWS, Publishers.**

Forever float that standard sheet,
    Where breathes the foe but falls before us,
With Freedom's soil beneath our feet,

And Freedom's banner streaming o'er us.[103]

Knoxville, Tenn., March 25, 1868.
The Kuklux Klan.

That there is in Tennessee such an organization as the one above named, no doubt can be entertained. It is true the Conservative press and party attempt to ridicule the idea, and to denounce and stigmatize as weak and over-credulous those who believe in the existence of the Kuklux Klan; yet, does such ridicule disprove their existence? Does it disarm them of murderous intent and wicked purpose? Can the rebel and Conservative press whistle high-handed murder and terrorism down the wind? Will derision and sneers give us back to life the pale victims of their fiendish wickedness? Yes, the Kuklux Klans exist. They are known to be formidable in Middle and West Tennessee. Their murderous, bushwhacking conduct in the counties of Dyer, Lincoln and Rutherford are now matters of history.

Their organizations have not appeared in force in many points in East Tennessee, but they are evidently organizing. As they burrow in darkness and skulk behind mysterious names and forms, they may think to escape detection, and even to elude suspicion. Yet they are observed, and their movements more known than they themselves imagine.

Who make up these organizations? They are rebels and Conservatives—men who fought in the ranks of the rebel armies during the war, and those who then sympathized with them, but who, through sheer cowardice, gave the battle-field a wide berth. Those Conservatives fully sympathize with the lost cause "now." They work for it, vote for it when they can, plan for it, and now, at last, go into

---

[103] Excerpt from *The American Flag* by Joseph Rodman Drake (1795-1820), originally published on 29 May 1819 by the New York Evening Post

Ku Klux Klans, to help by lawless violence, riot and murder, what can no longer be kept alive by fair, legitimate methods.

What are their objects? Precisely the objects that have animated the whole rebel crew, from Jeff Davis down to the verist pimp that buzzahed for the rebellion all along during the war. They hate loyalty, in black or white, is so odious to them, and especially in black men, that they cannot refrain from venting their hell-inspired malignity upon them. They took to compass their objects by intimidating colored men, and by wreaking vengeance upon white Radicals. Their objects are the overthrow of loyalty, which they loathe and hate, by any and every means, whether right or wrong, lawful or unlawful, honorable or despicable, true or false, and more generally by the latter than the former.

Union men, leaguers[104], beware of them! watch them! spot them! In nearly every county you have strength sufficient to make yourselves terrible to these midnight assassins and lawless desperadoes, and to visit swift and signal punishment on those fiends in human form who may break the peace of the country, and mob and terrify honest, innocent citizens, and if in any case you lack the numbers or the means to do this, there are more than a million swords ready to be unsheathed to avenge your fall, and to facilitate your victory. Especially in East Tennessee are you numerous and strong enough to hold the situation. Our counsel once for all is, that whenever these vile misecrants [*sic*] make their appearance among us, mounted, booted, and spurred, and however disguised, let the white and colored Radicals meet them promptly, and in the spirit of their lawless mission, and disperse them, and if need require this in dispersing them, exterminate them. At all

---

[104] "The Union Leagues were quasi-secretive men's clubs established during the American Civil War (1861–1865) to promote loyalty to the Union of the United States of America, the policies of newly elected 16th President Abraham Lincoln (1809–1865, served 1861–1865), and to combat what they believed to be the treasonous words and actions of anti-war, anti-black 'Copperhead' Democrats." (Source: https://en.wikipedia.org/wiki/Union_League, accessed 1 Sep 2021).

events, and at whatever cost, let these inhuman scoundrels learn that in East Tennessee, at least, they will not be allowed to carry forward this cowardly, miserably sneaking kind of warfare.

We speak earnestly, because the occasion demands it. But we are calm—we were never more so. Desperate cases require desperate remedies. If the Kuklux Klans attempt to run riot over our law, order, and the public safety, by these midnight raids, in disguise and darkness, then let force be met and punished by superior force. Pull off their viziers and expose their faces and their foul crimes at once to the light of the sun and to the gaze of merited scorn of an indignant, outraged public.

To prevent any misunderstanding as to the authorship of this article, we append our name.

THE SENIOR EDITOR.

The final entry for this appendix regarding the Ku Klux is the disturbing, confidential "A Letter of Advice" written by the Klan's first Grand Wizard, Nathan Bedford Forrest. Forrest was a well-known figure during and after the Civil War. Before the War, he was a planter, stagecoach company owner, and wealthy slave trader in Memphis, Tennessee. He was also a city alderman in Memphis as a democrat and served two consecutive terms. Additionally, he owned plantations in Mississippi and Arkansas. He rose to the rank of Lieutenant General for the Confederates States of America and is often admired as a brilliant tactician for the troops he led during the Civil War. Additionally, he became known because of the Fort Pillow Massacre. On 12 Apr 1864, Forrest's command surrounded a small Union installation on the Mississippi River, and his men killed Black soldiers who were attempting to surrender. During the battle and subsequent massacre, approximately 295 Union troops, most of whom were Black, were killed. "Remember Fort Pillow!" became a rally cry for Black Union Troops for the rest of the war.[105]

Forrest became the leader for the KKK starting two years after its founding, though he denied involvement during an 1871 congressional hearing. While he **publicly** denounced the violence of the KKK, and "ordered" the organization disbanded in 1869, he and the organization continued to be active. They espoused a belief in white supremacy and used threats, violence, and deception to accomplish their goals.

Here is the **confidential** *Letter of Advice* that Forrest wrote from Fort Pillow, Tennessee in July 1872, just seven years before Charley Peck wrote *Mary Anderson and Peacock the Mineralogist*.[106] While a person can state one thing publicly, what is said behind closed doors often reveals the truth of the matter. Forrest wrote the following letter four months prior to the 1872 presidential election between President and former Union General Ulysses S. Grant (Republican), and Horace Greeley (Liberal Republican). Notably, it is the only presidential election in which a major party nominee died during the election process. Greeley died on 29 Nov 1872, just 24 days after the election, and just one month after his wife died. Grant was easily re-elected for his second term in office. Charles Peck was 15 years old when President Grant was inaugurated his second time.

A Letter of Advice.

[CONFIDENTIAL.]

To the Grand Order---the K. K. Klan---throughout the U. States and Territories of America, Greeting:

---

[105] www.britannica.com/biography/Nathan-Bedford-Forrest, accessed 2 Sep 2021.
[106] "James M. Henderson Anti-KKK Oath," 1869, Record Group 319, 33961, Tennessee State Library and Archives, Tennessee Virtual Archive, https://teva.contentdm.oclc.org/digital/collection/reconaa/id/204, accessed 1 Sep 2021. Produced here to show the two-faced-ness of the KKK leadership, and the radical white supremacist agenda of its members. Original spellings/misspellings retained.

A Letter of Advice.

[CONFIDENTIAL.]

To the Grand Order---the K. K. Klan---throughout the U. States and Territories of America, Greeting:

FRIENDS AND COMPANIONS :—Four years ago, upon a similar occasion, I addressed you a campaign circular. And whatever its influence might have been upon the sentiment of the country, in its main object it was an inglorious failure ; that object being the defeat of that irrepressible humbug and impostor—U. Scalawag Grant, and the election of that model statesman and Christian—Horatio Seymour. I write you again at this time, for a similar purpose—namely, to defeat the same prince of damd scalawags and nuisances, and to elect a feller whom I acknowledge to be intrinsically, even more detestable than he; but for our purpose, as splendid and delectable as the Morning Star.

Let me explain. Our one grand scheme of re-establishment, the restoration of the old constitution as it was, and the honored institutions of the past, must never, no never, be lost sight of. All means to forward this truly pious work are as pure as the Virgin Mary, and holier than the holy Moses. Appropriation is not stealing. Killing is not murder—fire is purifying and cleansing. Now in tones of thunder I say to you that Horace Greeley must be elected. He is the man providentially raised up for our work and for our salvation. As things have bobbed the last four years, under Grant's infernal dynasty, the work for us to do has greatly accumulated. But, Farmer Greeley once elected, as we have sworn by the ghost of the holy confederacy he shall be, and this work will be dispatched by the double rule of lightning.

They purposes of heaven are inscrutable. As Pharaoh of old was raised up to save the Philistines and overwhelm the heathen Jews in the Dead Sea, and that against his cherished wishes and the deep laid plans of his life, so Horace is ordained as the harbinger of reform and the Star of Promise in the East, for our glorious and heaven-appointed Klan ; to restore the Bible institution of slavery, according to all the prophets and epistles ; to suppress the damd nigger, and to give us, once more, a white man's government. And all this against the life-long theories and teachings of the said philosopher, Greeley. Thus the overruling hand of providence will be visible—Horace's life work be happily turned upside down and crowned with inverted glory, and the wrath of man be turned to praise.

Horace Greely's history is like a beautiful rainbow, with all its separate and distinct colors and shades of color, in independent strips, fluttering in the breeze ; here the deepest red—there the greenest green—and yonder the palest, sickliest, damd nauseating yaller. He is like to an old rickety harp, strung up with all sorts of chords and wires, to be played on according to the fancy of the player. And if we elect him, as you bet your bottom dollar we shall, who will have the thumming of that crazy old harpsichord but our own precious selves

Butcher Grant has only one color, and a dull one at that; only one string, and a monotonous one of course. Nature intended him for a mere hostler ; and a mere wholesale manager of jackasses at that. Such another obstinate damd specimen of perversity, dyed in the wool, with fast colors, God never had ingredients enough to make. Our grand order has kept its secret agents for the last four years skilfully plying every art to soften and mollify the impervious hide of this untamed rhinosceros, but all in vain. His heart is composed of the purest virgin pot metal unadulterated, which never yields to external influences the millionth part of a hair's breadth. Nothing but Grecian fire will soften it ; nothing but gun-powder or nitro-glycerine will break it. The dishonest wretch uses all the money he can squeeze from the toil and sweat of honest labor, to pay off the villanous Yankee debt, and leaves all the sacred obligations of the Confederacy most insultingly neglected. Greeley will never be guilty of such bald-headed dishonesty as that. We have satisfactory assurances of it. Whatever else you may say of Greeley, every body knows that his honesty is a thing we can boast of.

Yes, Greeley has some bright spots in the grizzly ground of his character, and no mistake. First and foremost, when we felt it to be our religious duty to secede from the beggarly, sneaking, drivelling Yankee government, he frankly came forward and gave it as his opinion, (thus proving himself the great philosopher of the age, and great statesman of the Nation—which he is) that we had an inalienable and God-given right to go in peace. Then, by his officiousness in urging the Yankee army of idiots "on to Richmond," he made himself the immortal architect of Bull Run, the most glorious triumph on record. By this, and by his memorable Canadian diplomacy, and various other intermeddlings and interferences, he managed to protract the war, at least two glorious years ; and thus made himself the illustrious founder of our grand and patriotic order' which is destined, under Providence to restore our favorite institution, or split the Nation. Last, though not least, he scandalized the savage and ill-bred North, and honored our noble order, by bailing our beloved ex-President, and saving him from the vengeance of the rapacious Northern cannibals. *But*, whatever you may think of Greeley, and all his tantrums and peccadilloes, he cannot fail to be a far better tool for us than the hyena Grant. I therefore entreat you, nay, I *command* you, to labor earnestly for his election ; to labor both early and late ; to labor in season and out of season ; and to labor like the very devil ; without regard to yourselves or any body else; without regard to truth or principle or right, or any thing in God's world besides; place ourselves and our order in a position of power and extensive usefulness.

Take either horn of the dilemma you please. If he is the man of putty which we honestly believe him to be, then of course he is just the man we want, above all others. If on the contrary. he shall prove himself a tougher damd kustomer than we anticipate, still there is not even a homypathic possibility of the millionth dilution, that he possesses the quality and degree of bull-headed toughness and adamantine linkum vita willfulness, that constitute every fibre of body and the entire substitute for a soul which enter into the composition of the present egregious dastardly dam'd obnoxious autocrat of the Nation.

Upon these principles our old and tried Democratic friends all over the land are enrolling in the grand army of Greeley. And many soft-pated Republicans likewise, for reasons which God alone understands, (but whose votes will count as well as our own,) will swell the triumphant flood.

Greeley has promised us universal amnesty, and at least two members of his cabinet. With these advantages many others will follow as a matter of course. Brush up your disguises, clean your revolvers, sharpen your bowies, reconstruct your lodges, secure fleet horses, and be ready, at a moment's warning, for efficient service. And you well understand the meaning of that.

The butcher, no doubt, has some peculiar advantages, which we must not ignore. The National Treasury is within his reach. Now suppose for a moment that such an opportunity was placed within *our* reach! Wouldn't it be an important advantage to us ? Then all his countless myrmidons and toadies will move heaven and make a league with hell to beat us. They will also drag into their service all the cowardly, ignorant, ragamuffin, Yankee soldiery; which soldiery would have subdued the rebellion in one half the time it did, had it not been so stupidly brainless and cowardly. Then again, all the nigger persuasion, and all the psalm singing rabble, of Christian loafers, and shouting Methodists, must be counted on his side. With all this help, Grant himself must be written down an ass. In fact, his military successes were the result of ignorance, rather than true military skill. For if he had had only the gumption to perceive when his army was fairly and squarely licked, as was notoriously the case several times while on its murderous tramp to Richmond, he would have surrendered on the spot, as he ought to have done, by all the rules of civilized warfare. But his thick skull and indomitable mulishness saved him and his army, (though not worth the saving,) and have scourged the Nation with his tyranny for these four tedious years, and have also kept our beloved order in the back ground during all this tiresome period. His persecutions have been kept up with the most unparallelled ingenuity and un-mitigated cruelty—damn him. And unless we can escape them in the future, by consigning their author to political death and damnation, let him be gently admonished, by the fate of his illustrious predecessor, that another and an unfailing remedy is within our reach ; and when the decree goes forth can never be averted.

Some conceited upstarts may claim that Greeley is not safe—that the Democratic party cannot trust him—that his life-long labors have been on the side of the whining, disgusting, stingy black abolitionist, Yankee pick-pockets. Well I don't pretend to deny this. There would be no use denying it. But all this and lots of other things prove him to be a first-class coward ; which we all know Grant is not. Well, a coward is just what we want for the emergency. Greeley can be intimidated easier than any chickadee. And once let him *dare* to refuse us anything we ask of him, when he gets into the big chair at Washington and Gratz Brown will take his place in double quick time, and Gratz can surety be managed, either with one thing or the other, and the *other* means whisky. We propose to try all fair means first, after that the two black D's, Desperation and Despatch. But Greeley is cunning. He won't put us to any trouble. His whole game, for the last few years, shows him in his true character—that of an artful, ambitious, limber-jointed, damd hypocritic coward—exactly what we need, and just exactly the opposite of Butcher Grant.

Now a few words in regard to tactics. Four years ago we were too confident of success, and failed for want of this element. And the greasy--wooled, odoriferous African has been our master ever since. In the language of Solomon of old, Make yourselves all things to all men, in order to gain your points. During this campaign, let by-gones be by-gones. In the Northern States out-herod Herod in all the sickening, idiotic radical nonsense that offends your nostrils wherever you go. Where tee-totalism is rampant go the whole hog on Temperance. Wherever niggerism is epidemic hug and kiss the nigger and the nigger's wife and daughter. Take the lead and git excited on women's rights, when you can make capital by so doing. Go it blind on high tariff or free trade, as the case may be according to the direction of wind and tide. it will be impossible for us to make ourselves useful until we get the reins of government out of the hands of the nigger leaders. And all things are lawful, as Shakspeare says, while we are striving to gain a position of usefulness. This necessity will last but a few weeks more. Then we will resume our character of restorationists, and without gloves.

Why am I so bitter toward President Grant? President Devil! The reasons are too numerous to mention, and too patent to require mentioning. I will remind you of only a few.

1st, Fort Donelson ! 2d, Shiloh ! 3d, Vicksburgh ! 4th, 5th, 6th, 7th, 8th, 9th, 10th, 11th, and 12th, the Wilderness ! 13th, Richmond ! 14th, Appomatox Court House ! ! ! 15th, his abuse of President Johnson ! 16th, his persecution of our order and the entire southern people, with the exception of the lower classes ! 17th, his affection for the cussed niggers, which were the cause of all our woe ! ! 18th, his ungentlemanly treatment of ex-President Davis, and the officers and army of the Confederate States ! 19th, his refusing obstinately, and with chronic meanness, to give us office, or even amnesty ! 20th, his settlement of the Alabama claims, without fighting the loathesome, and conceited aristocratic English nation ! 21st, his refusal to pay even the interest of the Confederate debt, while promptly paying the interest and pegging away at the principal of the fraudulent and unjust claims of the disgusting, skin-flint Yankee murderers and robbers ! 22nd, his pigheaded refusal to remunerate the Southern people for their Slave property, of which they were so wickedly robbed by Lincoln and his thievish emissaries ! And 100 more equally unanswerable reasons.

But enough of all this. The spell is now broken. Grant is doomed and will soon pass into obscurity. A new era is about to dawn. The people are no longer to be ruled by tyrant, but by the Democratic party. And the Democratic party, as you know, is ruled and led by our order. Horace Greely, in this country, will sustain the same relation to the public service as Victoria does in England—that of a mere figure-head and automaton. While the selfsatisfied old philosopher, in his second puerility and early dotage, will flatter himself that he is the *de facto* president of this great nation, the power behind the throne will guide his hand by invisible machinery ; precisely as in the case of Andy Johnson. And you know how that was done, yourselves.

But the iron clad Grant, the atrocious, the infamous, the blood-thirsty Grant, is more than a match for the devil. If in the inscrutable councils which control human destiny, his re-election is pre-determined, contrary to all present indications, we shall have but one desperate alternative. You of course understand me. But when we resort to this, you know it is apt to react upon ourselves, as in the case of Lincoln ; and may set us back for years. It therefore must never be done except in the very last extremity. Smaller and less prominent obstacles may be removed without exciting much attention. The people are not very easily aroused. But when they do get mad they are mighty damd strong and unmanageable. So let us be wise as serpents, cautious as crows, and tenacious as the devil. If therefore, ill-fatedly for us, Grant should be re-elected, then before this great question is decided, I shall order a grand (Ecumenical Council of the Klan, and bring all our chiefs face to face to discuss the mode and means of his removal.

And now, with this caution, advice and exhortation, I must close. Not without much anxiety, I confess. The next three months are pregnant with a brood of mighty events. The air is thick with spirits of

all colors. Remember we are Restorationists ! Remember our motto—
Restoration and Re-instatement, or Disruption and Dissolution ! The
South must be avenged. The negro slave must not be our final
conqueror. Lee is dead—but Davis is alive, and Davis must be an
officer under the next administration, if not in the next cabinet. Once
give us amnesty, and he shall soon be either in the Cabinet or the
Senate. Once give us Greely, and we are sure of complete amnesty.

That the great Democratic party is to reach the sceptre again
through the medium and agency of its bitterest and most persistent
enemy is a puzzle the most mysterious, and a mystery the most
puzzling[.] History will treat it as the greatest political paradox of
modern times. It will stand as one of the most beautiful instances of
poetic justice in the annals of the world. But it is one of the ways of
Providence. He evermore employs his enemies in the upbuildment of
his cause. Horace Greeley the man, Horace Greeley, the black
republican, Horace Greeley, the bloody abolitionist, Horace Greeley,
the radical in everything repulsive to the Democratic Party, this
Horace, we detest, we spit in his face, we hold our noses in the
atmosphere of his presence. But Horace Greeley, the friend of
Jefferson Davis, Horace Greeley, the defender of secession, Horace
Greeley, the advocate of universal amnesty, Horace Greeley, the rival
of Grant and ferocious enemy of his entire kennel, Horace Greeley,
the champion of our glorious K Klux Order, Horace Greeley, the
hypocrite, Horace Greeley, the cowardly, crawling, dishonest,
candidate of the Democratic Party, this Horace we applaud, we
magnify his name, yea we honor and praise him.

And let every member of our grand invisible and invincible Order,
let every Democrat from Maine to Texas, shout, Amen ! And as many
black Republicans as are willing to join us. Amen and Amen !

FORREST
Worshipful Chief, K. K. K.

Fort Pillow, July, 1872.

K Klux Order, Horace Greeley, the hypocrite, Horace Greeley, the coward-ly, crawling, dishonest, candidate of the Democratic Party, this Horace we applaud, we magnify his name, yea we honor and praise him.

And let every member of our grand invisible and invincible Order, let every Democrat from Maine to Texas, shout, Amen! And as many black Republicans as are willing to join us. Amen and Amen!

FORREST,

Worshipful Chief, K. K. K.

Fort Pillow, July, 1872.

Figure 42 - The Republican chart. The nation's choice in war and peace Ulysses S. Grant / M.T. Boyd., 1872, Public Domain, https://www.loc.gov/pictures/item/2012648820/, accessed 2 Sep 2021.

Charley attended the Reagan High School for Boys in Morristown, Tennessee. The story of the school's building / land, and the educational institution it became, is included here to help us understand the time in which Charley lived. He was born in 1857, just 4 years before the start of the Civil War, and he graduated high school around 1875, just 10 years after it ended. Though East Tennessee had many Union supporters before and during the war, Tennessee joined the Confederacy. During Charley's life, racism, prejudice, and violence were exhibited by some towards the Black citizens in his community, and at times the White citizens who were friendly towards and helpful of the Black community.

The following article was originally found online at *Sometimes Interesting* and is reproduced here with permission.[107]

Morristown College: School of Freedom

Morristown, Tennessee, is rich in history. It was first settled in 1787, almost a decade before Tennessee became a state. The town played host to both Union and Confederate armies during the Civil War. It was also home to Morristown College, established in 1881 to offer former slaves opportunity

---

[107] https://sometimes-interesting.com/2016/05/16/morristown-college-school-of-freedom/, accessed 3 Sep 2021. Abridged, covering its founding until 1900, and concluding remarks. For more info on what the high school became after its land was sold, see the Citizen Tribune: www.citizentribune.com/news/history/back-when-morristown-hamblen-high-school-east-looks-to-its-100th-birthday/article_ac986ad0-b8d5-11ea-ae01-a3264998a33f.html. Morristown-Hamblen High School East traces its roots back to the Reagan HS For Boys.

for higher education. The school was fueled by donations and operated on a shoestring budget, yet managed to stick around for 113 years until it closed in 1994.

The buildings never found re-use and eventually landed in the lap of an unmotivated owner, who ignored redevelopment and rescue efforts. More than twenty years after closing, Morristown College's brick husks are still standing – albeit slowly crumbling – just blocks from the city center. A new owner hopes to change that, but development partners are needed before the plans can turn into a reality.

Are these decaying buildings significant and an important part of Morristown history, or are they merely blight? Are they worth saving, and if so, what can be salvaged?

Morristown and the School

The area known today as Morristown was settled by Gideon Morris and his family in 1787. Morris was granted a 400-acre tract by the state of North Carolina (Tennessee did not become a state until 1796), and on this land Gideon established Morristown – however it was not officially incorporated until 1855.

For the purposes of our story we fast forward to the fall of 1868, when the Freedmen of Jefferson County's Morristown district in Tennessee established a grammar school in a small church provided by the Presbyterians of Orange County, New Jersey.

In November of 1869 the school hired Mrs. Almira ("Miss Hattie") Stearns, a Vermont native and Civil War widow who served as a missionary after the war. Her calling was the education of the freshly emancipated slaves, most of whom were illiterate by law. Soon after her arrival Miss Hattie was teaching black students to read and write, 100 at a time. In 1880 Reverend W.C. Graves, the Methodist Episcopal (M.E.) Church's presiding elder of the Morristown District, partnered with M.E. Church Bishop Henry W. Warren, who shared his belief in a critical need for education beyond primary grades for blacks. The men "had the interest of the Colored people at heart," and "saw a need of a higher than ordinary school."

Graves and Warren represented the Freedman's Aid Society of the Methodist Episcopal Church, and together they set out to find a location to establish such an institution.

Figure 43 – Original building for the Reagan High School for Boys. "In this dim photograph, Judson Hill and his faculty in the 1880's pose in front of the structure that has served as a church, slave mart, Civil War hospital, and Morristown College's first building." Original Source: http://knoxheritage.org/wp-content/uploads/2014/05/A-School-For-Freedom.pdf, accessed 3 Sep 2021

The Reagan High School for Boys was a one-story framed structure situated on an acre and a half across a steep hill in Morristown, Tennessee. The building itself was constructed in 1830 and originally functioned as a meeting house. Later it served as a slave mart, then a hospital for both Confederate and Union soldiers during the Civil War. In 1881 it was purchased for $525 by Reverend Graves and Bishop Warren, with half of the funds coming from the Board of Education for Negroes of the M.E. Church.

The Church's plans were to improve access to education for non-whites, and it began with giving Mrs. Stearns and her pupils a permanent home in the former high school. A new entity was established. Reverend Graves became President of the Board of Trust

Did You Know?

The first black college in East Tennessee was Knoxville College in Knoxville, Tennessee, founded by the Presbyterian Church in 1875. Morristown College was the second, founded in 1881.

Figure 44 - Dr. Judson S. Hill, original source "Methodist Adventures in Negro Education" by Jay S. Stowell, 1922. Now accessible here: https://docsouth.unc.edu/church/sto well/stowell.html

of Morristown Seminary, and to serve as the first president of the seminary's new school, Graves and Warren selected Dr. Judson S. Hill.

Judson Sudborough Hill was a New Jersey native who relocated to Morristown in 1878 to fill the vacant pastorate of the First M.E. Church in Chattanooga, Tennessee. Upon his arrival, Dr. Hill also noted the need for education facilities for blacks, which led him to start a school in the basement of the church in Chattanooga.

This experience, in addition to his diplomacy in dealing with racial pressures, landed him the appointment as Morristown Seminary College's first president.

If enrollment was the measuring stick, the school was an immediate success. At the conclusion of the first operational year (1882), Dr. Hill and Mrs. Stearns hosted 190 students in the 60-foot-by-40-foot three-room building. Built in former Confederate territory, Morristown Seminary College became a moral triumph.

The bells of success rang proudly throughout the halls of the school; however they were inaudible outside its doors. Morristown was still rife with prejudice, and threats to both Dr. Hill and the school were not uncommon. Hill and his family found a less than cordial reception from the town's white community, who often hurled racial epithets at Dr. Hill and Miss Hattie in the streets. Stearns' daughter was treated poorly and spit upon. Hill often walked in the gutter to avoid being shoved off the sidewalk.

When the Civil War ended, the regional bigotry that had been cultivated for generations was not easily erased. One manifestation was ill-treatment in the streets, another was arson. Fires became all too common, forcing Dr. Hill and his staff to regularly rebuild and make repairs. The hate was not universal; when displaced by the fires, students found refuge in the homes of accepting white families in town.

Those responsible for Morristown Seminary College were not only driven, but resilient. Despite threats to their lives, Dr. Hill and Mrs. Stearns persevered with their mission to educate the oppressed minority. It was not a high-paying job. In the early and racially difficult years, the heartfelt gratitude and unwavering loyalty from the black community is what kept the educators going. For Dr. Hill and Miss Hattie, that was reward enough.

Morristown Seminary and Normal Institute.

RULES OF THE SEMINARY.

1.   Students immediately upon their arrival must report themselves to the President and adjust their bills at the office; and in no case must a student leave the Seminary without permission from the President.

2.   Study hours, embracing the recitation hours, will be published at the commencement of each term.

3.   Students' rooms shall always be accessible to members of the faculty. The occupants of the rooms are responsible for improper conduct occurring or tolerated in their rooms, and for all injury done to them or to the furniture while in their possession.   Nothing must be thrown from the windows.

4.   We strongly discountenance the use of *tobacco*, and any-one using it *will be cut off from the half term honor roll.   We forbid the use of it in the building or on the premises in any form.*

Frequenting places of amusement, drinking spirituous liquors, or entering places where they are sold, playing at games of chance, using profane, rude, or indecent language, immodest conversation or behavior, and all other practices opposed to morality and order, are totally forbidden.   Fire-arms, gunpowder, or fireworks of any kind, must not be brought upon the premises.

No student will be allowed to leave the premises after seven o'clock p. m. without permission.

Students who desire to leave town, or absent themselves from their rooms at night, must first obtain permission from the President.

Cleanliness and tidiness, both in personal habits of the students and in the condition of their rooms, will be rigidly exacted.

Students must sweep their rooms, depositing the sweepings in the box placed in each hall for that purpose, make their beds, and have the rooms present a neat and tidy appearance by seven o'clock a. m.

No gentleman, whether connected with the Institute or not, shall visit any person in the ladies' department without the permission of the President.

Students can not exchange rooms without the consent of the Matron. Students can not visit the kitchen, Matron's room, or dining-hall, or take a meal after the regular hour, without permission.

Students will be required to attend regularly such churches as may be designated by their parents, and also the Sunday-school connected therewith.

Occasional violations of these rules, through carelessness, will subject offenders to such penalties as the magnitude of the offense and the maintenance of discipline in the hall may require; but continued malicious infractions will render the perpetrators liable to expulsion from the institution.

Such other regulations as the President may make shall have all the force of these published rules.

Figure 45 - Morristown Seminary and Normal Institute "Rules of the Seminary", Original source "A School for Freedom: Morristown College and Five Generations of Education for Blacks, 1868-1985, Edited by JoVita Wells, 1986, Pg 10.

Morristown Normal Academy

Students began enrolling at Morristown's Seminary school by the hundreds. Initially the school was established as an elementary and secondary-level institution. The school offered Primary, Normal, and Preparatory courses which ranged from algebra and geometry to spelling. Due to its religious affiliation, Christian values were emphasized.

Figure 46 - "Student bodies during the 1880's and 1890's ranged widely in ages. For a brief period, it was possible for students to progress from kindergarten through college. Until 1898, the college campus consisted of frame additions to the original schoolhouse building." Originally from "A School for Freedom" by JoVita Wells, Pg 7.

Because its enrollment included students young and old, they were grouped by skill level rather than age. It was not unusual to see three generations seated together working on the same problem.

In 1883 the Seminary built the three-story, twenty-two room Stearns Hall dormitory for $2,500. The following year an Industrial Department was planned. Major advancement came in 1886 when the Tennessee State Board of Education recognized Morristown Seminary as a "normal school" (an institution for the training of teachers). Two years of high school level education were added and the name was changed to Morristown Normal Academy.

The *Women's Home Missionary Society of New Jersey* donated the funds to build a two-story model home in 1892. Its sixteen rooms were used to give instructions in dressmaking, housekeeping, millinery, and sewing. Known as the New Jersey Home, it is the oldest Morristown College building standing today.

Getting to School

Remember the grandparent story about walking five miles to school through snow, uphill both ways? Early Morristown students walked 10 to 12 miles to school – some without shoes – and several had to cross a river.

Figure 47 - Morristown College's model home: New Jersey House, circa 1900. This building still stands today and is Morristown College's oldest surviving structure. Original Source: "A School for Freedom" by JoVita Wells, Pg 18.

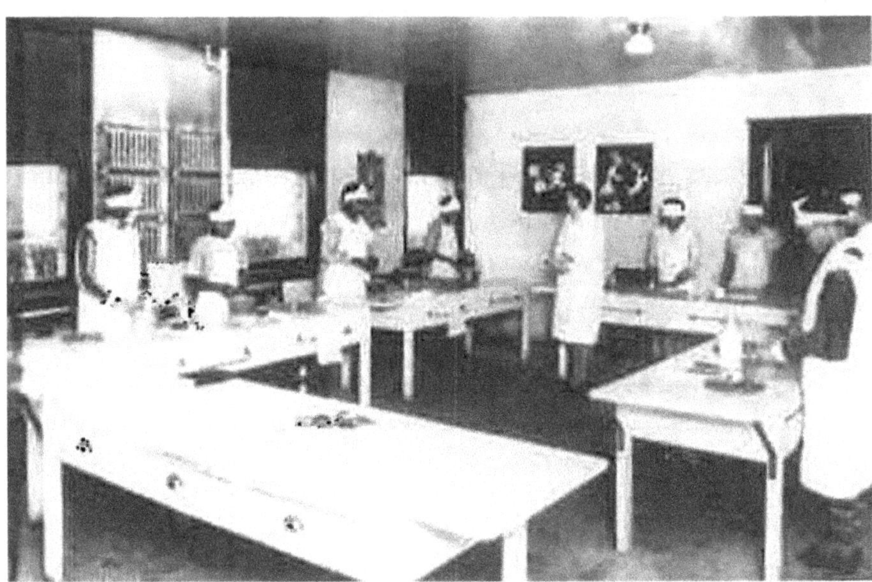

Figure 48 - A cooking class inside the New Jersey Home at Morristown College. "An important part of the Morristown College curriculum for women was cooking. Many young women worked in the homes of Morristown's white residents during the summer in order to earn enough money to pay their way through college." Ibid, Pg. 23.

Figure 49 - Morristown College faculty photo, circa 1898-1899. Miss Hattie Stearns is second from the left in the back row. Andrew Fulton, former slave and later teacher, sits on the far right of the first row. Ibid, Pg 9.

By the end of 1892 Dr. Hill had expanded the campus to 13 acres. He was not only a pious man, but a graceful diplomat and shrewd fundraiser. If there was a better candidate to smooth the district's obdurate race relations of the day, Morristown and the M.E. Church did not know of him or her.

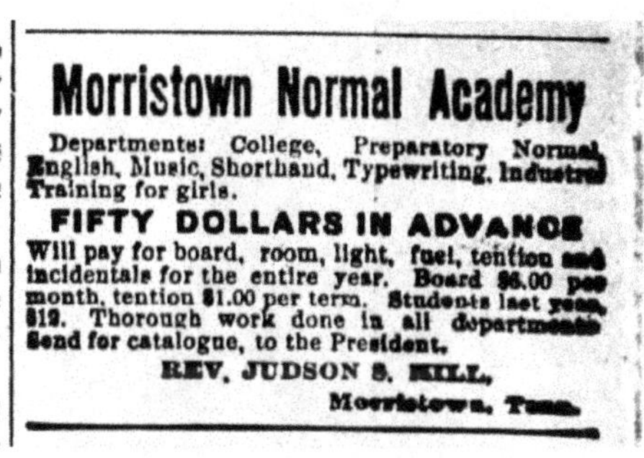

Figure 50 - Morristown Normal Academy advertisement. "The Appeal," St. Paul, Minnesota, 1 Sep 1894, Pg 2

Hill exercised an artful finesse when rubbing elbows with the upper-crust, and it was through his efforts that Morristown College was able to secure donations from philanthropists such as Andrew Carnegie, The McCormicks and Swifts of Chicago, and the Kelloggs of Battle Creek, Michigan.

Hill was even willing to bathe the feet of donors, as he did with Mr. Horace Crary, who was suffering with gout. Crary felt such relief he donated the remainder of the funds necessary to build Crary Hall, the school's first dormitory, completed in 1898 (see next page).

Hill's fundraising allowed for the addition of dormitories, classrooms, administrative offices, and a dining facility to the institution. A Music Department was added and "…arranged in three grades for the piano." In July of 1898 the school dropped the "Academy" and changed its name to Morristown Normal College.

A $15,000 donation by Mrs. Horace C. Crary upon her death in 1899 kick-started more expansion at the turn of the century. At the dawn of the twentieth century, there remained resistance among whites toward the movement to educate blacks, especially higher education. A compromise was the decision to steer them toward industrial and vocational education. This was not their preferred solution, but it was one endorsed by Booker T. Washington.

Figure 52 - Crary Hall, Morristown College, Circa 1910. Built 1898. Public Domain. Courtesy of North Carolina Digital Collections, https://digital.ncdcr.gov/digital/collection/p249901coll37/id/4348, accessed 3 Sep 2021.

- In 1901 it became Morristown Normal and Industrial College.
- In 1960 its name changed to Morristown College.
- In 1983 it was placed on the National Register of Historic Places.

Figure 51 - Newspaper Advertisement for Morristown Normal College, The Appeal, St. Paul, MN, 27 Jan 1900, Pg 3

Morristown Hero

From slavery to freedom, the story of Andrew Fulton

Fulton (pictured below) was sold in 1861 after a "lively auction" for $1,166 in the slave mart that later became [Reagan High School for Boys, and eventually] Morristown College. After being freed, Fulton studied in that same building under Mrs. Stearns, and eventually graduated from Morristown Normal Academy in 1887. Fulton then taught at Morristown Normal College for 45 years until his death in 1932, becoming one of its most distinguished educators.

Figure 53 - Andrew Fulton, Faculty Member, 1898-1999. Original Source: A School for Freedom, Pg 9.

The Andrew Fulton Story

"Andrew Fulton was born January 1855 to slave parents on the plantation of Lawson D. Franklin in Leadvale, TN. (White Pine) When Andrew was 7 years old, Lawson D. Franklin died and his estate was settled and his slaves were auctioned off at the Morristown Slave mart. Andrew and his mother were sold for $1400.00 and subsequently taken to Alabama.

Some twenty years later, Andrew Fulton returned to the same place where he and his mother had been sold and applied to the Morristown Normal Academy (previously the Reagan High School for Boys).

Judson S. Hill later described Andrew Fulton, "We had a revival a few weeks after Andrew arrived at Morristown Normal Academy. He came forward to pray and knelt and prayed for awhile then went back and knelt by a post and there he struggled and wrestled in prayer. In a moment, he jumped up and while clapping his hands, he shouted 'Glory! Glory! I am a free man!'" Later Dr. Hill asked Andrew why he had done that and Andrew said "Why Dr. Hill, it was right by that post where my mother stood holding me in her arms when we were sold as chattels. I came in here a slave to sin and I went back there that I might be made a free man in Christ."

In 1887, Andrew graduated and was immediately hired as a professor and he taught at Morristown Normal College until his death in 1932.

Andrew Fulton's family:

- Currie U., wife, b Apr 1865, NC
- Luther Fulton, son, b Aug 1879, TN
- Willie Fulton, dau, b May 1884, TN
- Nyunza Fulton, son, b Apr 1886, TN
- Clophas Fulton, son, b Jun 1891, TN
- Ruth T. Fulton, dau, b Oct 1893, TN"[108]

Morristown College Legacy

Morristown College featured moderately successful lower-division college football teams between 1906 and 1960; the Red Knights finished as co-champion of the Eastern Intercollegiate Conference in 1953. The school produced 15,000 graduates across several

---

[108] Information courtesy of Joe Moore, Hamblen County Historian, https://www.facebook.com/groups/HamblenCoHistory, accessed 3 Sep 2021.

generations before it closed in 1994. In the more than two decades since, its buildings have remained vacant.

Now the buildings are in extremely poor condition. The most beautiful and grand of the structures – the Kenwood Refectory and Laura Yard Hill Hall – have already been destroyed by fire. Gone are the students, classes, and pep rallies. Today the buildings host little more than meth chefs, stray animals, vagrants, and some youthful rebellion.

Untainted is the school's proud history, which includes notable alumni such as Marlene Clark, Shirley Hemphill, and of course Andrew Fulton, the subject of the school's unique milestone of being the first to matriculate and employ a former slave on the same site in which he was sold.

Morristown College was not the best, biggest, or even oldest school in the state of Tennessee. But it played an important role in post-emancipation opportunity, and ultimately, equipped its students for a better quality of life.

Maya Angelou once said people might forget what you did, but people never forget how you made them feel. Her words suit Morristown College, seen today by city planners and many neighbors as an eyesore. Yet to its alumni and former staff – some of whom still get together for reunions – the former school was a door to opportunity. It was where they met their loved ones, made friends, or experienced a first independence from home. And that made them feel great.

APPENDIX X. EVERY DAY POEM BY CHARLEY PECK

EVERY DAY.

Written for the Morristown Gazette.

Oh, trifling tasks, so often done,
    Yet ever to be done anew!
Oh, cares which come with every sun,
    Morn after morn, the long years thro',
We shrink beneath their paltry sway—
The irksome calls of every day.

The restless sense of wasted power,
    The tiresome round of little things,
Are hard to bear, as hour by hour
    Its tedious iteration brings;
Who shall evade or who delay
The small demands of every day.

The bowlder[109] in the torrent's course,
    By tide and tempest lashed in vain,
Obeys the wave-whirled pebble force,
    And yields its substance grain by grain,
To crumble strongest lives away,
Beneath the wear of every day.

Some find the lion in his lair,
    Some track the tiger for his life,
And wound them ere they are aware,
    Or conquer them in desperate strife—
Yet powerless we to scathe or stay
The vexing gnats of everyday.

---

[109] Bowlder = less common spelling of "boulder," meaning a detached and rounded or much-worn mass of rock

The steady strain, that never stops,
　　Is mightier than the fiercest shock;
The constant fall of water-drops
　　Will groove the adamantine[110] rock;
We feel our noblest power decay,
In feeble wear with every day.

We rise to meet a heavy blow—
　　Our souls a sudden bravery fills—
But we endure not always so
　　The drop by drop of little ills;
We still deplore and still obey
The hard behests of every day.

The heart which boldly faces death
　　Upon the battle field, and dares
Cannon and bayonets, faints beneath
　　The needle points of frets and cares;
The stoutest spirits they dismay—
The tiny stings of every day.

And even saints of holy fame,
　　Whose souls by faith have overcome,
Who move amid the cruel flame
　　The molten crown of martyrdom,
Bore not without complaint away
The petty pains of every day.

Ah! more than martyr's arriole,
And more than hero's heart of fire,
We need the humble strength of soul
Which daily toils and ills require;
Sweet patience, grant us, if you may,
An added grace for every day.
Chas. T. Peck. [111]

---

[110] Adamantine = rigidly firm : unyielding : resembling a diamond in hardness
[111] *The Morristown gazette.* (Morristown, Tenn.), 12 June 1878. Chronicling America: Historic American Newspapers. Lib. of Congress.

APPENDIX XI. CHARLEY'S LIFE AND TIMES TIMELINE

1857 Nov 16 (Age 0) – Charles Talbot Peck is born in Louisiana

1858 Oct 31 (Age 11 mo.) – 1st Cousin Adam Sharkey Peck (son of Cousin James Henry Peck) is born in Dahlonega, Lumpkin Co., GA

1859 Mar 27 (Age 1) – Oldest sister Ada dies from cholera at age 5

1859 Apr 13 (Age 1) – Mother Emma's cousin Horace Prentice, Jr. (son of Horace and Minerva Prentice) dies from typhoid fever[112]

1859 Oct 14 (Age 1) – Brother EDWARD JEROME PECK is born in Tennessee

1859 Dec 4 (Age 2) – Emma Peck writes to Emma Allen and says "Doc [Isham] does not do much else but settle church difficulties" and that it will take him until Fall 1860 to be ready to handle some of the "cases" he is taking depositions for.

1860 (Age 2) – Census lists family as living in Jefferson County, TN

1860 Jan (Age 2) – Father Isham's brother, Col. Wiley Hawkins Peck, member elect of the LA State Legislature from Madison Parish, shoots and stabs Charles N. Harris of Carroll Parish to death in the St. Charles Hotel in New Orleans[113]

1860 Jan-Feb (Age 2) – Father Isham travels to New Orleans to support his brother Wiley while he stands trial for murder. Wiley is acquitted. Isham returns to Oakland on 8 Feb 1860.

1860 Nov 27 (Age 3) – Mother Emma notes that Charley spells remarkably well "without knowing a letter"

1861 Jan (Age 3) – Uncle William Raine Peck becomes a signatory to the Louisiana Ordinance of Secession

1861 Apr 12 (Age 3) – Civil War officially begins when Confederate troops fire on Fort Sumpter in Charleston Harbor

1861 Jun 25 (Age 3) – Father Isham donates $1,000 to the "Peck Light Dragoons" of Jefferson County "to aid in their equipment"

---

[112] *Ada's Journal and Emma's Letters*, Pgs 52-53, 1 Jul 1859 Letter from Emma Peck to Emma Allen and https://www.findagrave.com/memorial/53256470, accessed 3 May 2020

[113] Ibid, Pgs 107-111

1861 Jul 7 (Age 3) – Uncle William R. Peck enlists as a private in the 9th Louisiana Infantry

1861 Aug (Age 3) – "Peck Light Dragoons" organized under Capt Benjamin M. Branner – Part of 4th Battalion, TN Cavalry (CSA), merged into 2nd (Ashby's) TN Cavalry Regiment May 1862

1862 (Age 4) – Brother Ashby is born in Tennessee (named after Gen Turner Ashby, CSA)

1863 Jan 1 (Age 5) – President Abraham Lincoln signs the Emancipation Proclamation declaring that all slaves are now free

1863 Mar 29 (Age 5) – Uncle Adam C. Peck writes to Charley's Grandma Sophia (Talbot) Peck from Strawberry Plains, TN and says that he has been preaching regularly at the Methodist Church.

1863 Jul 14 (Age 5) – 1st Cousin 1x removed Lafayette Peck (son of great-uncle Moses) dies in Tuscaloosa, AL as a Confederate Soldier

1863 Aug 1 (Age 5) – Great-uncle Adam Peck, Jr. enlists as a Private in the 11th Battalion, Georgia State Guards at the age of 72

1863 Oct 8 (Age 5) – Uncle William R. Peck is promoted to Colonel of the 9th Louisiana to succeed Leroy A. Stafford

1863 Dec 11 (Age 6) – Great-uncle Horace Prentice dies from pneumonia

1863 Dec 31 (Age 6) – 1st Cousin 1x removed Jacob Young Peck (son of great-uncle Adam) dies as a Confederate soldier in Atlanta as it is under siege

1864 May 25 (Age 6) – 1st Cousin 1x removed Mary Catherine Peck (dau. of great-uncle Adam) dies from cholera in Lake County, FL

1864 Jun 5 (Age 6) – Uncle Adam Clayton Peck dies in New Hope, VA in the Civil War Battle of Piedmont[114] [115]

---

[114] *Sawbones: The Life and Times of Dr. Isham Talbot Peck*, See 1876 *Morristown Gazette* article addressed to Sawbones where "Whitehead" says, "There are not many of us left. Adam fills a gallant soldier's grave, in the Valley of Virginia, where he fell in the battle of Piedmont"

[115] https://en.wikipedia.org/wiki/Battle_of_Piedmont, accessed 21 Apr 2020

1864 May/Jun (Age 6) – Brother "Big Peck" leads the 9th Louisiana in the battles of Wilderness, Spotsylvania, and Cold Harbor, followed by the Overland Campaign.

1864 July (Age 6) – Uncle William R. "Big" Peck leads his brigade as Senior Colonel and draws praise from his division commander, Maj. Gen John B. Gordon for his role in the Battle of Monocacy.

1864 Sep 19 (Age 6) – Uncle "Big" Peck is wounded in his right thigh by a shell fragment in the Third Battle of Winchester.[116]

1864 Sep 15 (Age 6) – Aunt Juliet Rhoton dies in Sneedville, TN

1865 Feb 18 (Age 7) – Uncle "Big" Peck promoted to Brig. General

1865 Apr 9 (Age 7) – Gen. Robert E. Lee surrenders his Army of Northern Virginia to Union Gen. Ulysses S. Grant

1865 Apr 15 (Age 7) – President Abraham Lincoln assassinated

1865 May 15 (Age 7) – Brother Louis S. Peck born in Tennessee

1865 Jun (Age 7) – Uncle "Big" Peck paroled in Vicksburg

1866 Jan (Age 8) – Uncle Wiley Hawkins Peck dies at the age of 43. He has a sudden "hemorrhage of the lungs" while visiting Big Peck at his "Mountain" Plantation[117]

1866 Apr 5 (Age 8) – Great-uncle Adam Peck, Jr. dies in Dahlonega, GA at the age of 94

1866 Aug 20 (Age 8) – President Andrew Johnson announces end of the Civil War

1867 Sep 22 (Age 9) – Grandpa William Henderson dies in Louisiana

1867 Nov 24 (Age 10) – Father Isham is in Louisiana working on the plantation, mother Emma is at Oakland. She expects Isham "home" before 1 Jan 1867. Many of the "negroes" die of cholera on Isham's Louisiana Plantation. 83 died on a nearby plantation close to Milliken's Bend. Things are terrible in Louisiana; people are selling their

---

[116] https://en.wikipedia.org/wiki/Third_Battle_of_Winchester, accessed 21 Apr 2020

[117] *Ada's Journal and Emma's Letters*, Pgs 65-67, Letter from Emma Peck to Emma Allen dated 1 April 1866 from Oakland, Tennessee

plantations for 50 cents/acre. One man moves to Honduras. Another tries to sell for $1/acre but no one will buy it.[118]

1868 (Age 11) – Aunt Eliza Jane Talbot dies in Sneedville, TN

1869 Mar 23 (Age 11) – Brother Paul Eve Peck is born in Tennessee

1869 Jun 10 (Age 11) – Grandfather Judge Jacob Franklin Clayton Peck dies at the age of 89

1870 (Age 12) – Census lists family as living in New Market, TN

1871 Jan 22 (Age 13) – Uncle / General William Raine "Big Peck" dies at the age of 52 at his plantation in Madison Parish, Louisiana

1871 Feb 27 (Age 13) – Older brother Willy commits suicide by laudanum at age 15

1871 Jun 4 (Age 13) – Grandma Sophia Westerner (Talbot) Peck dies at the age of 83 in Talbot, TN

1871 Nov 21 (Age 14) – Sister Helen Emma Peck is born at Glen Ada in Wolf Creek, TN

1872 (Age 14) – Charley begins attending Reagan High School for Boys in Morristown, TN around this time

1874 (Age 16) – The Women's Christian Temperance Union (WCTU) is founded and Memphis Chapter organized "out of concern for the destructive power and harmful effects of alcohol. They would meet in churches to pray, then march to saloons where they asked owners to close their bars."[119]

1874 Sep (Age 15) – Charley enrolls and attends Washington and Lee University in Lexington, Virginia as a first-year student

1875 (Age 16) – Washington and Lee students pull the wagon bearing sculptor the statue of Robert E. Lee to the campus, where it is stored for eight years until the mausoleum behind Lee Chapel is completed.

1875 May (Age 16) – Charley finishes his first year at Washington and Lee University and does not return to the school

---

[118] Ibid, Pgs 68-69, 24 Nov 1867 Letter from Emma Peck to Emma Allen written from Oakland, TN

[119] https://sharetngov.tnsosfiles.com/tsla/exhibits/prohibition/temperance.htm, accessed 10 Sep 2021

1874 Apr 29 (Age 16) – Brother Robert Lee is born at Glen Ada

1876 May (Age 18) – Charley starts his weekly newspaper, the Mossy Creek *Independent* (it is published off and on for 3 years)

1876 Sep (Age 18) – Charley sells the paper to his friend Capt. Ed Owens from Greeneville, South Carolina

1877 Feb (Age 19) – Charley "contemplates" reviving his paper

1877 Mar 5 (Age 19) – Charley stays at the Cain House (boarding house) in Morristown, TN

1877 Mar 19 (Age 19) – Charley stays at the Cain House in Morristown, TN with brothers Ed and Louis Peck

1877 May 19 (Age 19) – Ashby publishes his *The Mountain Boomer*

1877 Jul (Age 19) – Townsperson "Squire Simpkins" praises Charley's paper to *The Morristown Gazette*

1877 Nov 28 (Age 20) – Father Isham "visits his plantations in Louisiana"

1877 Dec 24 (Age 20) – Father Isham returns home from visiting Louisiana, headed to his home in Wolf Creek, and stays "at the Maxwell" in Nashville, TN. He is listed as having 30,000 acres of East Tennessee possessions.[120]

1878 Apr 24 (Age 20) – Father Isham endorses James Swaggerty, Esq. of Newport for TN Governor

1878 Jun 12 (Age 20) – Charley publishes his poem *Every Day* in *The Morristown Gazette* (See Appendix X)

1878 Sep (Age 20) – One "Charles Peck, Student" returns from a trip abroad in England on the ship Bothnia, a Cunard. He travels with George W. Peck.

1878 Oct 23 (Age 20) – Father Isham cannot visit his friend Maj Heiss in Nashville due to the spread of yellow fever throughout LA.

1878 Nov 20 (Age 21) – Family friend Maj Harry Heiss and Fishing Commissioner Col Akers visit Isham and fish on French Broad

---

[120] *The Daily American / Tennessean* (Nashville, TN) 25 Dec 1877, Page 4

1879 Feb 27 (Age 21) – His brother DR. EDWARD J. PECK graduates Vanderbilt Univ. Medical School at the age of 20 years old

1879 Mar 31 (Age 21) – Father Isham travels on the J. M. White boat so Ed can get better treatment. Ed is in "feeble health."[121]

1879 Apr 23 (Age 21) – Isham travels to Vicksburg, MS to care for Charley's brother, DR. ED PECK, who had a serious health attack (at the age of 20). Isham returns with Ed, "the invalid," and takes the train for his home. Isham is listed as being in "robust health" and Ed "as well as could be expected."

1879 Apr (Age 21) – Charley writes his novel, *Mary Anderson and Peacock the Mineralogist: The Back Luck of a Young Southern Girl*, during his idle hours, perhaps as he was home helping with Ed's recovery.

1879 Sep (Age 21) – Charley gives or sells 500 acres in Cocke County to his brother Ed

1880 Feb (Age 22) – Charley travels to South America, including Brazil, and returns by way of California and intermediate territories

1880 Nov 2 (Age 22) – James Garfield is elected President

1881 Mar 4 (Age 23) – Inauguration of President James Garfield. Charley cuts and pastes a clipping of a lithograph of the inauguration from an illustrated magazine into his form book.

1881 Apr 4 (Age 23)– Charley arrives in Knoxville, TN on the train

1882 Feb 18 (Age 24) – Charley is "stricken with an apoplectic fit" and prostrated in a street in Cincinnati. Officials telegraph for his brother Dr. Ed Peck to come from Atlanta, GA to help him.

1882 Feb 22 (Age 24) – Ed arrives by train just a few hours before Charley's death. Ed believes that if he had arrived 12 hours prior, he could have saved him.

1882 Feb – Ed travels with Charles' remains to Mossy Creek, TN

1882 Feb – Charley is buried next to his sister Ada and brother Willy in the Westview Cemetery, Jefferson City, TN

---

121 According to the *Vicksburg Herald* (Vicksburg, MS), 1 Apr 1879, Pg 3

INDEX

Cross Mountain Books

In addition to *Charley's Novel*, enjoy *Ada's Journal* and these forthcoming titles from Cross Mountain Books in The Pecks of Mossy Creek series.

Ada's Journal: The Civil War Era Journal and Letters of Emma Peck

Ada's Journal provides a window into history. Ada Louise Peck was a well-loved little girl (and Charley Peck's sister) who traveled back and forth between Mossy Creek, Tennessee and East Carroll Parish, Louisiana, starting in 1853. She experienced trials, health problems, and travel by railroad, steamboat, and stagecoach. This journal, recorded from Ada's perspective by her mom Emma, records the first two years of her short life. Edited by Andy Peck, over 70 photographs, maps, and historical references bring this true story to life in a powerful way. Journey with little Ada on a Mississippi River steamboat; keep your hands inside the train as you pass through the half-mile Cumberland Mountain Tunnel on the East Tennessee and Georgia Railroad; and enjoy the mountain hospitality at the Wolf Creek Inn as Ada visits with Mrs. Emma Allen, Peck family friend and hostess to hundreds along the French Broad River.

ISBN 9781955121002 (pbk) | ISBN 9781955121019 (hardcover)

ISBN 9781955121026 (ebook)

Sawbones: The Life and Times of Dr. Isham Talbot Peck

Between 1874 and 1886, Dr. Isham Peck (Charley's father, and grandson of Adam Peck, Sr., founder of Mossy Creek) wrote letters to the editor of *The Morristown Gazette* under the pen name Sawbones, and people wrote to him as well. *Sawbones* takes you on a deep dive into life in East Tennessee and Northeastern Louisiana during the years of Reconstruction after the Civil War and beyond. *Sawbones* expresses his thoughts on politics, agriculture, church, friendship, and fishing. Author/Editor Andy Peck includes the history of Isham Peck and family, including what is known about his pre-Civil War service in the U.S. Army as a surgeon. Allow yourself to be transported to places like Wolf Creek, Tennessee as the author includes a series of videos recorded at places where Isham and family lived. *Sawbones* is a journey worth experiencing!

ISBN 9781955121088 (pbk) | ISBN 9781955121095 (hardcover)

Cross Mountain Books
www.crossmountainbooks.com

He Loved the Folks: Dr. Edward Jerome Peck of Hot Springs, North Carolina by Andy Peck

In *He Loved the Folks*, learn how this doctor from Wolf Creek, Tennessee gently influenced the entire area around Hot Springs, North Carolina for good by his steady, faithful, medical care. Dr. Ed Peck (son of Dr. Isham Talbot Peck) was so loved at the time of his death, that the community came together and erected a monument to honor his life and love. He doctored Jane (Hicks) Gentry, the Appalachian folklorist and singer, and served important Hot Springs institutions including the Dorland Institute, Mountain Park Hotel, and the Southern Railway Surgeons Association. In *He Loved the Folks*, you will catch a glimpse as to why this man was so loved by the Hot Springs community, as he dedicated his life to them.

ISBN 9781955121040 (pbk) | ISBN 9781955121057 (hardcover)

Cross Mountain Books
www.crossmountainbooks.com

www.ingramcontent.com/pod-product-compliance
Lightning Source LLC
Chambersburg PA
CBHW070621310726
48982CB00001B/146